the pretender

rebirth

by

Steven Long Mitchell
&
Craig W Van Sickle

TELEMACHUS PRESS

This book is a work of fiction. Names, characters, places and incidents are either the product of the author's imagination or are used fictitiously. Any resemblance to actual persons, living or dead, or to actual events or locales is entirely coincidental.

THE PRETENDER—REBIRTH

The publisher does not have any control over and does not assume any responsibility for author or third-party websites or their content.

Cover design by Brightspark
https://thebampotpress.wordpress.com

Published by Telemachus Press, LLC
http://www.telemachuspress.com

Visit the author website:
http://www.thepretenderlives.com

ISBN: 978-1-939927-77-4 (eBook)
ISBN: 978-1-939927-78-1 (Paperback)

Version 2015.10.15

Printed in the United States of America

10 9 8 7 6 5 4 3 2 1

Table of Contents

Personal Message from Mitchell & Van Sickle   i

What readers and fans around the world are saying about

The Pretender—Rebirth   iii

Acknowledgements   v

Foreword   ix

Prologue   1

Chapter 1   3

Chapter 2   11

Chapter 3   15

Chapter 4   18

Chapter 5   22

Chapter 6   27

Chapter 7   29

Chapter 8   35

Chapter 9   40

Chapter 10   43

Chapter 11   48

Chapter 12   52

Chapter 13   56

Chapter 14   60

Chapter 15   64

Chapter 16   67

Chapter 17   70

Chapter 18   75

Chapter 19   79

Chapter 20   83

Chapter 21   86

Chapter 22   93

Chapter 23	94
Chapter 24	98
Chapter 25	103
Chapter 26	110
Chapter 27	113
Chapter 28	119
Chapter 29	122
Chapter 30	126
Chapter 31	130
Chapter 32	134
Chapter 33	138
Chapter 34	143
Chapter 35	146
Chapter 36	150
Chapter 37	154
Chapter 38	158
Chapter 39	163
Chapter 40	165
Chapter 41	171
Chapter 42	179
Chapter 43	182
Chapter 44	186
Chapter 45	190
Chapter 46	194
Chapter 47	195
Chapter 48	200
Chapter 49	205
Chapter 50	208
Chapter 51	211
Chapter 52	215
Chapter 53	218

Chapter 54   222

Chapter 55   225

Chapter 56   227

Chapter 57   229

Chapter 58   231

Chapter 59   233

Chapter 60   234

Chapter 61   237

Chapter 62   241

Chapter 63   245

Chapter 64   249

Chapter 65   251

Chapter 66   252

Chapter 67   257

Next for The Pretender   259

A Personal Thank You
   From Steven Long Mitchell and Craig W Van Sickle   260

Personal Message
from
Mitchell & Van Sickle

We love The Pretender and it's our life's passion to continue Jarod's story for all of the faithful fans and for the new ones just joining in.

We write for thinkers, creators, innovators and the curious who love to unravel a tale and enjoy the odd and unexpected, people who, like Jarod, know that 'life is a gift.'

If you are reading this you are one of them—one of us—and we are truly thankful you came along to join us.

*Writing for you is an honor and it would be an even bigger honor if you would write to us. If you like what we are doing with **The Pretender** it would mean a lot to us if you'd send a short email to us at centreinsider@thepretenderlives.com to introduce yourself and say hi. We always personally respond to our readers.*

*We'd also love to add you on our mailing list so you can receive notifications about future books, updates, contests and other information about all things **The Pretender**.*

*You can find us at **www.thepretenderlives.com**. We hope you follow this link and say hello so we can personally thank you for your readership and loyalty.*

What readers and fans around the world are saying about
The Pretender—Rebirth

"You don't have to be a fan of the show to love this novel, it's a fun, fast page-turner that pits the forces of power against intellect on an inexorable collision course. I recommend it highly."
Wendy F—San Francisco

"From the creators of cult-hit TV show, **The Pretender—Rebirth** *is the same characters we have missed for the past decade but in a fresh new light, answering questions and peeling back layers on a world we once were so curious about."*
Jeremy A—Paris

*"****Rebirth*** *is a captivating ride whose main character Jarod is brilliant, complex but very human all at once—the cunning of Holmes, the heroics of Bourne all in one."*
Dennis U—Melbourne

*"****Rebirth*** *is fascinating and incredibly engrossing …* **The Pretender** *is back with the series characters we love along with brand new ones. The chase is on! This is a must-read!"*
Jenna B—Hollywood

"A thrilling and fast-paced novel that I couldn't put down. Although I had never seen the television series, Jarod and Miss Parker (wow she's something!) immediately drew me in. I highly recommend **The Pretender—Rebirth** *both to fans of the show and everyone else.*
Laura H—Seattle

"Extremely well-written and memorable—I hope they will follow up with many more."
Sam V—West Palm Beach

"After 12 years since we last saw these characters, **The Pretender** *is reborn with a renewed strength and tenacity. Be ready for new secrets you didn't know existed and exciting insights into the lives of the characters you love so much."*
Vania A—Lisbon

"A perfect blend of the old and the new and yes—Miss Parker and Sydney are still hot on Jarod's trail. They want him alive—preferably."
Kris G—Maui

"Jarod's quest for the truth and secrets to his very existence continues to inspire as he discovers the world while fighting its wrongs and trying to stay one step ahead of his captors, The Centre. Can't wait for more!"
Mark M—Rome

Acknowledgements

Sincere thanks for your
time, knowledge, efforts and support ...

Jenna, Vania, Sam, Valerie, Ruthanne, Jacci, Kylie,
Leslie, Mark, Melissa, Wendy, Bob, Michael, Andrea,
Aridae, Wills, BG, Pete, Jeffrey,
Lupe, Matiana, Jeremy, Ella, Katie

rebirth

Foreward

My friends Steve Mitchell and Craig W Van Sickle have created a rich world with *The Pretender* that has touched people of all ages and backgrounds, all around the globe. From their fertile and wonderfully twisted minds they have created an anthology that is clever, deeply layered and inspiring. They have woven together a compelling story of action, mystery, and mythology with heart and humor.

It was a true honor for me to play Jarod for so many seasons. Bringing him to life has been one of my greatest joys. He has taught me lessons I will carry with me always, for Jarod is a great instructor on what is important in life. He teaches us to serve others selflessly and with great compassion. He shows us that random acts of kindness are way more fulfilling than money...or Pez. He reminds us to value our families and to retain the wonder and sense of adventure you had as a child. He asks us to rise up and stand for justice with unwavering conviction and bravery. He teaches us that no matter the adversity, despair, or cruelty you may have suffered at someone else's hand it is possible to rise above that pain and darkness and live in the light. He allows us the permission to become someone new while always being true to ourselves. Jarod is an inspiration for me and I hope he is for you too. He awakens the Hero in us all.

The Pretender would not have lived on so long without the best fans in the world. For your support and love I am eternally grateful.

Michael T. Weiss

Prologue

There are Pretenders among us,
geniuses with the ability to
become anyone they want to be.
In 1983 a corporation known as The Centre
isolated a young Pretender named Jarod
and exploited his genius for their 'research.'
Then, one day, their Pretender ran away ...

Chapter 1

LIKE A SLOWLY spinning top, the glass eye twirled on the metal table between an onyx ashtray and glass syringe. It came to rest staring at a man it no longer recognized.

Kaj stared back at the glass ball and realized he hadn't felt the backhand that had sent it flying out of his head and onto the rusty surface. The Libyan had lost feeling on the left side of his face hours earlier, after the twenty-eighth blow had fractured his occipital bone. Counting the strikes had helped him keep his wits. But his wits had flown out of his head in the same instant as the glass eye—the eye in which his face reflected.

What number blow had knocked it out? 115? 118? His short-term memory was nearly gone. He fought to regain a sense of what was happening, to remember why he was being tortured in the first place.

Kaj wearily rubbed his weathered face. A face much older than his 34 years and one that looked more like that of a goat herder's than an operative for hire. A face, just like his damp clothing, drenched in sweat that stank of his own fear.

Kaj wobbled in a wooden chair that was cut unevenly so as to purposely keep him off balance. The chair was maddening. So was the buzzing from the bare fluorescent tube in the ceiling. In fact, everything in the room that he'd been locked in since he was taken—*hours? days? weeks ago?*—was designed to be maddening.

A design that was working.

In his delirium, he watched the other man's hand reach down and pick up his artificial eye, staring at the sphere as it rose towards the other man's face. As the reflection of *that man* appeared in *his* glass eye, the throbbing in Kaj's head dissipated, replaced with marvel at the surreal vision he was witnessing. It was as if a drawing by Escher, like the ones in the picture books Kaj had always been fascinated with, had come to life before him.

The tall man, whose image glistened in Kaj's eye, was named O'Quinn. In contrast to the battered terrorist seated across from him, O'Quinn looked younger than his 44 years. Militarily fit, ramrod-straight spine, a shaved head, the swaggering alpha male was as much a testosterone machine today as he was in his youth.

In fact, O'Quinn's demeanor reminded the Libyan of another cocky bald man he'd seen in an old movie playing the King of Siam. But that remembrance was from a lifetime ago—a life whose memories began flashing through Kaj's fading mind. Recollections of a childhood spent playing in the dusty streets of Benghazi, of his mother serving warm—never hot—kabob. As a teen watching George W. Bush's effigy burning, of being promised "72 virgins" and getting his first taste of that kind of pleasure from an old whore missing her left incisor. Of watching the first car bomb he planted explode. And then the next.

Kaj was watching his life flash before his eyes—a life that would surely end if he didn't get out of that room—and soon.

O'Quinn rolled Kaj's glass eye between his fingers and began pacing. "A man with one eye can only see the world in two dimensions. Without the perception of depth he's never truly sure how close he is to another. Hopefully now you can see how close I am to you and that I was the wrong person to blackmail."

Adrenaline flooded Kaj's system, bringing him back to the moment. O'Quinn smiled. "Nice to see you're with me again, Kaj." But as quickly as it had appeared, O'Quinn's smile faded and his eyes filled with intensity. "Now, for the hundred and twenty-first time, where is my property?"

Kaj finally remembered why he was there and what O'Quinn wanted to know. He took a breath, trying to exhibit some measure of strength. "Why should I enlighten you with this?"

"I've given you a hundred and twenty reasons—and old friend, the truth is—you can't take many more of them." O'Quinn pointed at the syringe—"Or of these."

Kaj knew O'Quinn was dead right.

Key word, *dead*.

Kaj searched his brain for the right thing to say to save his life, but all he could come up with was "And you will release me when I tell you what you want to know?"

O'Quinn was not a malevolent man. He was a professional warrior of intense focus and in that way—in that one way only—he was honorable. "I could say, 'yes,' but that would be an insult to both of our intelligences."

Kaj felt warm liquid slip from his eye and down his cheek. He hoped it was blood, but knew it was a tear.

O'Quinn studied the pitiable figure before him. "Though you betrayed me, I will still make you a deal." He picked up the syringe. "Two of these will make it painless and quick—like going to sleep."

Kaj felt a lump forming in his throat. In his life, he had killed many people. Today though, he feared, it was he who would die.

"I—I have money ..." Kaj blurted.

Even in the Libyan's weakened state, the patronizing look on O'Quinn's face was not lost on him.

Defeated, Kaj continued. "I try not to buy freedom—that too would be an insult to intelligence. But blessed my soul would be if my mother were to receive this money—since ten years now she dream of owning her own Kabob stand—served warm—never hot."

O'Quinn placed a hand on Kaj's shoulder. "I'll ensure that she gets it."

Tears flowed freely down Kaj's cheek. He watched one drop land on the table near his right hand—a hand that had just begun to shake. "May I have one last cigarette?"

A shadow of a smile came and went across O'Quinn's face. Kaj raised an eyebrow. "Did what I say amuse you?"

"Sorry, Kaj. It's just—I've never heard someone say that in real life."

"Unless you have kabob, it is my final wish." Kaj looked at his ocular prosthesis in O'Quinn's hand. "And that ..." Kaj gazed downward, his vanity getting the best of him. "I'd like to look my best, when ..."

O'Quinn considered the request, then gently rolled the glass eye across the table. Kaj cleaned it as best he could on his sleeve and had just finished placing it in his socket when O'Quinn walked over to the heavy metal door and *Boom! Boom! Boom!*—banged on the wall next to it. Three times.

As if he were one of Pavlov's dogs, the sound of the three *Booms* immediately caused Kaj's body to tense—a conditioned reflex triggered by the anticipation of a series of events *he knew* would follow.

The Libyan looked to a midpoint on the door a split second before *he knew* he'd hear the sound of the slide bolt *slash—crack* to the unlock position. His eye then moved to the doorknob an instant before it turned, as if *he had seen* this happen a million times before. Or maybe just a hundred and twenty. The door opened and Kaj found himself *anticipating* the Glock 17's 9mm barrel the instant before it poked its nose into the room. As the gun guided the guard that carried it, Kaj's short-term memory began to return. *Three bangs on the wall and the guard with the grin like a butcher's dog enters.*

As he focused on the barrel and the *dried blood* on it, Kaj suddenly felt a wave of ice-cold anger and red-hot fear. He intuitively touched his cheek. As his fingers met raw flesh where the skin was split open, he was hit with a memory flash of being pistol-whipped by the sadistic butcher's dog himself. *Right. That was strike number sixty-four. I'll never forget that one.* Kaj exhaled slowly, his wits returning.

O'Quinn held out his hand to Dog. "Give me a smoke."

Dog patted his empty pockets, then stepped into the hall, yelling to the outer room. "Yo, Dick Face, you got any more Red Apples?" Kaj watched as Dog raised his paw and caught an incoming box of Marlboros.

Dog walked over to Kaj, flipped the lid and offered him one. The Libyan opened his cracked lips, accepting it. Dog fired a Zippo, Kaj leaned the tobacco into the heat and took a long, deep drag into his lungs—his one good eye never losing contact with Dog's two.

Desperate for a way out, Kaj knew if he was going to make a move, he'd have to make it now.

MOVE! his brain screamed. But who was he kidding? He knew in the shape he was in he couldn't take both O'Quinn and the mad Dog. And if he tried and failed they'd make him suffer more than he had up until now—and he couldn't take any more suffering.

So he sat and puffed.

O'Quinn motioned for his puppy to take a walk. After Dog exited, *slash—crack!* The bolt was slammed into the locked position on the other side of the door. As its echo died within the room, so did Kaj's hope.

O'Quinn moved the table aside, pulled up a chair and took a seat— knee to knee, eyes to eye in front of Kaj. "Now tell me what I want to know."

The terrified man took one last long pull from his cigarette, the hot embers burning brightly, giving his glass eye a sad but eerie glow.

As smoke slowly floated up from his lips, Kaj rubbed his brow with the shaking hand holding his Marlboro and began to speak in a low whisper. "I hid what is yours far away. It is being guarded by a friend."

"I can barely hear you, Old Friend." O'Quinn leaned in. "Now, tell me exactly where to go."

Kaj looked into the bald man's eyes and whispered. "Straight to hell." Moving insanely fast, Kaj grabbed O'Quinn behind the neck with one hand and shoved the red-hot cigarette ember into the bald man's left eye with the other. O'Quinn reached for his sizzling eye, but that was only the beginning of his pain as Kaj grabbed the onyx ashtray and smashed its sharpest edge into the screaming man's temple.

Before O'Quinn hit the floor, Kaj was at the door and *Boom! Boom! Boom!* banged on the wall next to it. His mind more intensely focused than it had been any second since he'd been kidnapped and brought to this hell-hole, Kaj peered at the midpoint of the door.

Slash—crack! The bolt unlocked. The door slowly opened. The Glock's barrel entered the room. And just as B Dog's elbow was almost inside, *Wham!*—Kaj slammed his body onto the door, breaking Dog's arm with a *sickening crack.* "Aughhhhh!"

Kaj caught Dog's falling gun before it hit the floor, then flung the door open to a small hallway outside. The K-9's grin had been replaced by shrieking agony.

And more was in store.

As Dog looked up from his shattered arm, Kaj kicked him in the throat. The blow sent Dog flying out of the hallway and into an adjoining room of what Kaj now realized was a small adobe cabin.

Kaj stepped over the Dog and immediately locked eyes with and rushed towards a man with a smoke dangling between the lips in his aptly named mug. Dick Face stumbled backwards, fumbling for one of the many pistols and automatic weapons hanging on a wall-mounted gun rack. But before he could grab one, Kaj's Glock was pointed directly at his dickish face. That was DF's first mistake.

His jaw dropped from shock. The cig fell from his lips. He glanced at the crumpled pile of Dog meat and pleaded: "I just work for them."

"You should rethink your career." Kaj shoved the Glock into DF's mouth and dragged him along the wall towards a window.

Kaj looked outside into the pitch-black night and saw two vehicles parked in front of the cabin, dimly lit by a porch light. A Mercedes S600 and a 4WD F-150 both faced away from the cabin, pointing towards a long driveway that led out into the sand. *Sand?* Kaj knew he'd been transported after being kidnapped in Philly, but he had no idea how far until he saw Texas plates on the vehicles. He hated Texas. Especially West Texas.

Kaj pivoted DF's face so he could see the cars. "Keys?"

DF gurgled, "Screw you." That was DF's second mistake.

Kaj spotted two sets atop the wooden table. Dick Face lunged for them. That was his last mistake. *Blam!* Kaj splattered the adobe wall with Dick Face.

The Libyan grabbed a set of keys, ran outside and flung the Mercedes door open. He hopped into the driver's seat and was struggling to get the key into the ignition when *Zing!—Shatter!* A bullet whizzed by his ear and into the side view mirror.

Heart pounding, Kaj looked back and saw the now rabid Dog shooting from inside the open door. O'Quinn stumbled up, grabbing Dog's Beretta. "I need him alive!"

Kaj fired two rounds, shattering the porch light. The men dove for cover. Kaj slipped in the key, fired up the ignition and rooster-tailed it the hell out of Dodge.

O'Quinn grabbed a MP5K from the weapons rack and he and Dog raced to the F-150. Dog got behind the wheel, O'Quinn in the passenger seat. "Go! Go! Go!"

The Mercedes screamed down the long driveway. Even with the head-lights blaring, Kaj could barely see. Squinting, he thought he could make out an asphalt road a hundred yards ahead that ended the driveway at a 'T'—but was suddenly blinded by the reflection of high beams in his rearview—the F-150 rapidly gaining ground.

Leaning out the window, wind buffeting his bloodied eye, O'Quinn was trying to steady the 5K to get a clear shot at the Mercedes. It was his turn now to not have depth perception.

Kaj caught only a fleeting glimpse of the machine gun's muzzle flashes before O'Quinn's shots blew holes through his trunk and spider-webbed his rear windshield. The Libyan looked over his shoulder, panicked at the sight of the truck quickly catching up. But when he returned his gaze forward he saw immediate trouble ahead of him—he was coming upon the 'T' where the driveway met the asphalt road—across which was a stone wall he was rocketing towards.

He yanked the 600's wheel, sending the Benz into a wicked power slide until *Wham!*—the car slammed sideways into a wooden mailbox post. The tires regained traction. Kaj floored it, began eating asphalt as he raced down the two-lane road. Up ahead he could see overhead lights of a free-way. If he could get there, maybe, just maybe, he could get away.

Dog pulled the truck off the pavement and into the desert. He exploded through prickly pear and tumbleweeds until he was parallel to the Mercedes—the only thing separating them, a roadside service ditch.

Kaj pushed the Mercedes for all it was worth, racing toward his free-dom. But Dog was not going to let the Libyan escape and veered erratically down, through and up over the lip of the ditch, landing hard in a flash of sparks right next to him.

The Libyan took a screaming right up the freeway on-ramp, hotly pur-sued by the F-150.

Dog swerved left, blazed around and up next to Kaj, jamming the Benz into the guardrail. As sparks flew, O'Quinn opened fire on the car's tires. Kaj returned fire until the Glock and his luck played out. He looked up to see he was headed straight at a concrete barrier. At the very last second, Dog slammed on the brakes as *Wham!*—the 600 flew right into the concrete barrier, which sent $160,000 of German engineering cartwheeling across the desert floor. With a sickening thud it finally came to rest on its roof.

The Dog and his Master rushed out of the pickup and ran to the Mercedes, just as an explosion erupted at the rear of the car.

O'Quinn glared at spreading fire and then to his one-armed underling. "I need him alive." Dog doggy-tilted his head as if O'Quinn was insane. "It's gonna blow." O'Quinn pointed his gun at Dog. "So's this if you don't move."

Dog cautiously approached the burning Benz. He found Kaj unconscious, dangling upside down in his seatbelt. With flames growing, Dog pulled his Whiplash knife and furiously sliced through the webbing until the Libyan tumbled onto the Benz's ceiling. With his working paw, Dog grabbed the terrorist by the collar and dragged him clear of the wreckage just as the flames reached the leaking gas tank.

The Mercedes exploded into a ball of fire, knocking the two men on their asses. O'Quinn rushed over, his only focus Kaj. "Is he alive?"

Dog put a finger to Kaj's carotid artery, then pulled out and shined a pen light into his one good eye. "Barely."

O'Quinn looked at Kaj's eyes, both of which were open. The glass one stared blankly into a place that no one else could see—while the good eye, with its dark pupil swallowing the retina, was now quivering spasmodically. "We can't let him die. I still need to know what's in his mind."

Chapter 2

THE DOVE-LIKE SOUNDS of a child singing a nonsense nursery rhyme, *"Kri Kraw Toads Foot, Geese Walk, Bare Foot"* echoed through the shafts of darkness and light in the shadowy space. The lilting voice was pure and innocent and carefree in the way only children's voices can be. Voices that don't know yet.

The song was coming from a paper-thin computer tablet, the glow of which illuminated the eyes of the man who sat in the shadows watching it. With unwavering focus the watching man stared at the screen, which was playing a high definition digital transfer of thirty-year-old surveillance film of the beautiful four-year-old boy whose soft voice was singing.

The images of the boy were reflected in the man's eyes, eyes that were vivid and brown, full of strength and pain, depth, sadness and hope.

It was through these soulful eyes he absorbed the child he barely recognized, the one he strained so hard to remember. Like his own, the boy's eyes were his most striking feature. They were both innocent and intelligent, but with that youthful sparkle that hadn't yet been dulled by the harshness of life.

Superimposed by an electronic chyron underneath the boy's image were the words: *JAROD 2/4/83, PSYCHOGENIC STUDIES, FOR OFFICIAL CENTRE USE ONLY.*

The watching man didn't have official use—he had stolen these and hundreds of other archives of young Jarod and was consumed with watching them.

Especially this one.

Because *this one was the first.*

As he continued to hum to himself, Young Jarod picked up building blocks—some sophisticated, some wooden, some plastic, some metal and placed them confidently on a structure that could not be seen in the surveillance footage from the current camera angle.

But there were many camera angles in the footage to choose from and the watching man switched to a different one.

Young Jarod looked to a side wall where projections of the Empire State Building, Times Square, the Brooklyn Bridge and other images of Manhattan flashed by. Young Jarod stared again at his creation and placed one last block. He then stepped back to take it all in. Satisfied with what he had accomplished, he stated in a sing-songy way, "I'mmmm finished."

Choosing another camera angle, the watching man saw that the last block the boy placed was a miniature radio tower atop a building. A building he recognized was an incredible scale model of the World Trade Center, Tower Two. The watching man widened the image so he could marvel at what this four-year-old boy had created from mere Legos and wooden blocks; it was not just the World Trade Center, but amazingly, in powerfully majestic and infinite detail, a forced perspective scale model of the entire skyline of Manhattan.

"Heeeellllllooooo?!" Young Jarod looked around the room for the location of his observers he knew had to be watching. The boy walked toward the camera and squished his face playfully against a sliding glass door—a door that any viewer would now realize was a two-way observation mirror looking into Young Jarod's workspace. He cupped his mouth so 'they' could hear. "I said, I'm finished."

The watching man switched to a much wider POV that revealed the space Young Jarod had been working in was actually a freestanding, rectangular-shaped isolation chamber built in the middle of a large warehouse-like space. The chamber was surrounded by dozens of remotely controlled observation cameras, all positioned to peer in through windows, sliding glass doors and even the glass ceiling of the structure, in order to digitally document Young Jarod's every move.

The sound of approaching footsteps from the footage drew the watching man's attention to the left side of the image. Appearing there was Sydney, a psychogenic experimental scientist in his late twenties. Distinguished and handsome in an academic way, his disheveled hair and rumpled tweed jacket were a testament to his many sleepless nights as he pursued his studies passionately. He walked to and stopped outside the sliding glass door that Young Jarod was pressing his face against. With an expression of excited amazement, Sydney gazed in at Young Jarod and then began adjusting the camera that was recording the boy's face through the glass.

The watching man switched to the perspective of a camera Sydney turned to and addressed straight into the lens. In his clipped but elegant European accent, he spoke directly to the voyeuristic observers somewhere at the end of this electronic umbilical.

"This one has only been with us 36 hours and he's already demonstrating more talent than any of our others. I'd like to keep him for myself." Sydney slid open the mirrored glass door, knelt down to be face-to-face with the four-year-old and in his kindest voice said, "Hi, Jarod. I'm Sydney. I'll be taking care of you for a while."

Young Jarod detected something in the Belgian's tonality that made him uncomfortable, something that didn't ring true and caused the innocence in his eyes to drain away and his voice to tremble with apprehension. "Why? Where are my mom and dad?"

The watching man replayed this moment over and over: *"Why? Where are my mom and dad? Where are my mom and dad … Where are my mom and dad …"*

With these words echoing in his mind, the watching man stared into the eyes of the four-year-old boy. The screen then went dark and Young Jarod's eyes were gone, leaving only the reflection of the eyes of the man Young Jarod had grown up to become.

Eyes that were no longer sad.

Eyes that were determined.

Eyes that had a job to do.

Chapter 3

SHE LOOKED JUST like her mother.

And like her mother, she was an alarmingly stunning, jaw-dropping beauty.

On a physical scale of 1 to 10, Miss Parker was a 13—a lucky 13. In her early 30s, she still had the body of an eighteen-year-old. It was a flawless body—the body of a dancer—the body of an athlete—the kind of body that artists carve in marble. But it was the face that turned heads. Framed in long brunette locks, she had the face of a goddess—just like her mother. The two of them, in side-by-side photographs at similar ages, looked like twins.

Identical twins.

Yet the beauty of Miss Parker's face was as much a dichotomy as was the nature of her inner being. In both, delicate features contrasted with sharp angles—none more so than her voluptuous full lips that were soft and enticing against her intelligent eyes that, like her heart, were known to go from engaging to predatory at the drop of a hat.

A lethal dichotomy.

It was her attitude that made her volatile. Miss Parker reminded many of those who knew her of a young Lauren Bacall mixed with a pit bull. She was the sexiest woman and the toughest 'man' <u>she</u> knew and many of the fools she refused to suffer insisted she was permanently PMSing.

That's what the chiseled nude Adonis beneath her was thinking while she was writhing atop him. Still wearing her black silk thigh-high stockings and Jimmy Choo Viper Calf Hair stilettos, the sweat dripped down her back in communion with her innermost basic instincts and pleasure.

He couldn't get enough of her. He was happy to be chewed up and spit out by her seductive power and wouldn't have traded his place in the world for anything—and couldn't if he'd wanted to, seeing as she had him shackled to her four-poster bed. When she noticed his eyes rolling back in his head she slapped, then forcefully grabbed his face. "Never lose eye contact!"

Her sexual sycophant nodded, submitting to her domination, which was exactly how she liked it. She needed that power, craved it. It was the only way she could lose herself. By being on top and in total control—figuratively and literally—she could forget everything else, flee into her most primitive, powerful, dominating self. The only thing that could pull her out of these escapist moments was a special ring on her cell phone.

Which is what stopped her physical grinding and pulled her mind back into the game. As she reached for her Bluetooth, Adonis scrunched his face, "Seriously?"

Miss Parker swung her leg over his chest, pinned his throat against the headboard with her spiked heel and for good measure, Kegel-gripped him into breathless silence. Then with a yearning childlike lilt, she answered the call. "Hi, Daddy."

She could immediately detect the stress in her father's usually upbeat and forceful voice. "Angel, I need you."

Those words—no, their tone, caught her off guard. "Of course, Daddy," she quickly recovered, "anything for you. I'll be there in ..."

Mr. Parker clicked off before she could finish, leaving her hanging. Leaving her stung. But that was okay. She understood her father was a very busy man, a *busy and important* man. She'd always known that. A million things clicked through her clever, cunning mind as she dismounted and unlocked one of her sexual chew toy's cuffed hands.

"Recess is over."

She looked at his face and searched the back of her mind, but came up empty. "What was your name again?"

"Peter," he said, feeling unappreciated and now a little degraded.

Miss Parker smiled to herself sardonically. "And the irony never ends." She placed the handcuff key on Pete's forehead. "Now get out."

His voice cracked with more whine than assertion. "But, I'm not done."

"I am." She got off the bed, lit a Pall Mall Red and looked out the window of her penthouse in Mid City, Blue Cove, Delaware. Ignoring her meaningless lover, Miss Parker puffed away as he freed himself and skulked off. As she gazed down upon the thousands of lights twinkling below in the city, she thought about one thing and one thing only—the phone call.

Her daddy *called her*. He *needed her*. He *was reaching out to her*. She was resolved in that instant that she would not fail him.

Chapter 4

WITH ITS SLEEK razor-sharp edges slicing through the azure blue waves and futuristic hull designed to limit wind drag, the Porsche R double F 135 Elegance was one of the swiftest speed boats to ever skim across the sea. None of which Miss Parker gave a damn about.

What she did give a damn about was that it wasn't fast enough for her. Miss Parker, as always, was terribly impatient. The middle-aged man at the helm next to her was not. He was enjoying every second of it. "Wonderful out here, isn't it?"

"Yeah, it's a regular day at Disney," Miss Parker said as she flicked her cigarette butt into the Atlantic. "How much longer?"

Before the captain could answer, a voice with a clipped European accent spoke up. "You'll have to excuse my partner; her sense of perceived purpose often interferes with her ability to enjoy life in the present moment or the beauty surrounding it."

Miss P shot a glaring look at Sydney—a look that, if it could kill, would have over the years left tens of thousands of bodies in her wake.

Though he was thirty years older than he was in the surveillance footage recorded the day Jarod had so impressed him for the first time, in his middle age Sydney was still very attractive and had an air of refined elegance about him. It was an *air* Miss Parker could stand about as much as she could stand his cologne. She stared at him with utter disdain as their eyes met. Sydney smiled at her in his enigmatic way.

Miss Parker hated enigma—especially his.

"Syd, only you could have created a big enough mess to put me back in the field."

"I am thrilled to be working with you again as well, Miss Parker."

"<u>For</u>. Not with. We're not *partners*. We're reluctant associates at best."

Miss Parker pointed at him with the same finger on which she always wore the square platinum wedding ring that had belonged to her mother. She pointed at people a lot. "And just so we don't get off on the wrong foot, let me clarify a couple things. I don't like you. Never really have. I've been sent to bring back your 'little experiment' and that's what I intend to do. So let's just put a stake in the 'chit chat,' shall we?"

Hiking one of her exquisitely sculpted legs onto the boat sill, Miss Parker leaned down to light another cigarette.

"Impressive sight."

Miss Parker slowly raised her face, meeting the Captain's smile. "Must have been at sea a long time, Captain Hook."

"Name's Hoke, ma'am, and it's not your gam that caught my eye. It's what's ahead."

Parker and Sydney looked and caught their first glimpse of the high-tech forest of wind turbines, hundreds of white windmills soaring up from the waves with their spinning blades harvesting energy blown from the heavens.

Hoke guided the boat towards the tallest of the mills, one built atop an oil platform-like superstructure that stood in the center of the others like a scarecrow in the middle of a mechanical cornfield. The back of Miss Parker's head nearly touched her shoulders as she looked up and up and up as the boat slowly approached, then slid beneath the towering edifice, the whole time Parker wondering what the hell Jarod had been doing on this thing.

As if reading her mind, Hoke explained that the structure, ten stories above them, served as both the control center for the turbines and the living quarters for the electrical engineer who maintained them. Hoke reversed the engines to stop the forward momentum and then hopped onto the dock platform and tied them in securely.

As he did he continued, "Monitoring the turbines is like running a lighthouse, solitary confinement really. But Jarod loved living out here. Said it gave him time to think."

Syd perked up, his psychoanalytical mind grasping for clues as to Jarod's temperament. "Did he say about what?"

Hoke offered his calloused hand to Miss Parker, which she flatly ignored, hopping out onto the dock under her own power. Hoke shrugged, then, leading them to the open-air elevator, answered Sydney.

"A million and one things. Especially the truth about what was really going on out here." Miss Parker shot Hoke an inquisitive look. "What truth was that?"

"The environmental damage caused by these twirlers that the company was covering up."

As they ascended, Miss Parker scanned the placid setting of pristine windmills churning clean energy and twisted her brow. "Enviro damage? Looks like an Al Gore wet dream to me."

"Looks that way on the surface—but it's what Jarod discovered below the waves that was the problem."

Syd asked. "And what was that?"

"That the company placed this wind farm right smack-dab in the hub of a whale mating ground and that the undersea acoustic waves the turbines generate were disrupting the songs of migrating whales that come here to reproduce. Jarod proved the noise was actually triggering an avoidance reaction in the males in search of mates. Because of what he exposed, the company's been ordered to shut down the turbines three months a year— gonna cost them zillions. But it's worth it for the future of the planet."

Syd smiled proudly. Miss P didn't. She deadpanned, "Certainly wouldn't want to interrupt the whale whoopee."

The elevator opened and Miss Parker blew past the men out onto the tarmac-like base of the platform. Hoke looked at Syd, who just shook his head. "She's a pistol, huh?"

Syd looked at him soberly, "Pressed against my temple."

As Hoke led them toward a metallic square building that served as the living quarters as well as the support base for the windmill's tower, he smiled. "Truth is, I'm glad Jarod blew the whistle on the company." Then he had a thought and his smile faded. "But, I'm sad too. I miss the guy, even if he was a little weird."

Miss Parker looked to the captain. "How so?"

"Everything with him was twenty questions and all about the same subject."

"Which was?" Sydney wanted to know. He *needed* to know.

Hoke got a confounded look on his face. "People."

Miss Parker raised an eyebrow. "Wait a minute, you're telling us Curious George isolated himself out here in Waterworld, to find out about *people*?"

Hoke stopped at the building's door and turned. "Yep. And he couldn't find out enough. 'What makes 'em happy?' 'What makes 'em sad?' 'What is love?' 'How does it feel?' 'How do you know if you're 'in it?'" Strange questions for an obviously brilliant man—which is why I have to ask you two one of my own."

"What is that?" Sydney asked, his mind captivated by these insights.

"Are you ribbin' me about Jarod not really being a scientist?"

Miss Parker looked to Sydney, then back to the Captain, "Why do you ask?"

Hoke scratched his head, confounded again. "Well, if he wasn't—how do you explain this?"

Hoke opened the door to the living quarters and when Sydney and Miss Parker saw what was inside, they had no explanation at all ...

Chapter 5

ENORMOUS MULTIPRONGED BOLTS of electricity exploded through the room of the main building that Hoke led Miss Parker and Sydney into.

Walking inside of the cavernous living quarters, Miss Parker looked up at the sparking currents emanating from an eight-foot diameter shiny metal orb hanging high in the far left corner of the room. The man-made lightning bolts flash-danced across the ceiling in psychotic fashion, until they were absorbed by a tall metallic column in the diagonal corner to her right.

Miss P hated lightning since early childhood and tried to keep her fear in check, but Hoke noticed the distress on her face. "Place used to freak me out, too. But not Jarod. He'd just sit there under these sparkers for hours."

And that is when Sydney first noticed it.

Precisely in the center of the room, directly underneath the electrical storm above, sat a Lazy Boy recliner. Sydney smiled warmly. To himself. He didn't want Miss Parker to know that it meant something special to him. Drawn to the well-worn, black-leather chair, he rubbed his hand gently across the headrest, across the spot on which Jarod's head had rested.

"Jarod had me bring that chair out here special." Hoke grinned. "And he'd just lay back in it for hours."

Miss P looked up at the lightning, then back at the chair, annoyed. "Just chillin' in the electric chair?"

"Yep. Spent all his time playing with the stuff in that box next to it and just—*thinking*."

Syd looked over to the side of the chair and saw the box Hoke was re-ferring to. But it wasn't a box—it was a wooden toy chest.

Hoke shook his head. "And just when I was getting such a kick out of the guy, he up and shipped out—and in a hurry too." Hoke pointed to an alcove in the near left corner of the room, where the flashing lightning bolts sporadically illuminated a cot, a nightstand and a half-packed duffle bag. "Left most of his personal stuff too."

Music to Miss Parker's ears, she shot a dismissive deadpan to Hoke, "You've been very helpful, Cappy."

Hoke got the message. "I'll, ah—wait for you folks on the Elegance."

As Hoke closed the door on his exit, Miss Parker noticed something: hand drawn on the back of the door was what appeared to be the numeral 8 lying on its side, the symbol for *infinity* which she knew to be The Pretender's favorite. Next to it were the hand scrawled words—*Jarod was here!*—and hanging just below them a small red notebook. She pulled it off the nail it dangled from and thumbed through its pages—pages that looked like something from a child's school project. With an eyebrow raised in wonderment, she closed the notebook, walked over to Syd and slapped it into his chest. "Shamu's savior left his calling card."

Syd opened the notebook and found dozens of printed internet articles documenting the wind facility being shut down and the mating grounds assured for future whale reproduction.

Parker 360'd looking for something and spotted it: Hanging on the wall in the far right corner was an electrical wall panel with a huge ON/OFF breaker switch. She bee-lined to it and yanked the lever, killing the storm above them. The bolts were replaced with normal lighting, which revealed all that had been hiding in the shadows: dozens of what looked like props from an old sci-fi movie—crude, hand-made electrical experiments of every shape and size.

Miss P eyed the room with dismay. "His decorating sense leaves a lot to be desired." Syd's look, though, realized what he was seeing and, like a proud papa, broke into a big smile. "Not decoration, Miss Parker—innovation." Syd called her attention to the metal orb and then over to the metallic column. "Including this magnifying transmitter, Jarod has recreated Nikola Tesla's most famous devices."

"Okay, Syd, I'm tapping out. Who's Nikki-T?"

"An innovator, futurist and rival of Thomas Edison's. An unparalleled engineer who invented some of the most important electrical mechanisms in the world. Though now recognized as a genius, during his time he was thought of as a mad man."

Miss Parker snorted. "How apropos."

Sydney shot her a defiant look. "Jarod is not mad."

"Yeah, that's why he spent days glued to a Barcalounger playing with his toys under 80,000 volts of fun."

Sydney sighed. "That red notebook and everything Jarod left here means something. If we hope to find him, we'll have to decipher what they are."

Turning his attention to the toy chest, Sydney beheld the three items he found inside. The first was a child's magnetic play set. Sydney examined the magnets with reverence, just as he knew Jarod would have. Sydney imagined the keen wonder in Jarod's eyes as he held the magnets and observed them attract and repel each other for the first time. Syd knew his Pretender always handled things that intrigued him with the inquisitive sparkle that most cease to possess soon after childhood and that this passionate, intellectual curiosity was something Jarod had never lost. Syd tried to discern what Jarod must have been thinking when he last held these smooth pieces of charged metal. He knew Jarod's thoughts had to do with Tesla, but he wasn't sure how or why, so he tried to work the problem out aloud.

"Tesla is best known for his extraordinary contributions to the development of electrical power. He invented the alternating current and because of it he is now considered the man who illuminated the world. But his true genius lay in electromagnetism."

Miss Parker rolled her eyes. "Let's see what kind of illumination your genius left behind before he blew this hellacious disco." Miss P walked to where Jarod's abandoned duffle was laying atop the cot, unzipped and began to search through it. As she did, Syd removed the second item from the toy chest, a rolled up poster that he unfurled. The magnets had confused him, but the images on the poster completely bewildered him.

Parker noticed Sydney's furrowed brow. "That pathetic look on your face is pure genius too, Syd—if only I could bottle it."

Lost in his thoughts, Syd didn't react to her. Miss P disliked not being reacted to, so she jabbed again. "You going to tell me what you found or just stand there looking lost?"

Syd turned the poster toward her. Printed on it was something that looked like a Rorschach test with multicolored neon lines, denoting pathways within. "It's a brain map of fruit fly neuron clusters."

Parker smirked. "Just like the one hanging in my closet." She continued digging though Jarod's belongings. "He definitely left in a hurry. Must've discovered Daddy sent me to bring him back."

Syd gazed around the room, trying to make sense of it all. "Tesla was a genius others thought mad and these are all his experiments. I think that's the message he was leaving with these—but the magnets and the neuron chart—have me baffled."

Unsatisfied with her slow progress, Miss Parker dumped the duffle contents onto the cot. "Try a misdirect, Freud. It's not Tesla he's thinking like—it's Houdini. Sleight of hand, *look over here, little monkeys. Now chase your tails while I'm really over there.*"

"You're wrong, Miss Parker." Syd contemplated the magnets and the poster. "These are bread crumbs he's leaving for me to follow. He wants to keep me close behind him."

"How sweet. Your teddy bear is out in the world but wants to make sure his emotional umbilical cord with his 'Big Daddy' hasn't been severed."

"He left these things to help me understand what he is doing, why he's doing it. He doesn't want me to be upset with him."

"You know, when the great shrinks of the world get through with you and Magnet Boy, they're going to have to redefine that whole Helsinki Syndrome thing."

Miss Parker's mood then suddenly changed. She spotted a business envelope, ripped it open, a big smile creeping over her face.

Syd caught Parker's expression. "What is it?"

With a spring in her step, she walked over and cockily slapped the envelope into Syd's open palm. "His bank statement, Syd-ster. I just found my way to track him down."

"No. *That's* a misdirect." She shot him a dismissive glare, but the Belgian continued. "Do you truly believe a man capable of making all this would leave something that obvious behind—by accident?"

"Syd, it's always the simple mistakes the smart ones, like your monster, make."

"Jarod is <u>not</u> a monster and he doesn't make mistakes. He's a Pretender—he can be anyone he wants to be."

"Whatever gets you through the night, Dr. Frankenstein. You created him. I just want to know where the hell he is."

Reaching into the toy chest, Sydney removed the last item that Jarod left behind—a college textbook. Its title sent a chill down his spine.

He looked at Miss Parker with trepidation. "I have no idea where he is—but I'm afraid I know what he's doing."

Reading the sudden anxiety on his face, Miss Parker snatched the text-book out of his hand. The title read: *TECHNIQUES OF MODERN SURGERY*.

Chapter 6

AS HE STOOD, the frayed hem of the Pretender's long buttoned-up coat rippled in the breeze, its upturned collar buffeting his rugged face as the wind ratcheted up to a cutting gust. His deep, intelligent, caring brown eyes, framed by his collar-length locks, peered out of the shadows of the alley.

He peeled off his thrift shop coat, leaving it to be found by someone in need. With his outer skin shed, the Pretender began to morph into someone more befitting of this uptown environment. With two graceful sweeps of his hands, his once unruly mane was shaped into a style similar to that worn by others who he had observed were in his new 'profession.' He tugged his clean, fashionably understated sweater into place and gave a subtle pull up on his slacks, transforming them from baggy to sleek and revealing the shine on his loafers that had previously been covered.

And while this transformation was by design, there was a flash of self-surprise on his face at the sight of his reflection in a storefront window, as if for an instant he was seeing between the blurred lines of his personas, catching a glimpse of his real self.

Of the real Jarod.

As he stepped into the light of day onto Second, Jarod's very physicality transformed as well. After several steps, his convincing wilted posture was gone, replaced with a stature of sophistication and the strength of a Manhattan professional. His jaw was set more rigidly, his eyes, though still warm, took on a mysterious glint now—his entire persona taking on an air of enticing mystery as he became focused on his next destination across the street.

Guardian General Hospital.

At 13 stories, the Gothic revival structure had lorded over this section of NYC for more than a century and with its looming shadow it was easy to see how it came to be known simply as *The Guardian*.

But Jarod knew better.

He knew if you looked carefully, you could see it was actually two hospitals in one.

And that's why Jarod was here.

He knew that behind the original towering stone edifice was a modern glass and steel Annex built atop the ten-story parking structure tucked in the shadows of The Guardian's hind end. The Annex was all but hidden from street view and seemed to lurk secretively behind its mother as if she were hiding it on purpose.

As he crossed the street and strode toward the Emergency Room entrance, how ironic it was, Jarod thought, that there would be two angels of alabaster standing watch outside this otherwise ominous-looking place.

And while both intrigued and comforted by these smiling angels, Jarod knew it was the *demons* who worked inside The Guardian that would pose the biggest threat to his monumental task at hand.

Chapter 7

IN ITS 113-YEAR existence, Guardian General prided itself in having never turned away a patient. Because of that reputation it was always busting at the seams with people in need.

This day was no different.

The injured and sick spilled out from the ER waiting room into the hallway, as did gurneys from overcrowded rooms. The noise of patients, loved ones, harried nurses, busy orderlies and the constant crackling of the PA system blended into a symphony of chaos. *"Dr. Su, please report to the ER, Dr. Su ..."*

~~~

Like an invisible Moses, Jarod walked slowly through the parting sea of the suffering masses. In a place like this, even with his impressive stature, he went unnoticed—just like so many of the frustrated infirmed who found themselves waiting interminably as the clock ticked backwards and their pain increased with every breath. *"Dr. Su, please report to the ER, Dr. Su ..."*

Jarod stopped in the middle of the mayhem, taking in everything he saw.

If Jarod had been noticed, an observant person would have wondered what that purposeful look was in his eyes. Was it empathy or guile? Honesty or deceit? He looked like a man surveying a situation—a man on a mission—but what mission was it? What *was* that purpose in his eyes?

"Outta the way!"

An orderly pushing a gurney with a groaning man writhing on top raced past Jarod. Running alongside and barking orders was an intensely focused African-American nurse, Gloria Pate. Having worn the white uniform for 27 years, 19 of them as the charge nurse, Gloria's appearance dated her way past her 40s—her exterior covered with hardened armor, her tongue stinging with the sharpness of ammonia, and permanent exhaustion etched onto her face. *"Dr. Su, please report to the ER, Dr. Su ..."*

"Tami! Where are those medipacs?!"

An earnest and flat-out cute 20-year-old candy striper rushed through the crowd with her hands full of medical pouches of solution. "Right here!" She offered them to Gloria. The veteran nurse brusquely placed them on the gurney and then told the orderly to "Get him to O.R. 5, stat."

As he whisked the patient away, Gloria turned toward Tami.

"Where the hell is Dr. Su?"

Tami shrugged. "We've been paging, calling him. Nothing."

Gloria shook her head. "Must not have cell service at the Mercedes dealership."

Before Tami could respond, a shriek cut through the commotion. Gloria looked down to where an older Hispanic woman in a wheelchair was tugging on her scrubs.

Gloria spoke firmly. "Ma'am, like I said before, we'll get to you as soon as possible." Gloria glared at Tami. "Didn't I tell you to deal with her?"

"I tried, but I—I can't understand anything she's saying." Tami pleaded.

"You wanna work here for real—you better learn how to problem solve." Gloria stomped off to the next crisis. *"Dr. Su, please report to the ER, Dr. Su ..."*

Tami leaned down to the Hispanic woman who moaned as she spoke, manipulating her fingers wildly. Tami was perplexed. "I'm sorry—I don't know what you're trying to tell me."

Jarod calmly approached. "She says she has intense pain—her abdomen—she fell down a flight of stairs—and she's been waiting hours to see someone."

Taken by surprise, Tami stood, immediately meeting Jarod's striking brown eyes. "You can understand what she's saying?"

"Not with her lips." Jarod wiggled his fingers. "With her hands. She's deaf."

Tami stepped back and watched in awe as Jarod knelt down, smiled to the woman and began communicating with her in sign language. "You're going to be okay. This young lady ..." Jarod looked up. "What's your name?"

"Tami. Tami Moore."

Jarod looked back at the woman. "Tami is going to help you."

As a tear rolled down her cheek, the deaf woman finally showed relief as she signed back. Jarod wiped away her tear. He signed, "No. God bless you."

Tami looked at Jarod adoringly as he stood. "On the surface she may not appear as bad as the others, but internally she may be worse. She needs to be x-rayed."

Still overwhelmed, she grabbed the handles of the wheelchair. "I'll have someone do that right away." As Tami wheeled her down the hall, the deaf woman looked back at Jarod. As they shared an expression of human connection—Jarod spun around to see the ER doors crashing open with a *BOOM!*

EMTs rushed in a gurney carrying a woman in critical condition—her clothes torn and bloody, her body covered in cuts and abrasions.

Gloria ran at full speed to join the EMT's. "Car accident, intermittent consciousness, BP is 80 over 40 and dropping fast. Pulse 110, rapid and thready. She's cyanotic."

Gloria flew into action, slapping a BP monitor on the woman's arm as orderlies and nurses began swarming in.

"Stall 3 NOW!"

As they hastily rolled the gurney into the treatment area, the woman let out a plaintive wail.

"Where the hell is Dr. Su!?" Gloria yelled.

Tami rushed up. "He's still not answering!"

Gloria gritted her teeth. "Get someone else!"

"There is no one else. Dr. Thompson is with a gunshot victim in 4 and Dodson is in the O.R. with an appendectomy."

Gloria looked at the BP monitor—70 over 30. "Then call Dr. Bilson! STAT!"

Gloria turned back to the woman, who was now gasping for breath and losing color. "Don't you code on me. Don't you code!"

Tami rushed to a wall phone, surprised to see Jarod coming in—rolling up his sleeves.

Gloria ripped the woman's shirt open, examining her injuries to determine the severity of her condition. But whatever was causing her patient's distress was above Gloria's pay grade.

"Start her on a two-liter of bag of Lactated Ringer's." The staff turned to see who had said this. It was Jarod, who joined Gloria and examined the patient while putting on latex gloves.

"Her cuts and bruises are superficial—search lower."

Gloria was dumbfounded, then blurted, "Get this man outta my ER— he doesn't work here!"

"Apparently neither do your doctors," Jarod responded evenly, as he began examining further down the patient's belly.

Gloria found Tami standing near the wall phone and snapped, "Call security! Get this man out of here and find me a doctor!" Tami hesitated for a moment, then followed her orders.

Jarod looked up definitively at Gloria. "I *am* a doctor!" He then directed Gloria's attention to a pulsating bulge below the woman's navel. "Abdominal aortic aneurysm—probably ruptured during the accident."

An alarm sounded on the BP monitor. The other nurse said, "60 over 20—we're losing her."

Jarod locked eyes with Gloria, his confident gaze flustering this woman who never got flustered. She looked at the bulge, her mind racing. "You need to CT that before—hell, we hafta be sure!"

"I am sure." Jarod turned to the other nurse. "I'll need a stent-graft package and the fluoroscopic x-ray."

Silent looks exchanged between the people in the room. No one knew how to react.

The weakened woman let out another moan.

Gloria was paralyzed with uncertainty, as the other nurse said, "50 over 15. She barely has a pulse."

Jarod stared intently at Gloria. "Are we going to do this or watch her bleed out?"

Everyone stood frozen. After a tense moment, the charge nurse nodded.

The ER circus exploded into action.

Jarod's requested tools were brought to him on a metal operating tray and an x-ray monitor was rolled in and powered up. Jarod immediately adjusted the mobile fluoroscope above his patient's torso that converted x-rays sent through the patient's body into a live endovascular image visible on an attached monitor. As the visualization of her internal injuries appeared, it was clear her aneurysm had ruptured and she was hemorrhaging massively.

Of all the onlookers, none was more focused than Tami. She watched, captivated, as Jarod took the scalpel and seamlessly made a small craniocaudal incision above the woman's right hip, then cleared the subcutaneous connective tissue to expose her femoral artery. Jarod then placed two loose ligatures around it and made a small incision in the artery between them.

He held out his hand. "Vascular sheath." Gloria picked up one of the flexible clear tubes from the operating tray and handed it to him. He slowly introduced it into the patient's artery to keep it from collapsing. As he worked, the woman began to whimper. Jarod scanned the staff. Everyone had a job except for the candy striper. Jarod startled her. "Tami, come here and hold her hand."

Tami looked around nervously—*me?* Then, swallowing her fear, she stepped over next to Jarod and gently took the distressed woman's hand. Responding to the comforting touch, the woman squeezed her hand back and seemed to relax just a bit. Jarod smiled. "Good. Now tell her she's not alone. When you're afraid, alone is the worst thing in the world to be." Tami was taken aback by his instructions, but she leaned down and whispered reassuringly into the woman's ear.

Jarod held out his hand, "SIA." She handed him the 'Stent Introducer Apparatus'—a stainless steel housing with a handle that controlled the flexible, guiding catheter.

Jarod slipped the tip of this soft plastic tube into the mouth of the vascular sheath and into the artery itself. Through it he introduced a thin wire, and using the x-ray visualization as a road map, Jarod remotely guided it within the twist and turns of the delicate artery.

As Jarod continued, two security guards stormed in along with Guardian General's Chief Administrator—an erudite, impeccably dressed man of 50 with a vexed look on his face. Dr. Jonah Bilson asked breathlessly, "I received a 911—about an intruder?" Gloria didn't have time for her boss now—instead of answering she SHUSHED him rudely, then gestured to Jarod and said, "He's working."

The peeved administrator spiked her with a nasty glare. "Who's working?"

Never losing focus, the Pretender said, "Dr. Bilson, my name is Jarod. I'm the guy who was supposed to meet you in your office five minutes ago, but I got hung up with this."

Bilson, irritated and now confused, looked at the monitor to see what Jarod was talking about. Within moments, the Chief forgot about the urgent call and everything else frustrating him and became completely absorbed with and impressed by what he saw. With an artistry that would take most men years to master, Jarod bypassed the fluid-filled sack, then expanded the stent-graft reinforcing the wall of the artery, cutting off the blood supply to the aneurysm.

The moment he did, the blood began flowing normally, the hemorrhaging stopped and before everyone's astonished eyes, the bulge on the abdomen slowly began to shrink. Tami looked at the woman's cheeks and grinned ear to ear. "She's pinking up."

The patient's eyes slowly flickered open. The first thing they found was Jarod's growing smile.

At that, the suffocating tension in the ER finally dissipated, replaced by an overwhelming appreciation for Jarod and a collective admiration of his work.

Few knew that Jarod's real work at Guardian General Hospital had only just begun.

Chapter 8

GUARDIAN GENERAL'S CHIEF Administrator Dr. Jonah Bilson's *raison d'etre* was primal greed and arrogance. The egotistical asshole was fueled by it, both inside and out. His haughtiness, though, wasn't a fault of his character—it was his birthright.

To some the term *Boston Brahmin* describes a group of wealthy 19th-century elitists infamous for their scholarly and pretentious nature. To Dr. Jonah Bilson, a 15th-generational member of this self-anointed Yankee aristocracy, it described *family* and he wore this progenal crest of inherited moral superiority as a badge of honor.

It was who he had been since birth and it defined his existence. Yet his self-infatuation wasn't something he was consciously in tune with. What he was self-aware of, however, was his attentiveness to details. He was currently concentrating on those details as he stood in the hallway outside the Emergency Room. Concentrating on himself that is.

"Dr. Su, please report to the ER, Dr. Su ..."

The conceited doctor stared at himself in the reflection of a hallway mirror and was quite taken with who he saw returning his gaze: a distinguished man of intelligence, stature and style. As he straightened the razor-sharp crease in his pants, Bilson reveled in the amount of pleasure he received by standing out from the 'huddled masses' and by how he accentuated that differentiation so purposefully with his fashion.

Bilson was decked out in an immaculate white suit, a high collar Jermyn Street dress shirt and monogrammed Hermès tie with a matching pocket square that screamed *Dandy*. Admiring himself, he then tended to the buttons on his coat sleeves. Buttons that he liked to inform others were not merely ornamentation or some kind of cheapie decoration, but *real* buttonholes with sleeves that actually buttoned up.

As with clothes, in every aspect of his life, details were what separated the purebreds from the mongrels. An innate practitioner of the odious art of physiognomy—the assessment of a person's character or personality from their outward appearance—Bilson took great pride in presenting himself impeccably at all times and appreciated that quality in others.

That Jarod shared a similar self worth was the first thing he'd noted when his new young doctor exited the emergency room. From his Canali flat front wool trousers, tan Italian dress shoes and caramel cashmere V-Neck—variations of which hung proudly in the older doctor's closet—Jarod was a perfectly blended composition of couture in brown. Bilson was also impressed with the confident manner with which Jarod carried himself. From head to toe, like Bilson himself, Jarod was self-assured and meticulous, even down to his manicure, where the shape of his nails perfectly matched his fingertips. Exactly as Bilson's were.

In fact, from Dr. Jarod Russell's impeccable Ivy League résumé to his experience in the field, Bilson could find no flaw in Jarod at all. Bilson actually felt he couldn't have possibly hired a better young doctor—unless he'd been able to clone himself.

Of course, Bilson didn't know Jarod had been following and studying him for a week, that Jarod knew where he lived, what foods he ate, what clothes he wore. That Jarod knew Bilson as well or better than he knew himself, that he knew everything about the grandiose bastard except what exactly it was that he did in the Annex wing of the hospital.

But he was going to find out.

Jarod rubbed his temples, still coming off the intensity of the procedure he'd just completed, not noticing Dr. Bilson approaching him.

"Nothing sharpens the senses like baptism by fire, eh, Dr. Russell?"

Jarod looked up, then quickly straightened himself and regained his composure. "Yes, sir—and I'm sorry about not making it to your office ..."

"Dr. Su, please report to the ER, Dr. Su ..."

Bilson chuckled ironically, hearing the page on the P.A. "Are you kidding me? You saved a life. Your curriculum vitae was superlative—but seeing you in action—well, let's just say that's the kind of dedication I've been looking for around here." He offered Jarod his hand. "Welcome aboard."

"Coming from someone as esteemed as you, that's quite a compliment. Thank you, Doctor." Jarod took it and shook firmly.

Gloria and Tami emerged from the ER and into the hallway. They spotted the two men and walked toward them. Gloria carried a clipboard and a determined look on her face, but Tami, upon seeing Jarod, was aglow like a schoolgirl. As they joined the doctors, Bilson continued with his accolades.

"And don't think your commitment to detail in that procedure went unnoticed—especially when you could have easily turned the *close* over to an intern or resident. Jarod, your performance was nothing short of outstanding."

"Well, I would say I was doing that to impress you, but the truth is, I needed to practice my stitching on a human patient." Jarod looked at Bilson with a deadpan expression. Gloria and Tami exchanged a quizzical look.

Bilson was taken aback for a moment until he convinced himself that Jarod was kidding and let go with his most charismatic Charity League chortle. "Very witty, Doctor. Your self-deprecating humor is refreshing as well. It reminds me of—well, *me*."

Gloria rolled her eyes and handed the clipboard to Dr. Bilson. "I need signatures on lines 14, 18 and 22." He took them and signed. "Dr. Russell, for future reference, when you need something around here, please ask Gloria. I may run this institution, but she is the boss."

Gloria looked at Bilson disdainfully. "If I was the boss I'd hire more than one new doctor, plus a whole slew of other help."

Bilson forced a supercilious smile. "The hospital then would be bankrupt. Not that I'd expect you to understand that." He dotted the 'i' over his name and handed the clipboard to Gloria.

"Dr. Su, please report to the ER, Dr. Su ... "

As the P.A. announcement made the same incessant plea, an Asian doctor entered the ER hallway. The slovenly Dr. Hiro Su was the antithesis of what one would picture a middle-aged Asian physician to look like—something that always irritated Bilson. But the Chief had hired him for other reasons and therefore overlooked his dumpiness and chronic tardiness as much as he could.

Tami was the first to see Dr. Su. She nudged Gloria, who looked up from her clipboard, then after spotting him, got a mini-scowl on her face. "So nice of him to make time to come into work today."

As Su approached, Bilson glanced at his Baume & Mercier watch, then at him. "Excuse my French—but where the hell have you been?"

Unaffected, Dr. Su flatly offered, "Sorry, I was in the Annex—or have you forgotten I'm not just a surgeon anymore?" Su then laid eyes on Jarod, gave him the once over and came up negative. "Who's the GQ model?"

Jarod offered his hand. "Dr. Russell. Please call me Jarod."

Su coldly left Jarod's hand hanging until Bilson interjected. "I'd shake if I were you and while you're at it, you should show a little gratitude. Dr. GQ just saved us from a multimillion-dollar lawsuit."

Su dryly took Jarod's hand and shook it. "Then I guess my work here is done."

Tami piped up. "You should have seen it. He was amazing!" The candy striper could feel the glare from Gloria before she saw it. She cringed. "I'm sorry."

"No reason. I knew Jarod was exceptional—which is why I brought him in." He stared down his nose at Gloria and Tami, his smile frozen on his face. "Thank you, ladies. That'll be all." Gloria gave Bilson an unnoticed disparaging look before ushering Tami back to work.

Su shot a penetrating glare at Jarod that the Pretender read as competitive, if not suspicious. "We don't usually get doctors coming to an inner-city hospital like Guardian with your kind of skill level or credentials. Which makes a cynic like me wonder, why did you?" Su half-smiled at Jarod and Jarod gave him the same in return—though neither man was smiling on the inside.

Inside they were sizing each other up.

Marking their territory.

Preparing to battle.

Jarod knew he could come at Su hard, but in deference to Su's herit-
age, decided on another approach. In Japanese the word *Judo* translates to
the gentle way and emphasizes winning in combat by using your opponent's
strengths as weapons against him—which is how Jarod decided to proceed.
"Dr. Su, I could tell you it was for the career challenge—but the truth is,
with the current healthcare quagmire, I wanted to go to a hospital that
offered additional *opportunities* for financial rewards."

Though not completely trusting, this was not a point Su could argue
with. Bilson seemed to enjoy the dynamic and beamed broadly at Su. "I told
you he was the right man." Bilson then turned to Jarod. "We do have other
opportunities. Some in traditional medicine, some in other more—
unconventional endeavors."

Su squelched Bilson's camaraderie. "But before we get ahead of ourselves, let's stick with surgery for now." He looked pointedly at Jarod.
"Ever done a Norwood procedure, Russell? We've got one scheduled tomorrow. It's yours if you want it."

Jarod stared down Su. The Asian doctor was going to be a harder nut
to crack than he'd anticipated.

"No." Jarod shook his head, "As a matter of fact I've never even
heard of one." Su smiled smugly, reassured he was still the top dog. That
was until Jarod added confidently, "But if there's a film on YouTube, I can
probably master it tonight." Su's smile dropped straight into deadpan.

Bilson lit up proudly and patted Jarod on the back. "An enterprising
spirit! Excellent. You're going to fit in around here just fine, Jarod."

Jarod smiled—to himself. That's exactly what he planned on doing.

Chapter 9

AS A YOUNG girl, back in the happy days, Miss Parker had once been out horseback riding with her mother. It had been a long beautiful day; they had ridden far from the main house on the Parker family's luxurious, hundred-acre gentleman's farm to one of Miss P's two favorite places on earth. It was the place she often went to as a girl and dreamt the dreams of children. Located a mile from the old abandoned church, it was a field of flowing heather overlooked by the grand old oak tree on the hill. It was a majestic old-growth hardwood that had been reaching for the heavens since before the Pilgrims landed and would still be touching the face of God long after the current settlers of this land were long forgotten. Time and again she rode out alone and climbed up and played in its branches. The oak was her old friend. She called it the grumpy old man. She felt secure in his huge creaking arms and she loved him as much as any human being—except her mother.

Miss P adored her mother and especially cherished the time they spent alone together. She wanted to be just like her in every way and had secretly wished her first name had been Catherine just like her mother's, but mother told her that only happened with boys. That she had a beautiful name in her own right and that Miss Parker should always cherish it as much as her mother did. Besides, she loved the secret nickname only her mother called her, "Little Miss." It made her feel special, and this was a special day. Her mother had awoken Miss P with butterfly kisses on her cheek that morning. And when Little Miss opened her eyes she saw that her mother had placed a gift on the pillow beside her.

The gift was wrapped in beautiful lavender paper with a deep royal purple bow— both of which were Miss P's favorite colors. She reached over to rip it open, but her mother said Little Miss had to wait until the next morning to open it, the morning of her 12th birthday. She told her daughter that the gift was something to take with her on their upcoming trip to France. A trip just the two of them were going to make. 'A time to be ladies together,' her mother had told her. A phrase Miss Parker had said over and over to herself the previous night. 'A time to be ladies together.'

Miss Parker had stared deeply into her mother's eyes when she had said those words. Her mother's eyes, once so joyful, but had of late taken on great strain and great sadness. A decision was brewing behind those eyes. A decision Little Miss knew mother was hiding from her. There was a hurt in those eyes the perceptive Little Miss knew mother didn't want her to feel. The first time Little Miss had seen that pain in her mother's eyes was the day she had snuck up on her mother while she was underlining a sentence in her diary she was always writing in: 'And under the hand of God, ye little children shall never be lost.' Mother was that way. She lived to protect people.

Especially little people, particularly her Little Miss.

Little Miss knew her mother loved her and that when she was with her she would always be safe.

Even with everything else that she knew, the things she'd buried deep in her young mind, that day, alone in her favorite place in the world with her mother at her side, made this one of the most perfect moments of Miss P's young life. But this would not be the first time in her life, nor the last, as Miss Parker reveled in a moment of pure joy, a storm would blow in.

In an instant, skies that had been brilliantly blue had turned dark grey and were angrily upon Little Miss and her mother. The wind suddenly whipped up, bending the branches of the grumpy old man until they began to crack, spooking their white stallions. That was the first time Miss P experienced what people meant by the heavens opening up. As the torrents fell, Little Miss was able to keep a steady upper lip, a brave face, as her father had always taught her. She really wasn't scared—until the first thunderbolt ripped through the sky and exploded above them. Then her fear took over. Even at a full gallop, Miss Parker knew they were too far from home to make it safely to the barn. She also knew, as did her mother who was circling around looking for options, that exposed in the pasture was the last place they wanted to be.

With her horse rearing up and whinnying nervously, Miss P began to panic—until her mother reached out and put her soothing hand onto Miss P's steed and calmed the frightened beast. Her mother then looked into her Little Miss's eyes and said, "We need to make it to the abandoned church. We'll be safe there." Her mother then smiled reassuringly. "No matter what happens, stay with me. I'll never let anything bad happen to you, Little Miss."

They began to ride and as they did, a lightning bolt erupted from the clouds. The bolt was so blindingly close, Little Miss could feel its heat as it sailed right above her head. She looked over her right shoulder just as it split the grumpy old man right in two.

Miss Parker didn't fear many things, but since that day, lightning was one.

Chapter 10

LIGHTNING BOLTS ERUPTED; a storm was coming from the East. Miss Parker peered out the window of the sleek black AS 355F Eurocopter as it sliced like a heat-seeking missile through the purpling sky toward the setting sun. Its TM-319 Arrius turbo shafts gave the state-of-the-art JetCopter a range with max fuel of 722km and a top cruising speed of 222 km/h, all making the 355F one of the finest pieces of airborne technology that a non-governmental organization could possess. None of which Miss Parker gave a shit about.

What she did give a shit about was what she was looking down at now. Her home away from home, a place known simply as The Centre.

High atop the bluffs on the Western-most edge of Blue Cove, Delaware, stood the stark, art deco, architectural creation that some thought looked like a prison, some like an asylum, still others like a fortress. In their own ways, all of these descriptions were accurate.

Built in the 1930's, the massive, limestone structure was anchored by two looming towers on both sides of its uninviting main entrance. By design, the four-story building was not softened by trees or shrubs of any kind, so that in the light of day no part of it would ever be in shadows. But shadows were the foundation that The Centre was built upon and within its labyrinth of corridors secrets were concealed behind every door.

Miss Parker had grown up in the ominous hallways that seemed to stretch forever out into the darkness. Her father had run The Centre since before she was born. In her mind she always looked at him as the king of this castle and she as its princess. Only natural since she'd been treated like royalty within its walls since her first breath and knew everything about this place.

Or at least she thought she did.

Pap Pap Pap Pap Pap echoed down the endless corridor as Miss Parker drilled holes into the marble floor with the spiked heels of her Christian Louboutins. Only a few of The Centre's 2,000 employees were still here at this time of day and those that happened to be, upon spotting Miss Parker, scattered like scared rats back to where they'd come from, as if suddenly remembering something they'd left in their office. Puffing furiously on her ever-present cigarette, she marched like a woman on a mission while Sydney, like a kite being dragged along in her turbulence, fought to keep up.

Miss Parker waved a printout. "We've put tracers on your prodigy's bank accounts and I was right. He's tapped them twice since he left the wind farm. When he hits them again we'll nail him."

Sydney picked up his pace as if hoping that walking next to her would make her listen to what he was saying. "He won't do that. Jarod has a gift and being stupid isn't part of it. If we are to catch him, we need to be patient."

Miss Parker slammed on her brakes, spun on a dime and thrust her pointer finger in Syd's face. "Listen, Rumpled-Coat-Skin, you may be satisfied in your little lab probing little minds, but I have career goals and they don't include schlepping around the world looking for boy wonder."

Miss Parker turned to move on, but Syd stepped in front. "He's playing a game with you, Parker. He always loved games, chess his favorite. I would've thought that if anyone remembered that, it would be you."

Syd's words hit their intended mark inside Miss Parker—something in her distant past. But she refused to give him the benefit of riling her.

"I'm not concerned with Jarod's games." She held up the bank account printout. "Besides, I plan to say 'checkmate' to your little Kasparov very quickly." She sidestepped Sydney and continued on, Syd falling in behind her just as she liked it.

"What Jarod left at the wind farm is merely the tip of the iceberg of what he's going to do to you." Miss Parker picked up her pace. "It's a reality you can't run away from. While you're making your second move of this chess match, Jarod has already conceived his fifty-first."

"It's not who's ahead in the beginning of the game—it's who wins in the end." Miss Parker stopped at a heavy carbon door. "Open it."

"Is this really necessary?" Syd argued. "I've been through his room a thousand times and found nothing."

"I haven't." She let out a lungful of smoke. "You think maybe—just maybe—because of your connection to Jarod, you could have overlooked something that someone less emotionally attached could find? Huh? He left a clue of how to find him at his windmill playground and I'll bet my sweet ass he's left one here. Now open sesame."

Miss Parker could easily have unlocked this door without Syd's help. Her security code could access anything in The Centre—or almost anything. Her code was second only to her father's and despite his lifetime of loyal service, many levels superior to Sydney's. No, she was demanding he open it as a reminder of her place above him in the corporate pecking order.

A reluctant Sydney removed his electronic card key and slid it through three separate readers. He then placed his left hand on a photo-volvic scanner and held it there while his right hand began punching an elaborate numerical and alphabetical code into the door's flat screen monitor keyboard.

"Miss Parker, I know this is none of my business, but since the accident, you've spent your life trying to prove to your father you're worthy of his affection. That you are a *good girl.*" He paused. "You don't have to do that any longer."

Miss Parker looked at Sydney as though he had read her innermost thoughts—"You know Syd, you're right." Then, like a light switching from ON to OFF, her look changed from contentment to contempt. "It is none of your business—and I damn sure don't have anything to prove. It also wasn't an *accident.*"

As the door unlatched, Syd studied Miss P. "You were such a happy little girl, what happened to you?"

She dropped her cigarette onto the immaculate marble floor and ground it out with the toe of her stiletto. "I grew up, Sydney—and so should you."

Just then a five-year-old girl rode past them on a tricycle, neither giving her a second look. They both then entered what anyone would consider an odd space—even for The Centre.

In the middle of this dark, yawning space glowed a sterile bio-chamber enclosed within a clear Plexiglass dome that looked very much like a modern exhibit in a zoo—with one disturbing distinction: The dome was surrounded by dozens of surveillance cameras, all designed and positioned to record everything that happened within.

Everything.

Inside, the dome was divided by clear glass walls into three distinct areas, like slices of a pie.

In the rear section, there was a small bed with white sheets, a white toilet and a shower with white fixtures—all of which were reminiscent of a prison cell. A white one. On the right, was a large white work desk piled high with white covered books, computers, an electron microscope, a 20-inch viewing screen for the microscope and other related tools. They too where white. *Everything* was white.

Except one thing.

In the third section, which was completely empty—in fact, eerily bare—there was a six-inch circular touch pad on the wall. The pad was the only color in the dome.

It was red.

Miss Parker entered and moved slowly through the unsettling environment. "Got to hand it to you, Syd, no one knows how to create *home-sweet-home* quite like you." Miss Parker looked up at the ceiling and was astonished to see that the 24/7 recording cameras were even pointed down into the shower and toilet. Miss P looked at the Belgian standing next to the touch pad and raised an eyebrow. "If I ever decide to raise my own sociopath and the Marquis De Sade is unavailable—I'm hiring you to design the nursery."

"Jarod is not a sociopath. This environment was specifically created to nourish his intellect, with controlled stimuli and input designed to best develop his pure genius."

"And yet somehow, your experiment developed a mind of his own. A bit of a failure, isn't it, Geppetto?"

She pointed at the touch pad. "Play Jarod's last simulation. I want to know where his head was before he flew the playpen."

Sydney shook his head at her insolence, then placed his hand on the red pad.

That's when the first explosion went off.

Chapter 11

THE FLOOR UNDER Miss Parker's feet jolted as a fireball raged through the fuselage of the 747. Chaos reigned and human tragedy played out as the terrified passengers around her succumbed to their reality. Some screamed. Some cried. Some prayed. Parker spied a young mother singing in comforting tones to an infant cradled in her arms, a baby she knew would not see her first birthday. She spotted a flight attendant watching the pilot fighting to keep the plane from plummeting out of the sky. The stoic look on the attendant's face told Miss Parker everything she needed to know: that every person aboard was about to die.

Except Miss Parker, everybody was horrified of this fate. She sauntered through the smoke and mayhem of the enflamed fuselage with nothing but disdain on her face.

Even when she watched a man doused in jet fuel screaming as he burned alive, Parker had no reaction. She didn't even recoil from the flames that danced up and around her miniskirt. In fact, none of the devastation surrounding her had any effect on her.

But nothing here was designed to.

Everything in this part of Jarod's living space was specifically tailored to stimulate his thought processes as a Pretender. In fact, the virtual reality Miss Parker was standing in was conceived and planned by Jarod himself, in order to get the most out of every simulation he plunged himself into. The Pretender had designed the room to be a completely immersive environment—for all five senses. Not only were the holographic images as precise as technologically possible, but also the pristine Surround Sound was of better quality than any THX system George Lucas had ever devised. The prodigious result fully stimulated both Jarod's visual and auditory senses in profound ways that were as real to him as if he were actually there.

But those were just the standard simulation conditions. Jarod's V.R. sim theatre was also equipped with temperature, smell and taste variances that, in this case, recreated the heat of the flames, the smell of the smoke, and the acidic tang of the jet fuel in the air.

Sydney joined Miss Parker in the middle of the disturbingly graphic cataclysmic event. "When the black box on this flight wasn't recovered, Jarod simulated a flight crew and passenger death projection and was able to factually recreate the final moments before impact."

As the plane crashed in an enormous explosion, Miss Parker hit the touch pad, killing the sim.

"Hell of an environment you raised him in, Syd. If he ever gets over the PTSD maybe we'll find him masquerading as a postal worker."

"Jarod doesn't masquerade. As I told you before, he is a Pretender. He can become anyone he wants to be."

"Whatever you say, Syd. The Centre should have stuck with computers for their simulations—they don't run away."

"But computers can't tell you what the flight crew was *feeling* as they lost power, what the man burning alive was *truly experiencing*, or how their emotions contributed to their fate. Jarod could. He could get into their hearts and minds and souls as if they were his living avatars—or he was theirs."

Dismissive of his ramblings, Miss P began scouring Jarod's living spaces with her expertly trained eyes.

Syd shook his head, dismayed at her arrogance. He knew he'd be wasting his breath if he tried again to explain to her that a Pretender is not just a genius with a photographic memory, but someone blessed with the use of nine percent more of their brain than the most gifted among us. She wouldn't want to hear again that Jarod's imagination was beyond parallel, that his savant-like qualities of extreme intelligence, coupled with a corresponding, hyper-focused psychological acuity, permitted him to see and experience the world differently. He knew that she would just ignore him if he told her for the hundredth time that Jarod was essentially Einstein as a human chameleon.

As he held his tongue, Syd observed a glimmer of curiosity in Miss P's eyes. Spotting something on Jarod's desk, she walked over to take a closer look. "Parker?"

Miss P leaned close to the desktop, seeing that it was covered in what looked like tiny pieces of sand. She rubbed her fingers through it.

"The Living Computer was into Zen gardens?"

Syd walked over next to her. "Those aren't grains of sand, they're Nano-Origami."

Miss P brought her fingers up, examining the microscopic creations. "You're saying these are paper swans?"

"Not swans. Angels. Jarod was obsessed with making them."

Syd found a pair of tweezers, picked up a single grain and placed it under the lens of Jarod's electron microscope. The image that appeared on the viewing screen was blurry, so Syd adjusted the scope's focal length. "For relaxation, Jarod folded hundreds of these in the months before he left." As the image finally came into focus, Miss Parker could now make out in great detail a winged Nano-Origami figure. Syd stared at the image. "Though I must admit, I still haven't determined the psychological connection of the angels to him yet."

A lightbulb flashed in Miss P's mind and a wicked grin formed on her lips. "That's because they're not angels, Freud—and Jarod didn't fold 'em to chill his jets. He made them as he was stewing in his angry juices." Syd had no idea what she was talking about and she liked that. She tapped her finger on the wing of the creature on the microscope screen. "Its wings are bent. It's Onyssius."

Syd stared, his face still blank. "Onyssius?"

Miss Parker raised an eyebrow. "Come on, Syd. The Greek God of retribution? He defends the weak and abused."

Sydney was truly taken aback. "I'm—I'm impressed. How do you know so much about Greek lore?"

"I did a lot of frat boys in college." Miss Parker reveled in her intellectual coup. "I told you I would find a clue, Sydster. Your sociopath thinks he's some kind of vigilante, getting retribution for the little guy."

Shaking her head as she walked out, she looked back over her shoulder long enough to ask, "Just what the hell did you teach him?"

Syd, now alone in the living dome he'd raised his Pretender in, was asking himself the very same question.

Chapter 12

JAROD STEPPED OFF the bus at 125th and 7th with a bag of groceries in his arm and a smile on his face. He turned left and headed toward
8th oblivious of the odd stares he was getting as he strolled through the
heart of Harlem. He was too busy enjoying the stalk of celery he was
chomping on and the sights, sounds and smells of this unique multicultural
environment. His attention was fixated by one sight in particular that
reflected it all—a marquee proudly announcing *THE APOLLO
THEATRE.*

While he was unaware of the phrase, *"There's no place like home,"* that's
exactly what he was feeling. For Jarod the sight of the name in lights made
him think of the quote, *"In NYC Harlem is the place-2-be."*

Those were the words that Johnny Boy Creed had spoken to Jarod the
same night he'd escaped from The Centre.

*The old black man was sitting in his 1965 Dodge Dart in the parking lot of the
MAMA store #302, on 4th Street in downtown Wilmington, Delaware. Sipping from
a can of Pepsi with a big smile on his travel-worn face, he was keeping a watchful eye on
a strange white man who just moments ago he'd witnessed jumping off a passing train
and who was now hiding in the shadows next to the convenience store.*

*The white man was peeking from behind a dumpster, staring at the store, seemingly
debating whether or not to go in. As he calmly sipped his Pepsi, Johnny Boy Creed noticed how the man kept anxiously glancing around as if paranoid someone might see him.*

Johnny Boy Creed watched with piqued interest as Jarod finally collected his courage and walked confidently up to the entrance of the store. Then something happened to make Johnny Boy momentarily lower his Pepsi and smile broadly. The old man's reaction was triggered by Jarod's unexpected one—as he reached to open the door, the Pretender jumped in a startled response when the door suddenly opened automatically for him, as if by magic! Jarod then took a timorous step backwards and was shocked again as the door closed by itself. This made Johnny Boy snort with amused disbelief.

Jarod nervously looked left, right and then through the glass door, searching for a logical answer for this phenomenon—but there was no one anywhere who could have made this happen. Then, gathering himself, Jarod cautiously took another step forward— only to freeze again and quickly retreat when the open/close cycle of the door repeated itself.

Johnny Boy thought about taking another sip but was afraid he'd blast Pepsi out his nose as he continued watching this hilarious show. He thought he'd witnessed everything in his 72 years, but what happened next as he continued watching the strange white man added to his list of done seen it all now's.

His mind racing to solve the mystery, Jarod's demeanor instantly shifted from stunned bewilderment to bold inquisitiveness. He slowly inched forward towards the door, taking very small and deliberate steps until Wham! the door opened for a third time. As it did, a lightbulb went off in Jarod's mind as a huge, corresponding knowing smile appeared on his face.

Johnny Boy looked on through his open car window and laughed. Jarod heard him, turned to meet the old man's eyes and, like an exuberant child, explained to him, "There must be some kind of sonar-like device that detects your presence as you ingress or egress from this establishment—it's very clever!"

And that's when Johnny Boy said, "You're not from around here, are you?"

Before Jarod could answer, a black Town Car pulled into the lot. Seeing it, Jarod slinked back into the shadows. Johnny Boy noticed the fear on Jarod's face as he watched the driver of the sedan get out and enter the store. The man was well built, dressed in a dark suit and carrying a photograph, which he showed to the cashier—a photo of a man that even from the distance Johnny Boy could tell was Jarod. Jarod saw this as well and he disappeared into the alley.

Johnny Boy fired up the Dart and rolled around the corner. He saw a visibly distressed Jarod quickly making his way down the alley, so he pulled up alongside and asked him if he could use a lift.

Jarod looked into his soulful eyes and immediately felt trust. He quietly replied, "Yes, please." Jarod opened the door and got inside the Dart. The Pretender had never driven a car; he'd only the vaguest memories of having ridden in one, but couldn't remember how or when. He did find this one comfortable and even liked the way it smelled. He decided in that moment that if he ever had an automobile of his own, he'd get a Dodge Dart just like it.

Johnny Boy looked at Jarod taking in this new experience and didn't even bother asking why he was so excited. There really wasn't time for that. He knew a man in trouble when he saw one. He'd been one many times in his own life.

But the memories for both men were washed away when they noticed the headlights of the Town Car slowly crossing the alley behind them. Johnny Boy noticed fear in Jarod's face and how his breathing got short as the headlights brightly illuminated, then faded away as the car vanished. He didn't ask Jarod about it. He just asked, "Where you headed?"

Jarod let out a huge sigh, then gratefully looked over at his savior. "As far away from here as possible."

With a nod and the biggest, whitest smile in the Western Hemisphere, Johnny Boy drove away into the night.

Johnny Boy Creed was the first person Jarod interacted with after his escape and he found the affable white-haired gentleman a Godsend. Jarod was more than resourceful enough to get himself to freedom, but it felt good to have human contact—it felt good to make a friend. Johnny Boy was in his 70's, but Jarod thought he looked 50 because he smiled all the time. In the two days they were on the road together, Johnny Boy Creed had made quite an impression on Jarod. In fact, it was because of him that the Pretender had chosen Harlem.

The way Johnny Boy had said it was "In NYC, Harlem is the place-2-be." He hadn't said the 'number two', but had flashed two fingers so Jarod believed that this would have been the correct spelling of it had it been written out and so he went with that as he entered it into his memory banks.

As they drove out of Wilmington, Johnny Boy told Jarod that he was heading to Memphis through Pennsylvania, Ohio and Kentucky and that Jarod was welcome to tag along as far as he wanted.

As he talked, Johnny Boy said that he had just come from New York City fresh from a gig at a place called the Apollo Theatre in Harlem.

Jarod was thrilled. He knew all about the historic Apollo project and all of NASA from the many lessons Sydney had taught him about the early days of the space program. "So this theatre has space capsules and lunar landers on display?"

Johnny Boy just laughed as he usually did. Either Jarod had a great sense of humor or he was mentally challenged in some way, but he didn't care. It came out that Johnny Boy was a musician—a blues man who had made his guitar wail with and for some of the greatest performers of all time, including the likes of Ella Fitzgerald, Sarah Vaughn and of course, Gladys and The Pips.

Jarod made a mental note to find out what exactly a Pip was, because he felt funny asking. Truth was, Jarod was even more riveted to music than he was with rocket ships. With music, he was fascinated with the infinite possibilities and unique combinations of notes and melodies and lyrics that could create powerful emotions within a person. While Jarod had never actually danced, he'd always wanted to and instinctively knew that music had to be a big plus when it came to that endeavor.

When Johnny Boy dropped Jarod in Cincinnati, Jarod gave his new friend a small harmonica he'd made in the car during their trip. Jarod named the harmonica the Little Pepsi, since the cover plates were made from the cans of the drink the music man was constantly sipping from. Jarod had found a dry, perfectly sized piece of birch for the comb in the parking lot of a Waffle House outside of Pittsburgh and scraps of copper for the reeds in the dumpster of a Dayton truck stop. The carving and piecing together of it all was a snap since Johnny Boy did all the driving and most of the talking. He was deeply touched by Jarod's gift and blew a sweet riff as they parted. Most of all, Jarod hoped to one day hear him play his Little Pepsi at The Apollo.

Jarod thought about Johnny Boy every time he walked past the Apollo, the glittering jewel of Harlem. He then took a left on 8ᵗʰ and headed into a whole different section of town.

Chapter 13

A FEW BLOCKS later Jarod stopped at an intersection that was the definition of urban decay.

Northeast and southwest were a burned out gas station and an abandoned jewelry store. Livening up one of the other two was a liquor store with heavily barred windows outside of which a half dozen men were drinking from large bottles wrapped in brown bags.

Crossing the potholed street towards the fourth corner Jarod pulled a second piece of celery from his bag. While savoring the crispy stalk, he noticed three young, curvaceous creatures wearing tiny, tight dresses, with their breasts bulging up and their inviting backsides hanging out, as they stood huddled together warming their hands over a trash fire. Considering the chilly weather, Jarod thought the people in front of the burned-out store had all made questionable wardrobe choices, and had they thought ahead and clothed themselves more appropriately to retain their body warmth, they wouldn't need to be standing near a can of flames.

Passing he heard, "Baby, I gots something you can chomp on dat's tastier than that rabbit food." He turned to the sound of heels clacking on concrete as one vixen, a thick, tall Puerto Rican Creole named Chaz, stutter-stepped on platform F-me pumps to catch up. "What's a big strong man like you in such a hurry for?"

"Just heading home." Jarod liked the way that sounded, *home*.

Chaz, who was wearing a huge flowing blonde Beyoncé wig and exaggerated, winged-out silver glitter eye shadow, fell in and started walking arm in arm with Jarod. "<u>You</u> live around <u>here</u>?"

Jarod recognized the concern in her face—but he had no idea why she was worried about him. To reassure her, Jarod grinned and said confidently, "In NYC, Harlem is the place-2-be."

Chaz grinned and playfully ruffled Jarod's hair. "You's a funny little Nilla wafer—ain't cha? You ever think about dunkin' yourse'f in some chocolate milk?"

Jarod tilted his head. "Nilla wafer? Chocolate milk?"

"Come on now, everyone knows that dippin' vanilla into hot fudge makes it so much sweeter, baby—don't you?"

Jarod looked at Chaz, completely drawing a blank. "I'm afraid Sydney didn't allow me sweets as a child, and therefore I am not familiar with what you are suggesting."

"Who the hell was Sydney to tell you what to eat? Your pimp?"

Jarod didn't know what a *pimp* was—and even if he had known, he wouldn't have been sure how to answer that anyway.

The vixen gazed into Jarod's brown bag, seeing it contained exclusively vegetables and greens. "Listen to Chaz, baby boy. Don't just shop the edges of the grocery store. In life, all the fun stuff's in the middle aisle. Even healthy boys needs 'em some adult dessert sometime. You feel me?"

She rubbed an acrylic nail down his chest. "Now—you ready for a treat?"

Jarod had read about the oldest profession and realized that was what this person did for a living the moment they'd begun walking together. And while that particular commercial exchange wasn't something he was interested in, there was something that fascinated him about it.

Sydney had once told Jarod never to judge a book by its cover. Jarod had taken that to mean 'never make assumptions at first glance,' but when looking at Chaz, Jarod had a hard time adhering to that rule. He cocked his head, thinking to himself, *something about both this cover and this book just isn't right.*

Jarod looked the sex hustler up and down.

Chaz was very large in frame, and under scrutiny, her long blonde locks didn't completely hide the bulky neck and shoulders beneath, nor the large bi and triceps. And most importantly the Adam's apple. Jarod looked at Chaz. "May I ask you a question?"

"Fire away, sugar lips."

"You are a man, wearing women's clothing, correct?"

"No. No, honey-boy. I'm a woman—I'm a real woman trapped in a man's body, wearing the clothing of the gender that I identify my true being."

That mouthful and what it expressed was a new one for Jarod. Chaz saw his perplexed expression and continued. "What? You ain't never watched *Ellen*? The experts say I experience what is known as gender dysphoria—a disconnection between my assigned and perceived gender. I'm like that Chaz Bono. She used to be 'Chastity'—cute as a button as a little girl—but she knew she had her a man inside. I'm the reverse. But I still named myself after her—wanted to give her props for being strong enough to be *herself as a him*."

The wheels still turning in his mind, Jarod hadn't reacted—out loud, and before he could, a loud bass rumbling caught his attention to his right. It was coming from a Cherry Red BMW 640i coupe riding low and blasting gangsta rap. Inside were four members of the Thrill Cru Boyz, a long established Harlem drug gang. As the Beemer slowly rolled past, their ringleader, a hardened gangsta with the nickname T-Dope leaned out the passenger window. "Hey, white boy, you better get you a *Man-Ho* cover if you gonna play in that skank ass sewer."

The other Cru Boyz cracked up wildly, holding their hands up to their mouths, one hooting, "*Damn!*" as they drove away.

Jarod could read the embroidery of emotions in Chaz's face. Seeing Jarod's expression, Chaz let out an exasperated sigh. "May as well join the party. You got clever shit percolatin' up in that head about who I am, then say it. Everyone else does."

Jarod, understanding that Chaz was a fellow traveler moving down a misunderstood path—just like him, smiled reassuringly. He had only one thing to ask. "Don't those pointy little shoes hurt your big feet?"

Chaz was taken aback a bit by this seamless acceptance. "Oh, baby boy—you has *no* idea." Chaz kicked off his killer heels and rubbed his huge, throbbing feet. "My dogs is howling—but a girl's gotta do whatta girl's gotta do for work—you feel me?"

As they rounded the corner, Jarod stopped and pointed to the decrepit warehouse building they were standing in front of announcing he was home.

"You live in this hood for reals?" Jarod nodded. She then took his chin in her hand. "Then you be careful, 'Nilla Man, wanderin' 'round, acting a fool is just low fruit for some bad souls." And with that and a grin, Chaz turned and sashayed back to work.

Jarod headed up to his apartment; he too had to get back to work.

Chapter 14

MISS PARKER WAITED quietly in her father's wood-lined office in the uppermost floor of The Centre's North Tower. She sat in the same straight-backed chair in which she'd sat many times as a child, also waiting for him there—quietly. The uncomfortable chair faced her father's imposing mahogany desk. The desk, it was rumored, had once belonged to a Duke, or an Archduke, who'd been a representative of one of the 19 factions that formed the Weimar Republic—or something like that.

Miss P could never remember. Her father hated when she asked a question twice and as a child, she'd been daydreaming when he'd answered her question about the desk the first time. She knew better than to ask again. However, she did remember that it was brought to this country by her Grandfather Parker, and that her mother hated not only GP Parker's mahogany desk but also everything he'd stood for.

It was for that reason she'd always found it unsettling that her mother's portrait was on the wall behind the desk, gazing down upon it, silently linked to it in time. Miss P knew her mother would have despised that irony. She'd once been brave enough to mention it to her father when she was 16, but only that one time.

Sometimes as a child when she sat in the chair in front of the massive desk, under her mother's gaze, she would be so intimidated by her father sitting on the other side that she'd forget what subject he'd called her there to be lectured on.

"There's my Angel." Miss Parker jumped as his startling baritone boomed across the room. She fixed her eyes on his six-foot-four frame moving confidently, his keen eyes twinkling and his thousand-watt smile on full display. She marveled, as she had a million times, that unlike the fathers of other children, her father radiated power and persuasion. In another life, in another time, the glow of his charisma was so strong he could have been a Broadway star.

But as quickly as he gives, Mr. Parker takes away. His smile faded under a stern look. "What took you so long?"

"Long? I—I—I'm sorry, Daddy, I came right over and I—I've been waiting ..."

Before Miss Parker could finish apologizing—as she always found herself doing—Mr. Parker's cell phone rang. He looked at it, then snapped his fingers at his daughter, instantly silencing her the exact same way he had done since she was a child.

"Ga-damned Africans."

Miss Parker's eyes never left her father's face as he answered with a warm effusion that did its best to cover his irritation.

As he spoke, Mr. Parker paced between his desk and the only other piece of heavy furniture in his office, his personal bar. Custom made of Kentucky white oak, it served one thing and one thing only, Maker's Mark. As he listened to the voices on the other end of the phone, it looked to Miss P that her father could use a stiff belt of his favorite bourbon right about now.

Mr. Parker, the boss of bosses at The Centre that his own father had founded, the domineering benevolent dictator that everyone both loved and feared, answered only to a group known as the Triumvirate. And his three sub-Saharan superiors on the other end of the line were not happy campers. She could tell they were grilling him about the escape of Jarod, and the severity of their concern was evident in his eyes. Miss Parker hadn't seen her father this concerned about the future of The Centre since the day her mother—well, since everything changed. And she knew exactly why. She knew exactly what was at stake if Jarod wasn't caught. She knew what could happen if The Centre's Digital Surveillance Archive recordings ended up in the wrong hands. The DSAs were the visual documentation of the entirety of Jarod's life, his simulations or *sims*—all the experiments he'd performed during his captivity—the same recordings Jarod had stolen copies of when he'd run away.

"I assure you, my friends, you have nothing to worry about. My best people are on it." Mr. P winked at his daughter. A wink that made her proud, as proud as she'd felt in years. It even caused her heart to flutter for just a moment.

He was counting on her.

Mr. Parker hung up. "That devious son of a bitch Zane with his two different-colored eyes has been stirring up our friends on the dark continent."

Zane was a bad man, a sinister man, a man who'd reminded her of an evil version of the serpent from *The Jungle Book*—the one that was a hundred years old and still in his prime who tried to hypnotize you with his eyes. He'd always seemed to appear in Miss Parker's life during times when things turned dark and evil. Zane was a man she associated with hissing, temptation and duplicity. He was also someone she called *Uncle*.

Mr. Parker paced back and forth, his mind, threatened with his survival, was clicking on all cylinders. "It's all part of the same power grab that ulcerous excuse for a human being Zane's been instigating for years. Now that he's solidified his control over the Brazilian arm of The Centre he's full bore trying to make this office his—wanting to control everything. It's the same poker game he's been hoping to get a winning hand to play since you were a baby. He thinks this is his way to go all-in, but he's not going to be raking in the chips."

Mr. Parker sat down, but not in his chair. He sat on the desk, squarely in front of Miss P. "The future here belongs to YOU not your Uncle Z— and capturing Jarod is the key to it all." Mr. Parker stood again, new thoughts firing—"Tell me, Angel, how is Sydney handling Jarod's escape?"

"Truth is he makes my skin crawl, Daddy, always has."

The look in Mr. Parker's eyes was mild amusement, but his tone was not. "He also knows more about Jarod than anyone else alive. So just keep that quack on a short leash, deal with him this one time, bring Jarod back and you'll never have to work with him again."

Mr. Parker then did something that shocked his daughter. He moved back to her, bent down and kissed her forehead. He looked into her eyes and said a few more things. But suddenly lost in the haze of the momentary physical affection he'd just bestowed on her, Miss P couldn't hear all the words he was saying. She only registered "make sure Jarod doesn't hurt us" and "the most important field assignment of your life." She was going to ask him to repeat himself, but knew better. None of it mattered, because the last thing he said resonated with her loud and clear: "I need you now more than ever."

Ever desperate for his affection, Miss Parker assured her father, "I'll get him."

"I know you won't let me down, Angel."

"Never. Daddy—I love—" but before she could finish, his phone was ringing and he'd snapped his fingers at her—silencing her yet again.

Chapter 15

BY MIDNIGHT THERE was only one source of light in Jarod's expansive fourth floor, bi-level Harlem warehouse loft. The bright glow came from behind a huge silk curtain he'd rigged in the upper-floor which made it easy to see that this space was far more *warehouse* than *loft*.

In Soho, Greenwich, or almost any other neighborhood in Manhattan, the monthly rent for this place would be in the high five figures and in realtor's parlance, would be considered to have *unlimited potential for the 'high-end entertainment-minded.'*

But in Harlem the rent was cheap. That's because with its rusted water stains on red brick walls, cracks in the large and filthy chicken-wired windows that covered one side of the space and more than a few sagging beams and saggier and soiled furniture, this pit was much better suited as the shooting gallery for heroin addicts who'd once lived there than a place for human habitation.

But Jarod loved it.

The only thing he changed about it upon taking possession was the addition of a Lazy Boy recliner that was placed in the middle of the vast main floor room.

To Jarod it was the nicest home he'd ever lived in—because it was *his*.

The kitchen counter, in the corner of the loft underneath the upstairs sleeping area, was cluttered with the remnants of Jarod's earlier culinary feast: a leftover serving of raw kale, an empty gallon bottle of spring water and a near-empty bag of celery—out of which crawled one of New York City's famous rats, carrying a piece of a stalk that he stopped to nibble on.

To most, the rat would be a pest, but to Jarod, from the moment the little creature had appeared, he had become a roommate, a friend, and a welcome dinner guest.

The rat finished his morsel and looked up, inquisitively sniffing toward the glow emanating from the curtained off area above. He then scurried across the counter and looked into the kitchen sink, which was full of Jarod's hair—clusters of loose strands left behind after Jarod had given himself a trim. On the counter next to the sink, several locks of the hair were now sealed inside a sterile plastic baggie.

The rat continued on his expedition, down the cabinet, to the floor and over a small pile of power tools and cut fragments of inch-thick Plexiglass sheets, tossed there from above.

He then found his way to the stairs and scampered up toward the light. Once there, like Toto in Oz, he curiously peeked behind the curtain—except in this case not finding a fraud in hiding, but a Pretender.

A human simulator in mid-process.

The large, boxy Plexiglass walls were designed intentionally to replicate, as best they could, Jarod's virtual sim room at The Centre. But the difference was that this space was rigged with intricate surgical lighting, a full array of flat screen monitors mounted on the red brick walls and surgical instruments on a rolling cart next to him. It was a virtual, full-blown operating room in every way, complete with O.R. sound ambience—*Hiss, Poof, Whirr, Beep*— *Hiss, Poof, Whirr, Beep*—that floated in from hidden speakers and washed over the operating table that was stationed in the middle.

There was even a patient on the table at this very moment. And that patient was Jarod.

He laid still, eyes closed, oxygen mask in place, his bare chest marked up with sterile surgical pen, indicating proper cutting areas. The instructional words and surgical images from a DVD were playing on one of the flat screens, its narrator thoroughly describing each precise step of a surgery that he referred to as *The Norwood Procedure. Hiss, Poof, Whirr, Beep—Hiss, Poof, Whirr, Beep.* Jarod was in a near trance as he *absorbed* the instructions.

The Norwood procedure is a complex, time-consuming operation that requires the use of a heart-lung bypass and a complete cessation of blood flow to the brain. It is used to reverse the rare, complex congenital heart defect in children known as Hypoplastic Left Heart Syndrome.

Jarod removed the oxygen mask, rose from his *patient* position on the operating table and continued listening as he began to dress himself in surgical garb. *Hiss, Poof, Whirr, Beep—Hiss, Poof, Whirr, Beep.*

The hybrid surgery returns the heart to proper function by allowing it to accept the high-oxygenated blood into the left atrium directly from the lungs and pump it through the right atrium to the body, while the low-oxygenated blood is rerouted passively through the pulmonary artery into the lungs to receive oxygen.

As the DVD continued to play over the course of the next two hours, Jarod seamlessly assumed the roles of every player in the O.R. He was not merely acting, but *becoming*—stepping into the skin of everyone involved in the surgery. Seeing him as them, *feeling* himself within them, completely submersing himself until the narrator's instructions ended and the last suture was stitched.

Because of its intricacies and its radical groundbreaking introduction, The Norwood Procedure takes several months to learn and master.

As Jarod shut off the DVD and welcomed his furry little friend to climb up into his skilled hands, Jarod knew *several months* wasn't a luxury he had. Truth be told, he was scheduled to perform this cutting-edge surgery in less than three hours.

Chapter 16

BOOM-BOOM, BOOM-BOOM, BOOM-BOOM, the heartbeat pounded in Jarod's ears as he calmly stood in the surgical theatre.

Boom-boom, boom-boom, boom-boom.

But Jarod wasn't acting in this theatre—wasn't on stage or in a simulation anymore.

Boom-boom, boom-boom, boom-boom.

As he looked down onto the operating table and the ten-year-old girl's heart as it beat in her open chest, he knew his previous E.R. experience didn't compare to the test he was in the midst of now—fail this and someone would die.

Ironically the thought of that made Jarod calmer still.

Jarod wasn't just pretending to be a skilled surgeon. In the last 24 hours he had *become* one. He had the confidence to know he would not fail his patient and the steely nerves to fully execute it.

While Jarod was being observed from the gallery above by a large audience, including Doctors Bilson and Su, Jarod wasn't acting, he was *being*.

Of all of Jarod's attributes, his ability to seamlessly *become someone else* had always impressed Sydney the most. Over the years Sydney filled notebook after notebook with his fascinated observations of how Jarod's very physiology changed when he assumed the psychology within his Pretends. As he now stood over his patient, Jarod thought that Sydney would have been quite fascinated. And he wouldn't have been alone.

The control Jarod felt over the quickening of his own pulse and the rush of his adrenaline pumping, the peaking of his senses and the precision of his mental focus in a real life Pretend was ultimately fascinating to Jarod as well.

Always had been, and yet what happened inside of him as <u>he became,</u> was a strange dichotomy.

As he worked his mind was firing a million synapses at once, yet his body remained completely calm and controlled. His breathing was as smooth and automatic as the photographic recall of the memorized techniques of the process itself: cut through the stratum corneum, then the stratum granulosum and finally through the basement membrane itself. The separation of the sternum next and then you will see the heart. *Boom-boom, boom-boom, boom-boom.*

Jarod had found that in all Pretends the memorized steps were easy to anticipate and execute. He was always calm executing the 'knowns.' In some ways though, he was also bored by them.

There were three other categories he factored into each Pretend— none of which were boring. The 'unknowns' were scary and were the reason he spent so much time troubleshooting and mastering the 'knowns.' Within the 'unknowns' lay improvisational opportunity—but more often than not they led to danger and needed to be avoided at all costs.

Then there were the 'unexpecteds' that got his juices flowing. Those and what he called the 'anticipatories' were where he found his excitement.

Today's *unexpected* was the jovial atmosphere of the surgical personnel around him. Their utilization of humor to blow off stress was something not mentioned in the academic instructions but an element that could only be discovered in action and one he found very satisfactory. Yet it was the 'anticipatories' he experienced that made his day.

The acrid smell of laser incisions to human flesh—as well as the sensation of human warmth on his fingers as he held them over the open body cavity in the cooled operating theatre were things he'd anticipated. In fact behind his mask he was now smiling like a child who had guessed the right answer for the quiz. These nuanced moments were what had always fueled his deeper curiosity within the simulations he'd done for Sydney over the years—over the decades. In these revelations he found his joy—the purity of wonderment validated.

The medical personnel surrounding him and peering down from above were having their wonderment validated as well. There were many shared looks of awe at the work of his nimble steady hands—and none more so than Dr. Bilson as he looked to an irritable Dr. Su. As Jarod sutured up his patient he glanced furtively up, seeing their smiles. Impressing them with his skills was the first major hurdle in gaining their trust. What he was about to do next was the second.

Jarod turned to the nurse to his right. "In ICU, give her 300 cc of Triexapan." The nurse looked at the other personnel, then back to Jarod. "I don't think we carry that." But Jarod assured her that "I ordered it especially for this patient—had it delivered last night."

Bilson and Su exchanged a glance. Dr. B punched a button on the gallery railing and piped in over the O.R. intercom. "There's a group of people up here not only engrossed in your remarkable technique but also curious about this Triexapan?"

Jarod smiled behind his mask again—this too was an 'anticipatory.' He'd bet Bilson would ask about this and had won. "It's a factor Xa inhibitor that I consulted on during its development at Dharma-Pharmaceuticals. It should not only help prevent clots from forming but also be mild enough not to cause added stress on this young one's kidneys."

Bilson shot Su an '*I told you so*' look. The Asian doctor shrugged in reluctant acknowledgment of the talents he'd witnessed. Still there was no doubt both of them were thinking about how this wunderkind MD could increase their bottom line. Jarod had anticipated this would be their reaction and had guided them toward it.

Bilson gleefully pressed the intercom button again. "Dr. Russell, I'd like to speak with you when you're finished."

Those words were as sweet a music to Jarod's ears as was the *boom-boom, boom-boom, boom-boom* of his patient's now healthy heart.

Chapter 17

JAROD HAD ALWAYS been intrigued by the effect a uniform had on his self-perception during a Pretend. He was especially fascinated how, when sliding into the skin of another, you assumed physical statures and mannerisms that were not of your own nature. Three hours earlier, the moment he'd first donned his surgical scrubs, he'd felt focused, confident and omnipotent. Now, showered, shaved and refreshed following his surgical triumph, Jarod felt an entirely different way.

As he caught his reflection in the mirror of the surgeons' locker room he was surprised how sophisticated he felt. His espresso Armani suit fit like a glove, his Dijon Hermes tie stood out subtly from his pale canary shirt, while his loafers completed the look of a confident professional and man-about-town. Even his self-induced haircut—brushed and lightly gelled made him feel impeccable as never before. While the idea of his style sense was part of his Pretend, devised to win over Dr. Bilson by targeting the vain man's vanity, Jarod nonetheless filed a small part of style's possibilities in his own personal-use memory bank.

It felt good to look good.

As Jarod left the locker room and emerged into the hospital hallway he discovered another sensation—one he'd not felt in any sim before because it was one that could only come in real world situations. It was the feeling of being admired.

When he'd walked into the hospital ER 24 hours before, he could have easily been invisible. But what a difference a day made. He'd assumed that by their nature as a closed specialized community, hospitals would be hotbeds of idle chatter and gossip—and was counting on that. He needed a reputation as an incredible doctor to precede him—to buy him time to achieve his true objective. And his assumptions had been proven correct. Today nurses and doctors nodded warmly as he strode down the hallway.

This was good.

But as he rounded the corner into an empty rear corridor his springy step abruptly slowed. He stopped cold and tucked into the shadows, unseen—because of what he saw.

This was bad.

Midway down the hall the candy striper, Tami, was speaking with Dr. Bilson while waiting for him to sign a clipboard of papers. To the casual observer, it wouldn't appear anything was amiss about this situation—a hospital administrator, doing his job while taking a moment out of his busy schedule to casually explain to a young medical wanna-be how things worked in the hospital she hoped to one day be a permanent part of.

But Jarod wasn't a casual observer.

While he couldn't hear what was being said, their respective body language made it clear their conversation was anything but casual. Bilson was berating the young candy striper for something and she was retreating under his ego and stature.

Gifted with an emotional acuteness few others possessed, Jarod didn't just see the dysfunction in the dynamic between the two—but also felt it. As he laid eyes on them a wave of unseemly energy radiated from the pair—one he was not completely grasping, but one he was certain was negative.

After having imposed a level of intimidation sufficient to have the young woman emotionally defenseless, Bilson suddenly softened his tone, then physically began closing the distance between their bodies.

From Tami, Jarod sensed nothing but fear and vulnerability; her temperament was timid and her movements, while slight, were reactionary and defensive.

Bilson's were the opposite. Calm, lascivious and predatory—as if enjoying her discomfort.

Which he was.

Jarod surveyed the situation in micro-seconds, dissected the intricate parts of everything he saw and sensed and reconstructed them into a mosaic not evident on the surface.

Bilson stood inches from her, then leaned in, erasing the space between them. Retreating, she tried keeping the forced smile on her face, but fearful, it began to falter.

Bilson's eyes flickered in response to her unease. But he wanted more. So as he pointed to and questioned something in the clipboard with his right hand, his left smoothly swept down the doorjamb coming to rest on her petite waist. When she pivoted away from his unwelcome physical advances he countered, blocking her escape—literally cornering her against the wall.

As Bilson did this, a quote from Jarod's past came to mind. It was from a story the 17th century French author Charles Perrault wrote that related to a little girl's observance of, and question to, a creature she'd mistaken for her grandmother—and 'what big teeth' she seemed to have. As Bilson smiled at the trapped young woman, Jarod could almost hear the fairy tale Wolf answering the little girl with the red hood: 'The better to eat you with, my dear.'

With a silent but deadly implosion within, Jarod decided he could do one of two things. Ignore this and walk away—or confront it head on. After all Tami was not what he was here for. He had bigger quarry in his crosshairs. But it wasn't in his nature to walk away from injustice, so Jarod instantly swallowed the anger rising within and bolted into the hallway. "Perfect! Just the two people I was hoping to find."

Bilson turned toward his new wunderkind MD and Tami used this opportunity to slide out from where he had her trapped. Jarod smiled warmly to her.

"I've been wandering these halls like a blind man. Think you could give me a tour of the hospital so I can learn my way around?"

Tami flashed a relieved smile. "I'd be happy to, Doctor."

Jarod then thumbed toward Dr. Bilson. "A tour I was hoping would include how to find Dr. B's office." He looked to Bilson. "You did say you wanted to see me after surgery, correct?"

"Yes, to say you were astonishing in that O.R., Russell."

"Thank you, sir—beginner's luck."

"*Luck* my beautiful bum."

Bilson pulled Jarod a bit further down the hall to a more private spot for the 'men' to talk.

"I never flatter to flatter, Russell. And Dr. Su is even harder to please and even that sourpuss couldn't deny the quality of your work."

"I'll take that as high praise then, Sir."

"You should." Bilson smiled, then turned more serious. "There is one thing, though. For financial liability reasons new meds are passed by me for approval before we use them in the facility, especially ones as expensive as I'm informed Triexapan is."

"No worries, Doctor. I made sure the patient's insurance covered 100%—and with my connection to Dharma-Pharmaceuticals the wholesale-to-retail cost structure makes for a great deal of profit margin for Guardian."

Bilson liked hearing this. "Any unintended side effects I should know about?"

Jarod grinned calculatingly. "Let's just say—nothing the hospital has to worry about."

Dr. Bilson returned the grin and changed the subject. "You look like a man who enjoys a good cigar and martini you could start a new religion with?"

Jarod played long. "Maybe not a new religion—but a cult following sounds good."

"Keep doing what you've been doing and I'll be wearing a saffron robe and leading the parade." Bilson put his arm around Jarod. "There's a club around the corner from Grand Central called 'L'Endroit de L'Homme."

Jarod smiled to the arrogant Dr. Bilson. *The place for the man?"* Jarod translated—"Sounds like the place for me."

Bilson was quietly impressed with Jarod's skills. "I'd like to have you as my guest—to discuss the 'other opportunities' Guardian General has to offer. Say tomorrow, 9:00ish?"

"Wouldn't miss it for the world."

"Perfect. Now go enjoy your tour." Bilson peeped voyeuristically over Jarod's shoulder to young Tami. "My guess is what the meek young lass lacks between the ears, she more than makes up for between the sheets."

Jarod threw a glance to Tami and like the 'Little' Bad Wolf learning from his elder looked back to Bilson—a lascivious twinkle in his eye.

Bilson winked, then walked away with the cocksure strides of a man who felt he had everything under control.

Little did he know.

As he studied Bilson, Jarod's smile faded and a wellspring of anger re-surfaced. *This is a man I look forward to ruining*, Jarod thought—*this is a man that, if pushed far enough, I could*—but Jarod's contemplation was interrupted by Tami saying, "Thank you for saving me."

Jarod looked to her, the corner of his mouth dimpling into a smile. "Is that what I did?"

"Dr. B is rather 'friendly' with the volunteers."

"Maybe he's just a friendly man?"

Tami didn't know if she should answer this question honestly, but something about Jarod made her feel secure. "Not really. He's always find-ing fault with what I do. I try my best, I really do. And I really want this job to turn into a career. But I wanna get it for all the right reasons. You know?"

"I'm sure a young lady as intelligent and honest and beautiful as you will."

Blushing, Tami looked into Jarod's eyes and asked the one question he feared most. "Are you really a doctor?"

Jarod froze. "Why would you ask that?"

"Because you're a human being and, well, I haven't really seen much of that in 'them.'"

Jarod showed his palms. "You got me. I'm a complete and total fraud. Promise not to turn me in to the authorities for at least a week though—okay? I'm on a secret mission." He flashed pearly whites. She couldn't hold back her own.

"Now, do you have time to show me around?"

The candy striper's crush on the Doctor grew until she was glowing.

Chapter 18

ELEVEN MINUTES LATER Tami was walking on air as she led her own up close and personal version of Dr. Dreamy on a makeshift tour around Guardian General.

Tami's favorite TV show was *The Bachelor.* She watched it every Monday with a group of girlfriends, all of whom prayed that a man half as gorgeous as one of the show's hunks would one day give them a rose. But none of the bachelors had ever been as hot as Dr. Jarod. Unlike the young men she'd 'dated'—if you could actually consider it that in the hookup culture of her generation, the outstandingly beautiful surgeon listened—really listened and focused on every word she said—like he was actually interested in someone besides himself. It seemed to Tami that Jarod, a man without an ounce of guile—or body fat for that matter—was someone she could live happily ever after with. And that's what had her so frustrated. This was her big chance, but as much as she batted her eyes and giggled, she wasn't getting his attention *in that way* and was quickly running out of both hospital and cute things to say.

As she lead him down the last corridor on the ninth floor of the 'creepy and old' part of the hospital and toward the 'cool new annex,' Jarod was surprised to note how often she seemed to either flick her hair or shrug coyly at him. He'd listened to a book on tape about flirting—an action akin to mating dances between exotic birds and realized that is what the candy striper was doing with him.

And Jarod found it fascinating.

He was amazed how her behaviors were changing right before his eyes and wondered if she was cognizant of them. Did she know that to compensate for the nervous excitement she was obviously feeling that she was mindlessly exposing her neck to him while unconsciously twirling the tiny diamond stud in her left ear? Was she aware that the pulse in her carotid arteries revealed that her heart was beating faster than normal or that her pupils were dilated larger than they would naturally be in the light ambiance they were standing in?

Did she have any idea that her very physiology was stimulating both of these responses and she was sending out signals of a courtship display? And if so, did she wonder if they had triggered a response in him?

Because they hadn't. At least not in the way she'd hoped.

While Jarod had a feeling of fondness for Tami, there'd been no involuntary change in his heart rate or rise in his pheromone levels as far as he could tell. And no arousal. The truth was he wasn't sure if this was flirting and didn't have the time to think it through.

His thoughts were on two other things.

First, he wanted to memorize the layout of the hospital as he had done with the streets outside just in case he needed to get in and out in a hurry. And second, he needed to know more about the part of the hospital she was leading him toward.

As they reached the end of the hallway, Tami stopped in front of a two-car service elevator that faced a glass security tunnel.

Like a see-through umbilical cord, the tunnel was the only go-between connecting the main hospital to the Annex on the rooftop of the parking structure behind the hospital.

The glass and steel atrium housed the specific place in Guardian General that Jarod needed to get into. A process that would be easier said than done.

In the middle of the tunnel was a security barrier that consisted of two distinct four-foot long security chambers separated by three sets of thick Plexi doors. On the doors leading into the tunnel from the hospital side were big red letters reading: *PSYCHIATRIC ANNEX—AUTHORIZED PERSONNEL ONLY.*

Tami motioned towards the tunnel like Vanna White to a new puzzle to be solved. "There it is." But Jarod didn't know who Vanna White was—and as he looked at the door he did, in his own way, need to buy a vowel.

He looked inquisitively to Tami. "Wow. That's some serious security. Who do they keep over there?"

"It's not just *who* they keep—it's *what* they *do* with them." Before Tami could answer further, *Ding*—one of the service elevator doors behind them opened and exiting from within was a nurse with a skinny body and a big head that seemed to swivel instead of turn. Her name was Nurse Kropski. Nurse Kropski liked to be called *Nurse Kropski* as if *Nurse* was her first name. *Nurse* was with Gloria and they both held post lunch, half-filled Quiznos bags. Gloria looked at Tami, then at Jarod, then back to Tami, contemptuously. "Play time's over, young lady, I need you in neonatal."

"Yes, ma'am. I'm on my way."

Gloria looked at Jarod again and said "*Humpf.*" She then tipped her head to Nurse K and walked down the long corridor in the direction Jarod and Tami had come from. Nurse Kropski gave Jarod the once over, then curtly nodded her giant head at him and said "Doctor." Ignoring the candy striper, she turned and walked through the security tunnel. Jarod's eyes never left her as she used a special picture ID badge she slipped through the first layer of electronic readers, then went into the first chamber where she leaned into a retinal scanner. The scanner scanned her eyes, which unlocked the second layer of doors, which allowed her through to the last chamber where she again used her ID badge at the final set of doors to gain access through and into the psych Annex itself.

As she vanished into unknown parts beyond, Jarod looked back to Tami. "What's a 'nice' lady like her doing in a place like that?"

Tami looked left—then right—and satisfied they were alone again—looked back and said, "I'm not 'authorized personnel'—but—and this is all very hush-hush—from what I hear they're doing pharmaceutical testing for new meds on the psychiatric patients—you know—to get FDA approval."

She raised her eyebrows knowingly, which Jarod took as a signal of trust. She quietly said, "And the ID badges and security clearance to get through the doors? '*Very special*'"—she actually whispered those words as if they had been italicized—then, pointed at the sign. "And only the authorized personnel get them."

Tami again looked left—and then right—and then back to Jarod and leaned in conspiratorially. Sensing that the corresponding action was for him to do the same, Jarod leaned in as well and as he did he saw something change in her eyes. She liked being that close to him—a lot. Her body couldn't deny it. Her skin began to flush. Her breathing became deeper and her nostrils flared ever so slightly. Tami took a deep breath, breathing him in and after a moment of savoring it, slowly let it out as a whisper into his ear. "They say the Annex is harder to get into than Fort Knox."

Jarod leaned back and looked into her eyes. And as she nodded 'Oh, yes' he made a face like—*Oh, my.*

But that wasn't the face he was making on the inside.

Jarod already knew how to get into and out of Fort Knox—he'd worked that problem out when he was a young child. In fact he used the same strategy he'd devised for the gold repository to escape from The Centre. But the barriers of the security tunnel keeping him out of the Annex were more difficult and time wasn't on his side.

Jarod postulated it would take five days before the people in the hospital would begin to realize he wasn't who he was pretending to be. He hoped that would give him enough time to earn their trust so he'd be allowed through the special security—because it was what was behind the psych Annex doors—in Room E913 that he was ultimately here for.

Chapter 19

THE CONSTRUCTION OF The Centre went on 24 hours a day, seven days a week and took exactly six years and one day to complete. It is rumored that, like the Pyramids at Giza, the Great Wall of China, or even Machu Picchu, many men died during its creation and were buried within its walls. Urban legend or not, it remained an unsolved mystery. But mysteries abound in The Centre, <u>one</u> of which was uncovered by Jarod himself.

Carved into the Delaware bedrock beneath The Centre's main structure were 26 sub-levels, at least 'officially' there were 26. Jarod once calculated the amount of material excavated from beneath the limestone complex and determined that it actually equaled the total cubic yardage required for the 26 levels that were commonly known about—and an additional one that wasn't.

It was deep in the bowels of this unacknowledged sub-level—SL-27— where the real Centre secrets were buried and where Miss Parker went to find the odd man with the big brain.

Cornelius only had one eyebrow. Black on each end and white in the middle, the collection of thick wiry strands was perched over his left eye and sloped upward at a slight angle toward what would have been his widow's peak—that is, if he had hair on his head or any other place on his body. When he was excited, his singular brow undulated in a way that made it appear that a zebra-striped caterpillar was crawling away from his ear. His appearance was caused by a genetic condition that most people would have taken as a curse, but for Cornelius, genetics had defined him. He wore his unique uni-brow and all it represented as a badge of honor. In fact he was convinced 'in the physical' that he was hot as 'sex on a stick.'

Deep in the bowels of The Centre, the odd-looking man typed away at his various desktops, laptops and notebook computers, commanding the eleven virtual screens that surrounded his circular workspace like a technological symphony. The average person would have no idea what he was even looking at—what all the flashing electrons that were organizing themselves into the images and words on his screens really meant. But Cornelius did. He was orchestrating it all for his own amusement.

"Catch me if you can, Beeyatch!"

It was Spy vs. Spy. Move vs. counter-move. Like Captain Kirk, Cornelius—'Yo, call me The Corn-man' or 'The Big C'—Compton, spun 360 in his Play Seat Office Elite Gaming Chair, immersed in a game of cyber tag he'd created and inserted inside of the National Security Agency's most top-secret mainframe, hundreds of miles away in D.C. An $87 million one-of-a-kind supercomputer, one that only six of the NSA's employees knew existed. The one that was 'impenetrable.'

But The Cornster had now turned their most prized receptacle for global intelligence gathering and information analyzation into an Elysian Fields for his pleasure.

Because he could.

When he wanted to, Cornelius could hack into any spy drone, satellite, 'eye in the sky' or secure feed transmitted between NSA and any location in the world—including the Situation Room in the White House. Today the keyboard gangster had turned his intrusion into a virtual game of hide-and-seek, pitting himself against a legion of NSA's finest counter-hacking experts. And each time the frantic people on the other side of the screen thought they'd found him hiding behind another electronic doorway, they instead walked right into an eyeful of sexcapades—starring some of the most influential, prominent and least attractive political and economic power brokers in the world.

Half of the cyber spooks in D.C. and Silicon Valley were trying to find him, trying to stop him. But no one knew who he was. No one knew that he was the person who'd really exposed General David Petraeus' illicit affair—by posting not only the X-rated sexting between the now-former

CIA director and multi-war hero and his naughty paramour—but as an added bonus, also included child-like animations of the two doing the horizontal mambo that Cornelius had created in his spare time.

But 'The Man of Corn' wasn't hacking into NSA's system to steal security secrets. Any moron with half a brain, or half of *his* brain, and a keyboard could do that. For Cornelius this was all personal. He was doing it to validate his very existence.

A child prodigy, Corn was the third smartest person born in 1987. Literally. As recorded by Mensa. And he hated that fact. A bronze medal finish that he was convinced *had to be a mistake* and until proven unjust, *wasn't worth a warm bucket of monkey piss.*

But it was these intellectual attributes that had made Miss Parker, that miserable bitch slave driver in a mini-skirt, offer him this job in the first place. She had almost made Cornelius piss himself when he exited the shower of his dorm room at Harvard and found her in the steamy bathroom, waiting for him with a business proposition. Miss Parker knew he was 'The Man.' He'd known that since the instant she reached into her bra and pulled out a business card—<u>her</u> business card—and handed it to him.

Even though she'd once referred to him as 'Gollum in Hugo Boss,' Cornelius knew she secretly desired him for more than just his big brain. All women did. Though for the life of him, he couldn't comprehend why, thus far, no one had ever made a move and acted upon those carnal desires.

Short, skinny, and with ears just this side of Dumbo's, Cornelius nevertheless had an innate sense of fashion that he knew would one day make the ladies swoon. Gone was the Hugo, now replaced with an exclusive Tom Ford wardrobe and all the must-have accessories.

All the bitches would soon be queuing up for this shit.

Technologically savvy, sinisterly brilliant, Cornelius could do things with bits and bytes others hadn't even conceived of—including the two geniuses who came in first and second in the IQ derby of '87. But unlike other hackers of real life and legend, he didn't learn to backdoor his way into the NSA's mainframe just for fun—he did it to prove a point. Turns out that the number two brainiac from '87, Silvio Cardonez, was NSA's counter-cyber-hacker expert. So, from time to time, 'The Big C' screwed with Silvio for fun as he did with the number one big brain from '87, whose identity he loved to brag about having stolen dozens of times—especially since that cocky bitch invented Life Lock.

Cornelius was finishing a jib-jab animated version of Hillary Clinton doing an unnatural reverse-cowgirl of biblical proportions on top of Donald Trump (set up to be found by the #1 and #2 counter-hacker investigators), when Miss P—who'd been standing behind him for how long he had no idea—cleared her throat, scaring the shit out of him. He hated when she just appeared. She always did at the worst times.

Then, without batting an eyelash about how weird he was, Miss Parker said six words that changed his life.

"I need you, you little freak."

He looked at her and his eyebrow undulated in anticipation of fulfilling her every desire.

Chapter 20

AFTER A GRUELING twelve-hour shift, the Pretender secured a tourniquet four inches above the venipuncture site of his final patient of the day. After tapping his inside forearm to encourage dilation, he lined up the blood collection needle and, making sure the bevel was up, plunged it into the median cubital vein. Jarod then attached the vacutube to the back of the needle and watched the blood pump in.

His blood.

Today, Jarod was his own patient.

Needles had never been a problem. From an early age The Centre doctors had done regular blood work-ups, constantly ensuring their prize was in tip-top shape. Today, alone in his office at the hospital, Jarod was gathering blood for a different kind of test.

Jarod switched to a second vial and as it filled he placed the first one on his desk next to a brand-new iPad he'd bought from a store in Times Square. He'd also purchased a red skin for it.

He'd considered buying one with characters from a television show called *Family Guy*. He found their images to be quite humorous, especially the cigar-smoking baby. He'd have been quite happy carrying it with him, but had chosen something more serious. He'd decided that iPads would become his new 'red notebooks' in which he would document all the reasons for the actions he was carrying out in the world. In retrospect he wished he'd had one when he was revealing the truth about what the turbine company had been covering up. The disruption of the whale mating songs could not be understood nearly as well on paper as they could be *felt* when hearing them recorded on an iPad. Serious work needed an iPad to look serious as well.

He settled on red because of tradition and to Jarod it was both a color of passion and honor. As he removed the second vial of blood he thought about honor and passion. Jarod was committed to passionately helping those who couldn't help themselves and in his own unique way, by doing so, was honoring humanity itself.

He sealed the blood vials and then took out three plastic bags that contained hair and put all five samples in a manila envelope with medical request forms he'd filled out earlier. As he was sealing it there was a light knock.

"It's open."

The door slowly swung inward and Tami timidly entered. "Dr. Russell, this is probably a mistake, so I hope I'm not interrupting anything, but I was told you wanted to see me."

"Why would my wanting to see you be a mistake?"

"Well, mainly cause I'm a nobody candy striper and you're like this incredibly cool doctor and well—like that."

Jarod gave a warm smile. "Tami, you can't be a nobody if I've been thinking about you all day."

Tami steadied herself with the door. "*You* were—thinking of *me*?"

"Yes."

"Really?"

"Really."

Tami's raised eyebrows were paired with a smile that conveyed she'd believe anything Jarod said just because it was he who was saying it.

"Now close the door."

Tami did as instructed, then stepped in front of his desk as if she were doing this to be a diligent worker—when in fact it was just so she could be closer to him.

Jarod met her adoring eyes. "I was hoping I could get you to do a couple things for me."

Tami actually blurted: "Of course, I'll do anything for you, Doctor." *Anything—and I mean anything*—she said—to herself.

"First, you can stop calling me Doctor. My name is Jarod."

Jarod thought he saw her right leg buckle. She was practically breathless. "Okay … *Jarod*."

He handed her the envelope. "Second, could you please run this upstairs to the lab for a full spectrum DNAP test? The orders are inside."

"Absolutely."

"Good." Jarod then lowered his voice. "And would you tell them it's very private—and a rush job?"

The candy striper's eyes went wide. "I'll wait for it if you want me to. I don't have any real plans tonight or anything I can't cancel."

"That's not necessary. But I'd like if you would get me the results as soon as they come in." Jarod stood, walked around the desk and held out a card. With a stunned expression she looked up from it and into his eyes. "Is that your—phone number?"

"Private cell. I'd appreciate it if you don't give it out." Jarod gave her the *can I trust you?* look.

Tami nodded at least seven times. "No worries. No one will see it but me, I swear."

"Good." Jarod rubbed her shoulder in a friendly manner. "Day or night—it doesn't matter."

Tami couldn't speak. She just kept clearing her throat and nodding as she backed out of the door.

"Tami?"

"Yes, Doctor—I mean—*Jarod* …"

"Thank you."

She looked at him blankly—made herself swallow, then recomposed, said, "You can count on me."

Tami made it out the door without further embarrassment.

Jarod rolled down and buttoned the cuff of his sleeve. He then put on his doctor's coat and picked up a clipboard with patient charts. His day job was now completed, but his night job was just getting started.

Chapter 21

DING. SEVEN MINUTES later the service elevator opened and Jarod stepped into the hallway facing the glass bridge security tunnel to the psych Annex.

The Pretender already had a plan in the works that would ensure he would get *into* the Annex. What he wanted to ensure—*needed* to ensure—was that he would be able to *get out*—and as he wasn't planning on leaving the Annex alone, it was imperative he had his escape worked out before the time came.

But there was an 'unknown' he wanted to solve.

On his first trip down this hallway with Tami he'd seen someone go from the hospital side through the security measures to enter the psych Annex, but he hadn't seen if the measures in the reverse direction were the same—specifically if the retinal scan was needed to leave the Annex or just to enter it and how long did that central door remain unlocked during passings.

Jarod performed his security door surveillance under the cover of doing his rounds and as all his recovering patients were on the same floor as the Annex, it made it easier to accomplish this task without raising suspicions.

Besides, for 'Dr.' Jarod, unlike many real MD's, doing his rounds was something that he actually enjoyed. He loved getting to know about his patients and was fascinated by their personal stories.

Mila Cahill, who was recovering from the aneurysm surgery, was a Special Ed teacher from Vermont whose entire class had made and signed a huge card full of well wishes for a speedy recovery and return.

Down the hall, Amanda King, the ten-year-old Norwood patient was being read a book about an inquisitive chimpanzee by her big sister, Penny.

But Jarod's favorite was Sylvia Zuniga, the deaf Hispanic woman who had fallen down the flight of stairs. She told Jarod that before her tumble she'd been making dinner for her husband, who suffered with Alzheimer's. Her husband no longer recognized her, nor could he remember how to speak in sign—but she had found a way to connect to him through his taste buds and so through her cooking kept her memory alive in his heart. She was determined to get back home as soon as possible to resume giving him that joy.

As he left Sylvia's room he turned to his right and walked down the corridor to the security entrance to the Annex. There was one other patient he wished he could check on this day—the one in Room E913 of the Annex.

During his rounds he had passed the security tunnel four times—but on all of those occasions no one was exiting.

He hit the elevator call button to give himself an excuse to stand there longer, then looked back across the tunnel. On the other side he saw a nurse with dirty blonde hair looking out from the Annex at him.

To Jarod, the nurse with the dirty blonde hair registered as 30ish. Her scrubs appeared to be a size too tight, accentuating a body that was feminine, shapely but ripped. While she was obviously attractive, Jarod found her beauty to have a slight emotionally damaged quality to it that included a long-time sad exhaustion in her eyes, as if she could never truly rest. Her hair looked hastily bunched and twisted atop her head and the very tips of her locks held traces of purple and orange—an odd choice, he felt, for a nurse. Calculating hair growth, he surmised she'd colored it some six months ago and it had almost grown out. She had a tiny scar curving around the edge of her lower lip—well healed and likely from childhood. And despite her attempts to pull down her too-short sleeves, she was sporting a tiny tattoo of an angel on her right forearm. Jarod liked angels and always had ever since he researched them for a long forgotten sim. The angel tat gave him a good feeling about her.

What she did next, however, didn't.

The nurse looked up at a wall clock, and then glared back at Jarod. Jarod perceived that she was wondering what he was doing loitering in the hallway, so to try and relieve any suspicions he smiled at her.

She didn't smile in return.

Jarod knew he didn't have much more recon time and staring at an empty tunnel was not helping his anonymity, so he took a pen out of his pocket and wrote a few notes in his patient charts to buy a few more seconds.

Then he got lucky.

A visually unique orderly with a pushcart of empty dinner trays struggled past the nurse with dirty blonde hair. The man had alabaster skin and long white hair that cascaded around his face from beneath a fedora. He walked with a pronounced hobble from a disabled left foot that folded inward and curled the ankle under. His nickname around Guardian was Albino Jude.

Jude limp stepped, limp stepped, limp stepped into the security tunnel to cross to the main hospital building. He stopped at the first set of locked Plexiglass doors and swiped his ID card. As those doors unlocked he limp stepped into the first four-foot security compartment, pulling the heavy cart behind him. He then leaned down awkwardly to get his face into a retinal device on the Annex side that scanned his pink eyes and unlocked the central doors.

So there is one, Jarod thought.

As Jarod was observing this, the elevator behind him *dinged*. But Jarod paid no attention as its doors began to open. His focus was on the doors Albino Jude was moving past in the tunnel and the ones he was approaching. Jarod also needed to know exactly how long the retinal door remained unlocked after activation and so began a countdown in his head. But as the orderly hobbled with his cart through the inner doors and into the equally small chamber on the other side, his cart got stuck in the closing retinal doors behind him.

Watching the frustrated orderly fumble with his ID badge in the electronic lock of the last barrier to his freedom, Jarod felt he wouldn't be getting the precise information he needed tonight.

Then something 'unexpected' happened that changed everything; the nurse with the dirty blonde hair blasted out from the Annex, snatched her ID hanging from a lanyard around her neck and whipped it through the reader to unlock the doors to the first chamber. This happened just as the ID door unlocked in chamber two and Albino Jude began to limp step out in Jarod's direction.

For one moment all three doors to the Annex were not only unlocked—but open.

As a thousand thoughts exploded in Jarod's mind at once he recognized that this very instant may be his best and only chance to get into the Annex at all. *Right now. Just go be polite, help the Jude with his stuck cart, say 'Good evening' to the nurse and slip through all three doors before they could close.*

Do that, and he could be inside the Annex and into Room E913 in less than a minute.

But just as quickly as Jarod had this thought, he decided not to act on it. He also realized if he got into the Annex this way and didn't accomplish his goal, he might never have another opportunity.

As the albino orderly's now moving cart unblocked and released the center door, the nurse stepped over to it and, very subtly, prevented it from closing with her shoe. She did it in a way the average observer wouldn't notice, but Jarod wasn't the average observer. As Jude and his cart trundled past him and headed down the hall, Jarod looked up to see the nurse in the first security compartment lean her eyes into the scan mechanism—*for absolutely no reason at all*—and then look up as if her retinas had been read. Then, with her foot, she flipped the door open as if it had unlocked. As she blew through the first chamber she looked up through the remaining Plexiglass security door at Jarod—she actually looked past him—then back into his eyes and yelled something to him he couldn't hear.

Jarod shrugged palms upward, the universal sign for *'huh?'* She grabbed her ID, slapped it through the reader while at the same time urgently pointing and shouting to Jarod a second time. More from reading her lips than hearing her diffused words, Jarod finally realized what she was saying.

"Hold the elevator!"

Immediately Jarod spun to the elevator doors, but they closed before he could reach them. The last security door had just unlocked and the nurse was emerging into the main hospital hallway as Jarod looked back to her and grimaced.

The nurse didn't grimace—she exploded. "I swear to God, I sometimes think this hospital is infected with stupid and I'm the only one with a vaccine."

Jarod was taken aback by this. "I'm sorry, I—"

"Sorry? What good does *sorry* do me?"

Jarod thought that was a strange way for a nurse to address a doctor and that he should in some way be offended by her behavior. But there was something about the dirty blonde with the ill-fitting scrubs and sassy attitude that intrigued him. Actually it wasn't intrigue—what he felt for the dirty blonde as she pressed the elevator call button three or four or five times in quick succession was more akin to fascination. And Jarod's fascination with her centered on one part of her anatomy. A part he could clearly see now. Her eyes. They were unlike any he'd ever seen before.

They were violet.

"In a hurry?"

"Yeah, I need to get downstairs and pick up something from the lab." Jarod observed her as she flipped a look down the long hallway to her left and just as quickly shifted to check out the one to her right. She then gazed up to the floor indicator display panel readout above the elevator which told her the lift had stopped three floors above them and was now in the down mode. For a person as seemingly self-confident as this nurse with the violet eyes, the way she shifted from foot to foot as she watched the numbers descend on the floor indicator belied the fact that she was actually quite nervous.

"I've only been here three days and even I know that the lab's upstairs—and so would every <u>real</u> nurse," Jarod said. The dirty blonde stopped shifting and stood perfectly still and looked into his eyes. Jarod smiled at her again.

"If you're going to make it out of here, you better get your lies straight."

Jarod had known the nurse with the violet eyes wasn't really a nurse since the moment he saw her block the middle security door with her foot and fake the retinal reading of her eyes. It was clear to him she too was faking her profession and that she was most likely a psych patient trying to escape her confinement. As an escapee himself, he found the quality in her of wanting to be free quite attractive.

Before she could answer him, a red light above the Annex tunnel began spinning and flashing and a low tone alarm sounded. On the far side of the tunnel several security guards and the very skinny woman with the hefty head—who was putting on an oversized scrub shirt and who Jarod realized was Nurse Kropski, burst from the inner Annex and rushed the first of the three doors pointing and yelling at the woman next to Jarod as they began making their way through the security.

Violet Eyes looked down both hallways and saw guards coming from each direction. She then gazed up to the floor indicator display that showed the elevator was about to arrive. She looked back at Jarod, who smiled at her and shrugged. The nurse who was not a nurse finally smiled back. "I guess you got me."

She then coldcocked Jarod with a roundhouse right, just as *ding*—the elevator doors opened and she rushed inside and into the waiting arms of Dr. Bilson and Dr. Su.

"No, no, no!"

She struggled for freedom as they emerged with her.

Jarod stood up, rubbing his chin, just in time to see Nurse Kropski in the big scrubs rush out of the tunnel. She looked at Bilson with embarrassment and then with fury to the violet-eyed escapee. "Bitch hit me with a bedpan and stole my ID."

Bilson and Su handed her over to a couple of guards, who she continued to struggle with, Bilson asking her, "Have you not been taking your meds, Skylar?"

"No! And it's because I'm not crazy and I don't belong over there!"

"You're a persistent thing, I'll give you that."

Jarod looked deeply into the violet essence of her unique eyes. "Skylar, huh? What a pretty name. It means strength, love and beauty."

"Yeah, right now it means 'screw you.' I shoulda known you were one of them!"

As the guards took Skylar back into the security tunnel and toward the Annex, Jarod realized non-nurse was the most unexpected 'unexpected' he'd ever encountered.

And for some reason he liked the girl with the violet eyes immediately.

Chapter 22

"I'LL SHOWER YOU with riches." That had been Miss Parker's quote. Her exact quote. The one he'd written down. Help her bring back Jarod and that's what she'd do for him. Shower him with riches. And that's when he realized riches were his missing link. God knows he had the style and the swag and the pimp roll—but the bitches couldn't resist the Benjamin's and he'd soon be rolling in them too. Then he'd be sitting pretty—able to attract all the sexy shorty-flies to his honey. All he had to do was match wits with The Pretender and he'd be doing the back-stroke in the briny juices of the big ass oyster that would soon be his world.

Just like the first time he'd stolen Miss Lifelock's identity and had $3.2 million charged to her various credit cards for electronic water-resistant sex toys, this was going to be easy.

Alone in his little corner of SL-27, thinking of the bigger things in his future, Cornelius licked his pinky finger, wiped his eyebrow slick and smiled the smile of winners. He had a plan and was shocked when it fell into place so quickly.

Chapter 23

IT WASN'T THE music floating through the air—(which he found out later was a recording of an instrument called a calliope) that made Jarod so happy that day. Nor was it the bright sunshine that enlivened the small town Americana Main Street of Tourne River, New Jersey, where he was standing. It wasn't the oversized, brightly colored painting of the man with orange hair and a red ball on his nose that covered the entire outside panel of the truck—though Jarod did find him amusing. It wasn't even the eight-foot-long, funnel-shaped object that appeared to have been dropped atop the truck by some enormous giant—and out of the top of which a make-believe gooey pink substance was seemingly melting and dripping down the sides.

No, what had Jarod fascinated with complete and utter wonderment wasn't on the outside of the soft serve ice cream truck that was sitting next to the sidewalk across the street from Riverside Park at all. What had totally captivated him was what Jarod was staring at through the window of the truck—the magical frozen confection that was being extruded from the ice cream machine itself.

Like a toddler amazed at a soap bubble flying through the air, Jarod was equally enamored every time the grumpy man with the paper hat lifted the silver handle and a rope of the creamy cold dessert flowed out and slid into the base of a conical-shaped receptacle that Jarod had just discovered was made out of some type of hard pastry. As it dropped down, the grumpy man twirled the edible container slowly in his hand as the ice cream filled up the inside of what the man referred to as a cone.

As he handed it to Jarod, the Pretender's smile was as wide as a mile—his eyes twinkling with anticipation. Jarod took it from the ice cream man. He stared into its millions of ice crystals and multitudinous folds that he knew were bursting with flavor. He then chose just the right spot for what he wanted to do next.

Jarod took a lick from his cone—his fourth of the day—and as its taste exploded in his mouth, he closed his eyes in total and utter bliss. Jarod was overwhelmed by the delicious decadence of the forbidden treat.

He was amazed that it could be light yet dense and at the same time, simple yet complex. He reveled in the exquisite creamy texture, the vanilla-bean taste in which he could detect a million tastes at once, including the essence of custard, subtle caramel and maple notes.

He savored the confection as if enjoying a first kiss. He then opened his eyes and smiled at the dumbfounded ice cream man—his mind bursting with a million thoughts and questions.

"Do they whip in air to make it so fluffy?"

The grizzled soft serve veteran looked at Jarod as if he was from the moon. "I don't make it—I just sell it."

Jarod took another taste—still finding each one better than the first. "It's very good."

"Does your mom know where you are, friend—or did you just miss the short bus by a long time?"

Jarod took no offense.

In fact his mind was now off on another tangent—suddenly captured by what he had been standing there waiting for, for the last hour.

The green SUV pulled into the parking lot across the street.

Jarod slowly lowered his ice cream cone as he watched the lithe, well-dressed woman climbing out. Her name was Cassandra Hearns and every day for the last eight weeks she performed this same ritual. At 4:18 every day she parked in the same spot and stared out at the river as sadness filled her 33-year-old eyes.

The reason Jarod had come to New York was Cassandra Hearns.

The reason he was Pretending to be a doctor was because of this sadness in her eyes.

Jarod watched her grab a bundle of daisies from her passenger seat. He sensed in her a lonely despair he gravitated to.

He pulled from his backpack his iPad with the red skin and turned it on. It opened to a story he'd downloaded from his favorite news site, Instapundit. The article included a picture of a distraught Cassandra Hearns clutching onto a framed photo of a ten-year-old boy with the caption: *CAR FLIES FROM OLD TOURNE RIVER BRIDGE—FATHER INJURED—SON VANISHES IN RIVER*. Next to the story was a photo of a broken guardrail atop the small two-lane Tourne Bridge as the wrecked BMW that had crashed through it was being fished out of the water.

Jarod looked back up to Cassandra, who held the daisies as she wound her way out of the parking lot and out of sight down the trail that led into the woods.

Turning off the iPad, Jarod followed her down to the river's edge. He kept a respectful distance, partly to stay out of her sight, but mainly because he found in his short time out in the world that people showed their truest colors anonymously. His clandestine observances always showed him their reality, be it the Wall Street broker kissing his wife good-bye only to rendezvous with his girlfriend moments later or the homeless man he followed who gave his beggar's money to someone worse off than he. The truth in people was often a lonely affair and Jarod quickly drew the connection between getting into their heads via the hundreds of sims he performed for The Centre and getting into their heads out here in the real world.

He stopped behind a cluster of birch trees as Cassandra arrived at the riverbank beneath the two-lane bridge from the photo Jarod had been looking at—a bridge with a newly repaired guardrail where her husband's BMW plunged through weeks earlier.

With a silent prayer she laid the daisies into the water stem by stem. They floated languidly downstream, presumably just as her son had, to a fate she had not yet accepted. Jarod was clear this was not a mother ready to let go and wouldn't until she saw her son, dead or alive, with her own eyes.

But the moment here was not hers alone.

It was Jarod's as well.

As he watched Cassandra cross herself, kneel down at the river's edge to pray, he knew that he was not merely observing one mother's heartbreak for her son, but that he was watching every mother who had lost a child—including his own.

A mother he could only vaguely remember.

As Jarod observed Cassandra, a question began to play over and over in his mind and as he listened to it, his eyes began to brim with tears.

The question was one he'd asked his mentor when he was but a child.

"Sydney, is it possible for a person to forget the ones they love?"

Chapter 24

HOLLOWED BY TIME, Young Jarod's voice echoed through Jarod's hospital office. "Answer me, Sydney. Is it possible for a person to forget the ones they love?"

Jarod was seated at his desk deep in thought staring at the screen of his paper-thin notebook computer from which a distinctive Belgian accent answered Young Jarod's question, "Focus Jarod, we're working now."

If adult Jarod's new existence and whatever the future held for him was the window he now viewed life through—his massive collection of DSAs and their specialized player he stole during his escape from The Centre were the dark mirror that pulled him back into his cloistered and unique past. Literally a catalog of every single day of his life there since age four, Jarod knew his dark mirror was one that saw all. Nearly every moment of his past was at his fingertips. But while home videos may stir warm memories in the hearts of the world's masses, for Jarod a DSA was more likely to swirl up distressing anxiety or, depending on the Sim, unsettling discomfort at the very least. But now, free and as an adult, Jarod knew he couldn't shy away from his past, that these DSAs were a treasure—a living, archived diary.

Alternatively, this powerful tool also gave him invaluable insight into The Centre's motives and activities. Yes, it was often disturbing the paces Sydney would put him through in the name of The Centre and 'for the good,' but it was also hard information that, now seen through adult eyes, provided Jarod with clues to discover his captor's secrets.

Most importantly, he hoped to mine more clues about who he really was and where he came from. *Where are my mom and dad? Where are my mom and dad? Where are my mom and dad?*

Jarod refocused on the simulation he was watching on his DSA time machine, its screen glowing in his eyes as he gazed back at himself through time.

A clear plastic orb filled the DSA screen.

Surrounded by darkness and a growing shroud of steam, mounted on a motorized platform and lit from above, the Plexiglass orb was eight feet in diameter and fully enclosed. Packed in tightly within this claustrophobic cocoon, an agitated 8-year-old Jarod wearing a space suit, helmet and headset was breathing heavily and sweating profusely.

As the surveillance cam pushed in tighter on the image of his younger self, adult Jarod's pupils began to expand, his eyes riveted to the screen where electronically superimposed underneath the boy's image were the words: *JAROD 1/28/86, PSYCHOGENIC STUDIES, FOR OFFICIAL CENTRE USE ONLY.*

Jarod's throat began to constrict as he watched.

Young Jarod's eyes darted fearfully around the inside of his 'capsule,' noticing something distressing—ice crystals forming on the glass—here, here and here—a revelation that greatly alarmed him. He shouted into his head mic: "External temperatures are too low for launch. I repeat—too low! Control—are you listening to me?"

Jarod switched to a different camera angle—one that showed a Young Sydney in the shadows eyeing rolling data on a computer monitor, careful to remain behind YJ as to not distract him.

A voice crackled in YJ's headset.

"T minus ten seconds and counting."

The countdown continued as steam began enveloping the capsule. "Wait—there's a problem!" 'Eight—seven—six ...' YJ squirmed anxiously. "Wait!"

Jarod looked at his younger self, pleading to be heard.

"Sydney, why didn't they listen to me?" Young Jarod braced himself against the Plexi. "Didn't they read Morton Thiokol's report? 31 degrees is on the edge of parameters—they needed to abort!"

"We have lift off." Suddenly the orb lurched and rolled back from the hydraulic arms that controlled its movement. Heavy steam and mist fell away as YJ was slammed into his seat. The orb began to vibrate intensely, simulating the thrust and shimmy of 4.4 million pounds lifting up to the heavens and its corresponding G-forces pressing downward onto the boy astronaut. Even though the physical stresses were enormous, the Young Jarod remained calm, implementing the tasks of a shuttle commander just like he was trained.

"T plus seventeen and looking good, Challenger."

YJ lifted his head, scouring the darkness of the Sim lab, his in-command demeanor returning to that of a frightened little boy.

"Sydney? Sydney? Where are you?"

Sydney remained planted in the dark, "Focus, Jarod."

"I just want to know if it's possible, Sydney."

Annoyed, Sydney looked up from his control monitor. "Is what possible?"

"Can people forget the ones they love?"

Sydney rubbed his temples, "We'll talk about this later, Jarod, we're in the middle of—"

But Jarod wouldn't be put off. "Like a mother or a father forgetting their child." Jarod exhaled. "Or a child forgetting its parents?"

Sydney's sigh was long and frustrated. "We've gone over this Jarod and I'll answer your questions as soon as you're finished. We're on a deadline, you know that."

YJ didn't like the non-answer, but resolved to it instantly and slipped back into his pretend persona of the Challenger commander; shoulders squared, every movement confident, his eyes steely again with focus, he activated the sequencing on his control panel.

"T plus twenty-four, Challenger at 30,000 feet."

Suddenly a huge jolt rocked the orb. Young Jarod looked out and down—a sudden unexpected plume of smoke could now be seen.

"T plus sixty-eight—go with throttle up."

Resolved to his fate, Commander Young Jarod obeyed by increasing booster power. At T plus seventy-two, pull away began but quickly jolted the crew capsule again, lurching laterally on the hydraulics, instantly alarming YJ— "Uh-oh."

The death knell tolled out of nowhere.

Warning alarms began blaring followed by a thunderous explosion. The heat was as intense as the flash of light in his eyes—but it was the enormous jolt that sent Jarod's head slamming back against the Plexi. The orb capsule began bucking wildly, sending it and the young Pretender into a crazed prolonged spin. Amid the chaotic din, Young Jarod kept his cool, checking gauges and error messages until suddenly there was silence and no power, the capsule spinning wildly now, still shooting upward from sheer momentum—the control panel reading 68,000 feet, when suddenly the orb reached its ascendant apogee—and seemed for a second to just be floating in air—until the gravitational forces of the earth slowly urged it back downward, pulling Young Jarod and his imaginary crew faster and faster into their death spiral.

Young Jarod as commander, resigned to his fate, continued with his disciplined training procedures. "Control? Control? If you can hear us, we've lost all power. No emergency bailout. Oxygen systems shutting down. We're in free fall."

And with silence all around, the Sim lab backdrop changing from darkness to light again, YJ began to hyperventilate for real—his oxygen shut down—so intense was his simulation he literally began to suffocate as the hydraulics spun the orb violently, tossing and spinning Young Jarod in his cocoon until with a sudden crash simulating the impact into the Atlantic—it was over.

The Sim lab lights came up. Sydney unlatched and opened the orb. "You did wonderfully, Jarod. I am proud of your work."

But Jarod wasn't proud, he was frustrated. He shoved Sydney's hands away as tears welled. "I told them they shouldn't launch! That it was too cold and that the O-rings weren't spec'd for that—but they didn't listen, they didn't—" Young Jarod's voice fell away. Young Sydney stared at his charge.

Jarod, in his hospital office, zoomed in on Young Sydney's eyes, trying to decipher the emotion within them.

Young Jarod remained silent. Sydney knelt down and lifted his chin. "What was he thinking about, Jarod? The Commander—as he plunged to certain death?"

Tears flowed down Young Jarod's cheeks as he looked back at Sydney. "That he'd never see his family again. Ever see the ones he loved. They were all he could think about as he left this world." Young Sydney's eyes began to well with tears of his own.

Jarod clicked off the DSA. As the sounds of his past in The Centre were replaced by the sounds of his present in the hospital—*Dr. Su, please report to the ER, Dr. Su*—Jarod reflected for a moment about what emotions he had witnessed in Sydney's eyes. He clearly felt the loss Jarod was questioning him about—but why? Was it personal—or theoretical? Whose pain was Sydney feeling?

Jarod reached down to the side of his desk and brought up his backpack. He opened it and looked inside to where he had a dozen throwaway cell phones.

Releasing his own heavy sigh, he grabbed one, sat back and wondered if he could actually make the call he was about to.

Chapter 25

SYDNEY'S CAVERNOUS, 200 year-old, French Colonial home echoed with a deafening silence that screamed *emptiness*. The rooms were devoid of any sign of life. The furniture draped in white sheets, the bookshelves empty, blank spots where art had once hung.

It was as though no one lived within its walls.

In the kitchen—where there had once been all forms of crystal and glasses, utensils and silver—there remained but one simple piece of earthenware. A goblet that served as both a bowl and drinking vessel for coffee, water and the occasional pouring of his favorite *Vin de pays des Jardins de Wallonie*, a wine from the rural Wallonian countryside of his youth. Sydney often had a large serving of this wine before he went off to slumber.

He slept in a chair in the middle of the great room—on those nights when he was able to sleep. It was identical to the Lazy Boy Jarod had sat in under the electrical storm at the windmill farm. Sydney wondered how Jarod discovered that he slept in the chair. Wondered if Jarod had come by his house the night he escaped, looked in the window and saw him snoring in it. Wondered if Jarod had subsequently purchased his own so that he could remain symbolically close to Sydney, connected to him. It couldn't have been a coincidence, could it? The Belgian thought deeply about whether he'd ever told Jarod about why he slept in the chair. That he couldn't sleep in a bed comfortably since the incident.

He thought about everything he'd ever said to Jarod. Going over and over in his mind what he could have done or said that could have triggered

Jarod to leave him. Sydney hadn't felt this hollow since the incident so long ago.

It took him three months afterwards before he'd find the strength to go into Amelia's closet and even look at her belongings, and three months more until he found himself gently folding the clothing his Spanish born wife had worn on her tender cinnamon colored skin.

Piel canela.

Sydney wrapped the canvases she had painted in paper, boxed up the books whose words had long filled her imagination, along with the crystal and china she'd inherited from her mother. He tenderly placed all of her things, the pieces of her and all the little things that reminded him of their life together, in the back of the old Volvo with the squeaky, unreliable brakes. After a long drive on a very cold day, he came to a high-pitched stop in the Goodwill parking lot in nearby Pilcher's Pointe. After three minutes of unloading, her entire life had been donated to others.

But Sydney couldn't donate the crib.

It still sat in the nursery where it had been collecting dust for over 30 years. Syd rarely ventured in there, but for years after the incident he often stood in the doorway and looked inside, peering into a time long past when joy and the laughter of his beloved Patrick filled the long silent home. The hole in his soul from losing his son was one he thought would never be filled.

That hole was now empty again.

~~~

Sydney gave up on escaping into sleep and drove the old Volvo back to The Centre. He took the long walk back to his lab. Back to where he found contentment—to where his purpose was.

Atop his desk was the toy chest Jarod had left at the offshore windmill farm. The toy magnets, the book on surgery, and the poster of the fruit fly neuron clusters that he still hadn't determined the significance for. He knew they all meant something to Jarod—and if they meant something to him, they meant something to Sydney. He was determined to find out what it was.

Syd walked over to where a photo of Jarod hung on the wall, next to the observation window that looked out to the floor below—to the domed living space where his brilliant charge had been raised.

The picture was of Jarod the day he'd arrived. The day the beautiful little boy with the tender brown eyes had blown Sydney's mind when he'd built the skyline of Manhattan.

The day Sydney found hope again.

Since the night Jarod had run away, Sydney often found himself here after hours. Alone he would walk into the space where Jarod had lived and worked. Where *they* had worked. Where the most fulfilling joy in Sydney's life had occurred. And here he was again, wandering through Jarod's space, the world where Jarod had made so many discoveries, where his genius had amazed Sydney on a daily basis.

Sydney opened a white cabinet filled with red notebooks—Jarod's hand-made reports of his simulation work—the reasons he did them—the chronicles of the discoveries he'd made—the discoveries only he could have made. Sydney closed the cabinet of these memories and moved on to other personal items of Jarod's. Sydney ran his fingers over the keys of Jarod's computer, over the blanket that had kept him warm at night and the pillow that had supported his head as he slept.

Syd was lost in his memories when his cell phone rang. He removed it from the pocket of his tweed jacket and was surprised to see on the screen the call name "Slate." Syd joyfully sat down on the bed and answered.

"*Slate* is an anagram for Tesla. Very clever, Jarod."

"That's what you taught me to be," Jarod replied solemnly.

~~~

Jarod was still alone in his office at the hospital, staring at his computer notebook open in front of him on his desk. In his thoughtful *knowing* eyes were reflections of these images from the bright screen, frozen images of his boyhood self, looking out of the Plexi-sphere at the younger version of Sydney.

On the other end of the call Sydney felt the weight of their short silence. He took a hopeful breath. "Must have just missed you at the cemetery. The flowers were still fresh."

Jarod had no emotion in his voice. "My parents died 30 years ago. It was about time I was allowed to say goodbye, don't you think?"

Syd rubbed his eyes in guilt and frustration, then answered quietly. "It was wrong of me not to have taken you there in the past."

Jarod closed the DSA, removing Young Sydney's image from his sight. He then began opening other files into several windows.

Syd couldn't take the silence or hold his emotions in check anymore and didn't want to. All he wanted was his Pretender, his son, to return to him and thus found himself suddenly pleading. "Jarod, I want you to come home."

A sardonic look crossed Jarod's face. "That's an interesting way to put it, *Home.*"

Sydney was genuinely emotionally perplexed. "Jarod, I—I don't understand what's going on. Please tell me—why—why did you leave?"

Jarod couldn't believe the naive totality of Sydney's question. "You're the shrink, Sydney. But if you want to know the truth, it's because of the lies. *Your* lies."

"My lies?" Sydney stood abruptly, adrift in this conversation. "Jarod, what are you talking about?"

"I found out the real application of my simulations, Sydney!" Jarod's eyes remained fixed on his notebook, where various windows were open and playing Digital Surveillance Archive recordings from the cameras that had surrounded his living dome—each recording showing different versions of his younger self. In one DSA, a mid-teens Jarod Pretender was standing in front of a scale model of the Muir Federal Building, explaining where the structural weak points would be if someone was to place a large enough explosive—and exactly how the building would come down.

"Counter-Terrorism Simulation 32. They took my results and turned an office building into a pile of rubble. One hundred sixty-eight people didn't go home that day."

Sydney ran his hand through his thick grey hair and began pacing anxiously. "Jarod, listen to me ..."

"No, Sydney, you listen!"

Jarod referred to another window on his screen, where Young Jarod, at 7, was wearing an isolation suit and working with test tubes full of blood. "Outbreak Simulation 14, 87 people died of Ebola in Zaire."

His eyes moved over to a third DSA that showed the Pretender at yet another age, walking through virtual blueprints of an industrial complex as he explained the design flaws in Chernobyl's nuclear reactor and how the Soviets should be warned. That it could be sabotaged and made to appear as an accidental core meltdown. Jarod stared at one last window—a news report about the terrorist bombing of the USS Cole.

"Simulation Number 142, 89, 268 ..." A tremor of emotion broke through Jarod's voice as he was overcome by the totality of the atrocities he had unwittingly been a part of.

Syd, flustered, terrified of losing Jarod in the sea of these horrible truths, stopped pacing and again pleaded into the phone. "Those were military contracts, Jarod. I didn't know about their ultimate applications."

Jarod could feel tears welling in his eyes, tears that burned with guilt. "How many people died because of what I thought up?"

"You need to come back, Jarod. I'm worried about you. I've been walking around your room. It's ..." Syd wanted to say *lonely*, but instead said "empty."

"Can't say that I miss it, Syd." He paused. As one side of his mouth turned up in a slight smile. "And by the way—ice cream *is* good."

Suddenly the lights came on in the outer lab, startling Sydney. He turned to see Miss Parker and Cornelius slink into the dome. Miss P, her cell phone in hand and intently tuned into one earbud, looked over the bald imp's shoulder as he sat down in Jarod's desk chair and fired up the laptop he'd brought with him. She then quickly walked over to Sydney and whispered in his ear.

"Keep him talking, pops." She placed the second earbud in her other ear and looked at Sydney, waiting.

Syd, confused but following her directive, uncomfortably returned to the conversation, the hesitation layered over his voice. "This is serious, Jarod, they've brought in Miss Parker."

Jarod's razor-sharp intuition had already zeroed in. He could instinctively feel *them* listening. "Of course they did, Sydney. Nothing gets past her—but happiness."

If Miss Parker had any reaction to hearing this, she didn't show it—yet Sydney guessed she did. But his focus was on something else right now. Increasingly stressed, he turned away, tuning out the two intruders staring at him.

"I'm worried about you, Jarod."

Jarod's voice was calm and even. "If you're so worried, why don't you go to the authorities?"

Sydney's voice was barely a whisper. "You know I can't do that."

"Why? Because you love me—or ..." Jarod looked back at the DSAs still playing on his computer screen, "... you're afraid of what I know?"

Sydney looked over his shoulder at Miss Parker, who nodded and motioned for him to keep talking.

All the while, Corn concentrated on his tracking screen, which was displaying the honeycombed-shaped cell phone tower grid that electronically blanketed the USA. The longer Jarod stayed on the line, the more time Corn had to pinpoint the exact location of the origin of the call.

Jarod continued, in complete control. "I know you can't answer that, Sydney. Hell, I can hear Miss Parker pulling on your leash from here. You're right, you know—she really is a total bitch."

Miss Parker raised a fierce eyebrow at Sydney until Corn suddenly piped in. "He's east of the Mississippi."

Knowing he only had moments left, Syd was disconcerted, his mind muddled over what he needed to say most. "Jarod, I don't know why you're doing what you're doing but ..." He paused. "One man can't right all the wrongs in the world."

"You raised me to believe nothing was impossible. I have to go now, Sydney."

Miss Parker shook her head adamantly eyeing Corn's tracking screen, which began illuminating everything South and West and finally— "Northeast Corridor."

Sydney was now near frantic. "Jarod, I don't know what you're up to, but I do know you are *not* a doctor!"

"Sure I am, Sydney—as a matter of fact, I'm due in surgery right now." Jarod hung up.

Miss P was pissed. "Little bastard had it timed to the second. What a clever, clever boy." She looked at Cornelius.

"But not as clever as me, Miss Parker." The Big C turned his laptop to show his boss. "He scrambled his origin, but I unscrambled it. He's somewhere between North Carolina and Maine." He smiled wickedly. "Catching him is going to be fun."

Sydney cast a stern look at Cornelius. "Catching him is not a game." He then stood to face Miss Parker, incredulous. "You tapped my phone?!"

"Don't soil your Depends, Syd, I knew your teddy bear would call eventually."

"If you think a simple phone trace will lead you to Jarod, you're sorely mistaken." There was a hint of pride in Sydney's voice. "He'd have anticipated that."

"Of course he would. But a simple phone trace isn't how One-Eyebrowed Jack and me are going to find him." Miss P turned to her. "Right, Jack?"

Cornelius just giggled.

Chapter 26

PSHHHHHSSSS! DEEP IN the heart of Harlem, the door of the bus opened and Jarod, carrying a bag of groceries, descended the three steps out onto the broken curb below. Jarod turned back to the older black lady bus driver with a smile—"Love the new color, Coleesha." The bus driver raised her hand from the steering wheel and waved her florescent pink nails that looked to Jarod like fuchsia snakes climbing out of the tips of her fingers. She then looked at him with a serious look, like a concerned mother dropping a simple child off at school—"You be careful out there, shugga."

Jarod reached into his own brown bag and came out with a vanilla wafer from a box he'd just purchased at the Pathway Market, right there in the middle aisles where Chaz had told him all the fun stuff in life was.

As Jarod crossed the street to where the Streetwalkers in their tiny out-fits where warming their hands by the trash can fire, he took a bite. The tasty crisp-baked cake brought an immediate smile to his face and he just knew his roommate rat would love it too. But the smile on his face was quickly replaced by disappointment when he saw there were only two ladies of the night. His transgender friend with the huge flowing, blonde Beyoncé wig and two-inch by four-inch sweeps of silver glitter eye shadow was no-where to be found.

So Jarod continued on toward the building that contained his *more warehouse than loft* abode. As he turned left at his corner he heard the familiar loud bass of Gansta rap and turned just as the Thrill Cru's Cherry Red 640i slowly rolled past, T-Dope again riding shotgun, miming a pistol with his fingers, then aimed at Jarod and said *Bang*.

"Don't let them muthas screw with you, 'Nilla boy. They just punk-ass bitches need to be learnt a lesson." Jarod turned to the voice and at first didn't realize whom it belonged to. Oh, he could tell it was coming from the person holding a sign that read: *VETERAN—WILL WORK FOR FOOD*, but seeing as the person was dressed in a WWII Women's Army Corps uniform—khaki skirt, matching coat, shirt and tie complete with an officer's hobby hat atop a retro 1940's Andrew Sisters-like victory roll hair-do, he was confused as to why. Upon closer inspection he noticed that this Andrew Sister was six feet tall—weighed in at 230 and had a Puerto Rican Creole accent.

"Chaz?"

"Hey, 'Nilla man—how's it shaking?"

"Good." Jarod held up the cookie. "I took your advice and you were right. But they're not as good as ice cream. Ice cream is good, very good."

"Glad to see one of us living the dream." Chaz held up the sign to a passing car, the driver of which shouted out something rude and unseemly. Jarod took this all in. "You're not selling sex anymore?"

"Been forced into a different profession. Demetrius, my pimp, ran me off the corner for a younger ho—says prime real estate belongs to the prime beef. You feel me on that?"

"Yes, I do. And I'm sorry."

"Don't you never mind yourself. Chaz'll be just fine, 'sides, the Khaki's warmer and these WAC ankle-high eight-eyelet two-inch heels are much more agreeable with the puppies."

Jarod looked at his/her sign. "This says you'll work for food. But will you work for money?"

"Why? You got a job you need me to do?"

"Yes, tomorrow at noon." Jarod pulled out a fat wad of hundreds.

Chaz's eyes went wide as saucers. "What you done did boy, rob a bank?"

"Not yet." Jarod offered him the cash. "Will this be enough?"

Chaz raised the bill on her hobby hat. "For damn near anything, boy."
Chaz took the cash and as she began to count it, asked, "What you want me
to do?"

"I want you to murder me."

Chapter 27

"A SKELETON …" THE sickly young girl with the hollow eyes thought about it a bit longer, then continued, "with a crushed skull."

In the shadows of Sydney's lab, five-year-old Dara, the tricycle girl, sat in an isolation booth. Behind her on a screen she could not see were various projected images. In her black cotton dress and with straight black hair, Dara looked like the orphaned child of a Salem witch. Many in The Centre were sure that she was.

Syd, standing next to her, looked at the screen where there was in fact a photograph of a human skeleton laying in a shallow grave with an indentation in its cranium.

"Verrrrrrry good, Dara."

Syd switched from the skeletal image to that of a fuzzy little chipmunk. Intuitively sensing something joyful, a smile began to spread over Dara's face. But when the lab door behind her opened—which was also out of her line of sight—Dara's smile faded, replaced by an uncomfortable darkness. She pointed over her shoulder as she looked at Sydney. "I don't like her."

From the doorway Miss Parker poked her head in, snapped her fingers at Sydney and impatiently motioned for him to join her.

~~~

Moments later, Miss Parker puffed on her ever-present Pall Mall as she rocketed down the hallway with Sydney at her side. "We got an ATM hit on

Jarod's bank account. He's accessing as we speak." She rounded a corner as sharp as her intensity. "He's panicking, Syd, making mistakes—he wants to be caught."

Sydney knew better. "Actually, it's just the opposite. He's showing he has no anxiety or fear about being apprehended. He wants to keep us near. It's an emotional game."

"Yeah, well, it's a game he's going to lose." Followed closely by Sydney, Miss Parker entered into a computerized theatre packed with technicians and dozens of computers that made it look like the Martian Lander control room at JPL. She spotted her boy standing in the middle of it all. "Cornman, make my day!"

Miss Parker walked up to the maestro conducting this technological orchestra. Cornelius wasn't wielding a white baton, but he did have an overly eager look of excited anticipation on his face—the exclamation point of which was the black-and-white eyebrow that jiggled above his left eye. "Satellite feed will be up in fifteen ticks on the tock."

Cornelius, as a planned afterthought, then blithely acknowledged the Belgian shrink, whom he thought of as inferior. "Top of the morning, Doc-a-doodle-doo."

Sydney exchanged a mutually disparaging look with the physically unappealing human being who had, from day one, catalyzed an uneasy feeling in his gut—and not just from his appearance. Sydney had analyzed Cornelius and warned The Centre's powers-that-be of the odd narcissist's psychologyical profile long before he was hired.

Syd's report stated, among other things, that Cornelius was a man with a fragile ego looking for meaning to fill up the emptiness he felt inside. That as a child, he'd disconnected from himself and as a result had no inner sense of 'self' which resulted in him needing constant validation from others to remind him of his existence. Because of that enormous emotional void he felt inside, if hired, The Centre would become that surrogate for him.

Of course Cornelius, with his hacking skills, had read the report before it had even been opened by the PTB's and had decided that Syd was someone to get even with—when the time was right.

For Cornelius that time was rapidly approaching. But right now, it was time for him to preen his plumage. "Jarod is clever, but not quite clever enough. I'd love to get the Mensa statistics for the year he was born. I'd bet he was in the top 500."

Cornelius turned around and brushed the back of his hand beneath the honey-bob ponytail and across the exposed shoulders of a cute, but nerdish little technician, who ironically both he and Miss Parker always patronizingly referred to by her hair color: *Blondie*. She blanched at his touch, his chronic bad breath and his annoying voice as he instructed her, "Blondie, give Syd a visual aid to help him comprehend 'the what's' I did."

Blondie, whose name was really Daphne, pushed her Wicked Wendy rhinestone cat-eye glasses back in place and swallowed the little bit of puke that rose in the back of her throat every time he touched her.

She called up a visual of the globe on the large flat screen that dominated the room and Cornelius took to the spotlight. He explained, "Jay-rod bounced cash from bank to bank to bank using Trojans, Back Doors, Phantoms and a little thing I call 'Old School ID Exchange'—which seem apropos for him, given his chameleon-like talents. But I too can sim, so I put myself in his mind and anticipated his each and every move."

Daphne pointed and directed everyone's attention to a corner of the flat screen where a window appeared, showing real-time bank camera footage of Jarod at an ATM machine in a dusty sparse town. "He's in Santa Fe, New Mexico."

Miss Parker's smile was delicious. "What did I tell you, Syd? It's the smart ones that always do something stupid." She looked at Daphne. "Call the hanger—tell Vania to get the jet ready."

But as quickly as Miss Parker spun on her heels to exit, Daphne piped back up. "Wait a minute, Miss Parker—he's—he's not in Santa Fe. He is in Rome."

Miss Parker whipped back around and looked at the screen. "Rome?"

Another computer window popped up on the big screen. It showed Jarod at an ATM with the Trevi Fountain in the background. Then another window opened—and another. One in Rio with Sugar Loaf over his shoulder. The other in Brussels.

Syd smiled proudly as he explained that the house seen across the street from that ATM was the home he'd grown up in as a child.

"Chicago, Manila, Barcelona!" Impressed with his brilliance, Daphne couldn't hold back the thoughts running through her head. "Wow, he scrambled the *entire* global ATM system. He could be anywhere!" Miss Parker killed Daphne's excitement with a single wrathful glare that quickly erased the smile off her face.

Then something suddenly took over all the open windows on screen—something that left everyone in the room confused and disconcerted. On each of the ATM cameras, seemingly shot from around the world, a masked woman wearing a nun's habit entered frame and pulled a gun on Jarod.

With fear in his eyes, Jarod raised his hands and BLAM! BLAM! BLAM!—he was blown away. Murdered before their eyes.

The room went silent. Sydney blanched white. Until, on each image, Jarod sat up, pulled out two hand-written signs he flashed to camera: *DON'T YOU JUST HATE THIEVES WHO STEAL YOUR MONEY?* The nun with the gun removed her mask revealing she was Chaz, who smiled and took a bow. Jarod then revealed the second sign: *MAKES YOU WANT TO STEAL THEIRS.*

Miss Parker watched the screen, completely irritated and non-amused. "What's that supposed to mean?"

All of a sudden an alarm sounded on one of the computer monitors. This was repeated in a nonsensical sequence as an alarm began sounding on another monitor in a different section of the control room, and then another and another, until every monitor in the room had joined the chaotic choir.

As the techs scrambled to make sense of it all, the main screen in the front of the room turned red.

Vivid red.

Cornelius's eyebrow began to quiver hysterically. "Blondie, what the hell is happening?"

Daphne surveyed her desktop's screen and shrugged. "Don't have the slightest."

Sydney began putting two and two together. "Red is Jarod's favorite color. He's telling us something."

The words *PROJECT Z-17 COMMODITIES SIMULATION RUN 2522* suddenly appeared on every computer screen in the tech theatre along with commodity ticker symbols from every trading market around the world. The mood of the room suddenly chilled. Something was wrong—*very* wrong. Daphne typed frantically, then turned to Miss Parker and Cornelius, fear in her eyes. "I'm locked out. We're locked out."

As the global commodity prices began to shift abruptly from positive to negative territory, Cornelius's caterpillar eyebrow came to an abrupt halt. "Oh—my—God."

Miss Parker was now the only one in the panicked room who didn't seem to know what was happening—and she damn sure was going to find out. She slapped the back of the clammy head of the nervous man beginning to sweat through his Tom Ford suit. "Cornman. What the hell is going on?!"

Cornelius yanked Daphne out of her chair and took command of her keyboard.

"Talk to me!" Miss P shouted.

"A special client of your father's hired us to secure the commodities market from manipulation," Cornelius mumbled, sailing from keyboard to keyboard, trying desperately to stop the oncoming avalanche before it could bury them.

But Miss P's answer came from Sydney—"Jarod spent four months on the simulation and found a way to do it." Sydney announced proudly. He then looked at the hairless man who was about to make creamed corn in his pants. "That was after you'd assured the PTB's that it couldn't be manipulated, was it not, Cornelius?"

It was Corn's turn to blanch now. He was in a losing fight and his mind was furiously racing for a way to save face. The feeling of coming in third place *again* washed all over him—*how freakin' smart was this Pretender?!!!* As he futilely typed and typed and typed, trying to stop the inevitable, he grumbled to no one in particular, "There must be a mistake—somewhere."

"Yes." Sydney confirmed, "And you just made it."

Syd turned to the bewildered Miss Parker and explained, "The Centre decided to use Jarod's manipulative technique to double a one-day investment. $100 million. Jarod knew today was the day of the manipulation. It's happening now."

Cornelius stood up, dazed, his eyebrow laying back down horizontally over on his confused eye. "Everything was going according to plan until we were suddenly locked out by 'someone on the floor' who started manipulating the manipulation." Corn gave up on the keyboard battle and now found himself trying to swallow a bit of puke that had suddenly found its way to the back of his throat.

As Miss Parker stared at the main screen on which the commodity market was collapsing, she felt like a trapdoor under her feet had just been released. She began spinning herself into pre-fury. "Are you saying this *someone on the floor* is in charge of The Centre's $100 million?"

Daphne sat back down in her chair, grossed out by the damp warmth left behind by Cornelius but amazed by what she now saw on her computer screen—"Yes, Miss P, and whomever that *someone on the floor* is," Daphne said knowingly, "he just stole every penny of it."

"I guess you were right, Miss Parker." Syd said as he smiled sideways at Corn. "It *is* the smart ones who make the stupid mistakes."

"But look on the bright side," Daphne piped in. "At least we know what city he's in."

Daphne accessed the 'eye in the sky' surveillance camera grid that was secretly installed all over NYC after 9/11. She zeroed in on the New York Stock Exchange, just in time to catch Jarod walking out. In real-time, Jarod looked up at the camera and winked at Miss P, who he knew would be watching.

If Miss Parker knew what Jarod was really planning, she would be the next to blanch.

Chapter 28

JAROD'S HARLEM RAT now had the handle Oscar. At least that's what his two-legged roommate had taken to calling him. Truth was, Oscar didn't care how Jarod referred to him as long as he kept the goodies coming. In the last few days these goodies greatly improved from the original celery and kale to the current Nilla Wafers and chocolate milk—with an occasional taste of soft serve ice cream thrown in. Today had been the best for Oscar, who emerged from an empty Nilla Wafer box that was lying on its side atop the table next to the Lazy Boy recliner. If rats could claim a Thanksgiving, Oscar's had just gone down in October.

For the last few hours, before he'd gone upstairs, Jarod had been sitting in the Lazy Boy, staring at the flat rectangular plate that glowed in his face—the one with the red skin on it—just thinking. When Jarod thought, it made Oscar happy. The rat had learned early on in their relationship that his new roomy was a creature of habit and that when he sat in the recliner to *think* he always ate. And when Jarod ate—*he shared.*

Oscar enjoyed being the beneficiary of Jarod's largess—but at the same time felt that he was responsible for Jarod's epicurean generosity. In his little mind, Oscar was convinced Jarod could read the gastronomic thoughts Oscar had sent out to him—as if his human friend understood the words he was speaking to him telepathically—in rat-speak. Whether or not the human was really comprehending him didn't matter to the happy rodent, what did matter were the results—the absolutely satiating results.

It happened like this the first time.

Jarod was staring at the flat rectangular plate 'thinking,' when he absent-mindedly reached into the box of Nilla Wafers and tossed one into his mouth. As the human was savoring the taste of the delectable treat, the self acknowledged 'smartest rat in Harlem' telekinetically sent him a message—*'give a cookie to Oscar.'* Truth is, the rat didn't know what to expect from his interspecies communications experiment, but lo and behold, right after Oscar sent the message, Jarod reached into the box and handed him a wafer.

Friggin A, thought Oscar.

At first Oscar did have doubts that his rat thoughts were actually being heard, his prayers being answered, by a human no less. So, as Jarod was pouring himself a glass of the chocolate milk, Oscar decided to test his theory and sent out an additional *suggestion* to his roommate.

And his test was very successful. His roomy clearly had been influenced by this second telepathic message because as soon as his glass was full of chocolate milk, he then poured some of the silky brown goodness into a plate for the rat as well.

Oscar didn't believe in coincidences and certainly not two in a row. Mere moments later, his rodent thesis having been proven correct again, Oscar ran in a circle three times to the left as he always did when celebrating.

Oscar stretched out his growing rat body and let out a sigh. Life for the wily rodent had taken a turn for the better since Jarod moved in. Hell, if he could figure out how to plant a hypnotic message for his human pet to discover gummy bears, peanut butter and cheese, he'd be the fattest rat in Harlem. And who knows, maybe some female attention could be put in the mix.

Oscar sniffed the air and looked up to the elevated space above the kitchen in their *more warehouse than loft* apartment, to where Jarod had gone when he had finished his thinking and the box of cookies. As much as Oscar liked his new two-legged roommate, he was still bewildered by the space behind the hanging sheet where the cookie man went and did all that *weird stuff.*

The same place where Jarod was currently doing that *weird stuff again.*

The Harlem rat looked up to where the glow seeped through a huge silk curtain Jarod had rigged in the loft. Oscar hopped off the table, scurried across the rough honed wooden floor, then loped up the stairs to see what that crazy homosapien was up to this time. But when he arrived at the loft landing the little rodent stopped. His tail instinctively rose above his body and flicked twice to the right as his head tilted to the left—and it wasn't just because of the glowing sheet with the human images projected onto it from inside—but because of the *sound* he heard as well.

It was a sound Oscar remembered from when he was a baby rat—on 125th Street: the *clickity-clack* of wheels on metal, on the Harlem train line.

Oscar slowly slinked up to and then under the silk curtain and into his roommate's makeshift sim lab.

There he found Jarod experiencing his first Christmas morning.

Chapter 29

THE PRETENDER WAS sitting next to a roaring fireplace by a noble fir decorated with ornaments, sparkling lights and glistening tinsel. He was enjoying the kind of dawn most people experience on the 25th of December. No, Jarod hadn't recreated a scene out of *It's a Wonderful Life*, he couldn't have if he'd wanted to as he didn't know that movie existed. Jarod was inside of a different movie of sorts—one that Cassandra Hearns had videotaped and then posted on Facebook less than a year ago. A video Jarod had downloaded onto his red-skinned iPad and projected onto one of the Plexiglass walls of his makeshift sim room—an enclosure Jarod had designed to replicate, as best he could, that of his learning space within his living dome at The Centre.

The Pretender had placed himself in the midst of the Hearns family in happier more innocent times. He wanted to *feel* what it was like to be part of this family—to be part of any family for that matter.

Cassandra had placed their video camera on a tripod to record this time with her two men. She sat on the couch in her robe watching the two of them share a very special moment. Luke was wearing pajamas with a big, green, very muscular half-man half-monster on them who Jarod would find out later was a superhero. But in Luke's mind there was only one superhero in this room and that was his father.

Jarod marveled at the joy of little Luke's face as he and his dad sat under the tree playing with his new present—a toy train set that was zooming along over the metal tracks—*clickity-clack—clickity-clack*.

This wasn't just any toy train, as Roger Hearns explained to his son, but an exact scale replica of a Maglev bullet train, the train of the future. Luke smiled with adoring reverence to his father as he lay on his belly and watched the sleek engine—that looked more like a rocket ship on its side or a wingless fighter jet—pulling its long line of passenger cars quickly around the track. Roger placed his thumb and forefinger onto the train's joystick acceleration control, then looked at his son with an anticipatory grin.

"Now, watch the magic." Roger ticked the stick to full power. Luke watched intently as the train sped up, going faster and faster until the *clickity-clack* went silent as the wheels of the train lifted off the tracks ever so slightly—so that the Maglev was *floating above them.*

Luke turned and looked at his father with amazement. "It's flying!" Roger ruffled his son's hair lovingly. "It's just like your science project, buddy. One day you'll make magic like this too." The ebullient Luke hopped into his father's lap and as the boy took control of the train's joystick, Roger leaned back against the couch and into the loving embrace of Cassandra.

Jarod stared into the eyes of this couple, the eyes of a husband and wife sharing an incredibly simple, yet intensely loving moment of connection in their lives—in the life of their family.

But in life, as Jarod knew oh so well, joy is balanced with sorrow.

Oscar watched as the Pretender stood and moved to the other side of the cube to face the parallel Plexiglass wall onto which a different story was being projected.

A local newscaster with just a bit too much hairspray was walking slowly across the Old Tourne River Bridge. With the sincerest fake sincerity Jane O'Donnell could muster—"Reporting from the scene of a terrible tragedy—where a family's life was changed forever in an instant." She sighed and paused in all the right places for emphasis, "A father—a son— one rainy afternoon." The reporter stopped at the point of the bridge where Roger Hearns' car had crossed over the opposing lane of traffic and crashed through the guard railing. "A loss of control." She stared down into the waters below, adding melodramatically, "And a crash into the dark, churning waters below."

Jarod wasn't focused on the bubble-headed bleach blonde, his attention was on the railing and the severely curving tire marks on the concrete where the reporter stood. "The driver of the car, 35-year-old Roger Hearns—was fished from the river by a passerby with only minor injuries—but his ten-year-old son—whom he had picked up from school less then 20 minutes earlier—nor his little body—has yet to be found."

A haggard police spokesman appeared on screen.

"All of the seat belts in the recovered vehicle were undone. So both father and son were able to free themselves. We have dive teams scouring the river now. Fifteen miles of strong currents till it dumps into the Hudson and then it's out to the ocean. But we won't give up until we find the child."

Jane O reappeared facing the camera—"But what happened to young Luke isn't the only mystery in this story."

In another clip a police investigator indicated that "the skid marks left by Mr. Hearns' car when he lost control showed he'd been driving well over the speed limit—well over 90 miles an hour."

Oscar scurried across the floor and jumped up onto the table next to the red-skinned iPad as the report cut back to Jane on the bridge. She was now kneeling on the concrete curb next to the broken railing with a somber look on her face as if she understood something none of her viewers were intelligent enough to figure out for themselves. "Well over the speed limit—in the rain. Why?"

The news report shifted now to a shot of the slightly bandaged, terribly distraught father exiting the hospital with his grieving wife Cassandra, clutching onto a framed photograph of her missing son. The emotional confusion both parents were struggling with was only exacerbated by the intrusion of the large crowd of people with cameras and microphones who awaited them outside. Over this action Jane told her audience that "Roger Hearns, the father who lost control of the family car, is an engineer who, in a tragic irony, is currently working in the field of transportation safety."

Jarod stood still and stared into the eyes of Luke's parents as they faced the cameras and the ignorant question that came from one of the genius reporters. "How are you feeling right now?"

Roger was too anguished to speak. But Cassandra answered in the only way she knew. "I just want to know what happened to my son."

Jarod reached down and hit replay on his iPad. He picked up Oscar and petted him as he watched this last part of the interview a few more times. *"I just want to know what happened to my son—what happened to my son— what happened to my son ..."*

With the warmth of another life in his gentle caring hands—Jarod imagined the grief Luke's mother and father were going through knowing the life of their son had been ripped from theirs. It resonated within him in ways he couldn't quite grasp.

From the very moment Jarod first came across the image of the little boy who had been swept away from his parents and the resulting pain in their eyes, something had begun stirring in Jarod's soul—and since that first instant, Jarod had instinctively been compelled to delve into this tragedy.

Jarod was resolved to discover the truth about the pain in the eyes of Luke's parents and ease it if he could.

But that would be harder than Jarod had anticipated. Ironies abounded in this story, one in particular ticked at the back of his mind, a question he couldn't answer in this room. It was something he knew he'd need to sim a different way.

Chapter 30

TWENTY-SEVEN MINUTES LATER Jarod was on the corner of East 124th Street and FDR Drive outside the Wagner Houses where he'd discovered the Thrill Cru Boyz hangout was located. Jarod took a peek in through the ground floor window of the housing project and could see the bangers inside with several ladies—breaking the law.

They were working with large quantities of a white powder he assumed was cocaine, mixing it with baking soda and cooking into tiny rocks of crack. Jarod was happy to see this. Not that they were making drugs, but that they were occupying themselves with an activity that would keep their attention focused—while he was outside—breaking a law of his own.

Jarod slinked away from the window and moved ten steps toward the street. There, unnoticed by those few out at 3:00 a.m., Jarod slipped into the front seat of a parked car—a car he'd had his eye on for several days now. The Cherry Red BMW—the exact make and model of the car Roger Hearns went off the Tourne Bridge in.

Jarod was quick with his hot wiring work and within seconds the Beemer rumbled to life with a throaty growl.

Jarod didn't get to see the dumbfounded look on the gangbangers faces as they rushed out of the housing project letting hot lead fly. He didn't have time for that. He had something special he needed the car for—a real life sim he had in mind.

~~~

Nineteen minutes later as he exited off Highway 3 west and turned onto New Jersey State Route 1947 north, Jarod had two thoughts. First, while this was only his second time behind the wheel of a car, he was pleased with how he was catching on very quickly and feeling proficient as a driver. He liked the freedom driving gave him, the control and the power of self-determination. This was a new feeling for him in general and one the act of driving enhanced. As Jarod merged onto the 118 east heading toward Tourne River he decided then and there he would get his own car one day and set out on the road like Johnny Boy Creed.

But for now he had a job to do—which brought him to his second thought: about Jane O'Donnell and what the bubble-headed reporter had been saying as she walked across the Tourne River Bridge, the bridge he'd be driving across in less than a minute and the one Roger Hearns was driving on when he lost control. *"Well over the speed limit—in the rain. Why?"*

Jarod felt that particular statement was the only thing the overly theatrical reporter had proffered that was worth a second thought. Had Roger Hearns been going the posted speed when he lost control, his car would not have been able to jump the concrete curb and crash through the guardrail, sending him and his child to the water below. Why indeed would a father be driving that fast in those conditions with his child in the car? Especially a father for whom transportation safety was his very job.

A quarter mile ahead Jarod could see the long left-hand curve the two-lane road made as it approached the Old Tourne River Bridge. It was actually this long left curve that was the reason there was an old bridge and a new one downstream. The curve slightly obstructed the driver's view of what was coming at him over the bridge in the opposing lane. As Jarod passed the 45 mph speed limit sign he instinctively felt he should be slowing down—*for safety*. But Roger Hearns had not slowed down, he had been traveling in excess of 90 mph as he crossed the bridge.

Jarod punched the gas, accelerating the Beemer accordingly and when his speedometer hit 80 mph Jarod noticed the first of a two-part problem. The more the car's speed increased, as it proceeded around the left-hand curve, the less control Jarod had over it. As he got nearer to the bridge, Jarod was fighting mightily to keep the cherry red rocket 'between the ditches'—as Johnny Boy Creed had once said—but the centrifugal force while curving to the left was pulling the BMW to the right.

As he hit 85 mph, closing in on the spot on the bridge where Roger Hearns had gone over the rails, the second part of the two-part problem suddenly lit up Jarod's mind.

The Pretender postulated that with the centrifugal force pulling him so profoundly to the right—to send a car this size and this heavy not only into the oncoming traffic lane but to also jump the six-inch concrete curb and blast through the guardrail itself—a driver would also have to turn the wheel to the left as hard as he possibly could at precisely the right moment.

And that's exactly what Jarod did.

With all his might he jerked the wheel left and power-slid right. With rubber tires *screeching* as they desperately tried to cling to concrete for traction, the BMW *roared* across the roadway until *BAM*—its undercarriage *exploded* with sparks, *smashed* into the curb and lifted the front end up sending the coupe *crashing* through the brand-new guardrail and airborne out into the night.

Knowing that gravity pulls objects down at a speed of 9.8 m/s2 and disregarding air resistance, Jarod hung tightly onto the steering wheel as he calculated it would take 1.5811 seconds to hit the water. He was right about the timing of the fall to the millisecond. But the violent impact into the river was much more intense than he'd anticipated. The water's chilling temperature was also a shock to the system, which only added to the confusion and immediate fear anyone would have had in this crash situation and one that undoubtedly was experienced by the passengers in Roger Hearns' car that fateful afternoon.

In much less time than Jarod concluded the stunned crash victims would've needed to recover from the initial shock and release their seatbelts, the Beemer was completely submerged into the murky currents. To re-experience what the passengers would've, Jarod stayed in his seat until the car had touched bottom and was twirling on its axis, only then releasing himself from his seatbelt and the car itself.

Jarod's lungs felt like they were exploding with fire as he swam higher and higher and higher until he finally broke the surface and took in fresh air.

But his ordeal wasn't over.

The current was swifter than it appeared on the surface and Jarod was quickly sucked down stream. Unable to swim to the side, he found himself at the mercy of the river. But Jarod soon discovered just how unmerciful the Tourne was, when along the way, he hit the first of 35 submerged obstructions he could not see or anticipate. *Tree stumps? Boulders? Submerged cars?* He wasn't sure. But the massive obstacles he'd slammed into had only stunned the Pretender; he knew they could have easily knocked a small boy of seven unconscious—or much, much worse.

As Jarod was washed downstream he thought of the fear and terror Roger Hearns must have felt. The fear of not knowing where his boy was— and the terror of wondering if he'd ever see him alive again.

He also thought about something else.

There was something about this 'accident' that didn't make sense to Jarod. Something he'd experienced while driving in the 640i that defied logic: During the long left curve as he was approaching the bridge and his car being pulled to the right, he'd had to do a very unnatural act to recreate the 'accident.' It took all his strength yanking the steering wheel to the left to make the car crash through the railing and fly out into the river.

To his mind that was an action no one could refer to as 'an accident' as Roger Hearns had reported it. But when he was found battered and stunned on the bank down river, that's what he had told the police. Why would he lie? Had he been drinking? No alcohol was found in his system, but his blood was tested hours later, so it could have been gone. Had he simply lost control? Had he blacked out?

As he floated with the current, Jarod knew that whatever the cause, the result of the accident was that a family had been torn apart, a young boy was missing and a mother had an unanswered question. *"I just want to know what happened to my son."*

Jarod was determined to answer that question for her.

Chapter 31

"JAROD, I DON'T know what you're up to, but I do know you are not a doctor!"

"Sure I am, Sydney—as a matter of fact I'm due in surgery right now," Jarod's voice echoed through the room.

Mr. Candycorn was alone in the tech theatre except for Daphne. He needed someone to boss around—someone to blame for his epic failure. One of the loser tech idiots, one of the data-processing wage-apes who worked in this room had screwed something up, had pissed on the cupcakes of *his* debut, so he wasn't going to let anyone else mess up his perfectly planned dream any further. The straight-laced gal with the straight-laced outlet mall wardrobe and honey-bob ponytail sitting diligently at her computer station was the perfect focus for his ire.

"Play it again, Blondie."

As she cued up the digital recording of the traced phone call between Jarod and Sydney and began playing it again, Cornelius thought he had only felt this humiliated once before—though he didn't overtly show it then and refused to show it now. No one could know he had any self-doubt, especially the voice in the back of his head that had tormented him his entire life.

The last time he'd felt this mortified was when the second place finisher in the '87 Mensa IQ Derby had bested him at a six-month immersive, virtual adventure online game called *Snap Dragon* that he himself had created. Cornelius' babe-bedding, sharkskin suited, alter-ego 'action hero'

Avatar had been left with egg on his face, as number two's lame, boring 'kid investigator' Avatar had solved the Black Dahlia-like mystery and saved the tattooed nymph. The angst of that continued to rile him to no end.

But the *Can'o'Corn* hadn't been feeling well the day the game ended—the swelling under his right armpit had flared up again and that'd always distracted him. Yeah—that's what he'd been that day—*distracted*—distracted by something out of his control—which was what he convinced himself had happened in the tech theatre earlier. Someone had screwed up—one of the mopes who ran one of these monitors had done something wrong and he was going to figure out whom and summarily have them terminated. Not killed—he didn't have that clearance at The Centre—yet. But fired, out on their ass for having failed him. But the truth can be an annoyance, especially to a self-liar like Corn who soon discovered it wasn't anyone's fault but his own and Jarod's.

He'd try to explain to the PTB's what Jarod had done, but the odds that he could put it in simplistic enough terms for the people with the miniscule intellects who ran this place to grasp were not very good. Basically, Jarod had screwed him over on the manipulation by using a simple, yet ingenious 'New School' logarithmic program allowing Jarod to be one step ahead of what was basically a rigged game anyway.

Touché, Jarod. Clever, man. I tip my hat and wiggle my brow to you.

But *Alpha-Corn* was also ingenious. He decided to go 'Old School' in order to put himself a step ahead of the human Chameleon—which is why he was now painstakingly going over and over the digital recording of the traced call between Jarod and *that imbecile*, Sydney.

Cornucopia employed an infrared forensic audio enhancement that he'd perfected—one that changed digital sound to light waves so that he was able to peel apart every hum, echo, vibration and frequency, one layer at a time. It was the same method he'd imagined using on all the hotties he'd soon be picking up in the bars around Blue Cove, to get to the bare essence of what was underneath.

The details others would overlook.

The details that would ensure he'd catch Jarod and get the hundred mil back, less a slice for himself, and put him in line to capture an even bigger prize than the inked seductress of Snap Dragon. That prize was the affections of the princess of the new game he was a human Avatar in. The woman who haunted his dreams. And he wasn't thinking of that ponytailed blonde bitch in the chair in front of him who wouldn't give him the time of day, as good as he'd been to her—but the ultimate woman. The sultry Mistress of the namesake of where the game itself was played. A place called The Centre and a prize called Miss P.

"Roll it again, Blondie."

Daphne looked over her Wicked Wendy's at the maniacal freak barking orders at her with hidden disgust and then executed the audio playback. But what was 'rolling again' was her stomach.

To say that Cornelius creeped her out would be the understatement of all time. His lascivious glances undressing her with his unlashed eyes and then painting her 'imagined' nude body revolted her. The way his right nostril both flared and whistled when he was turned on nauseated her, literally. But the thing she hated the most was his proclivity of always finding her exposed skin and touching it with his clammy fingertips.

Even on days when she wore a turtleneck, a long skirt and high boots as protective armor, he'd somehow find a way to brush his psoriasis-laden hand on the back of her knee. Then he'd let out that grunting little sigh of his when his synapses fired with the sexual connection and she'd feel her stomach lurch.

Once after a particularly patronizing encounter with her harasser, where he rubbed his dank digits across her freckled shoulder blades (on a day she'd mistakenly worn a sundress) and ordered her back to the blender to remake his special juice smoothie that she'd 'incompetently screwed up the first three times,' Daphne added a secret ingredient to the ocher-colored concoction he swore by. A huge handful of laxatives that had kept him glued to porcelain, out of The Centre and more importantly, away from any of her exposed flesh, for over a week. It still made her smile when she remembered the instant that his eyes went from 'dictatorial dick' to—literally 'oh shit'—as something bad was about to happen in his Caraceni linen slacks.

She was thinking about doing it again when his phlegmy voice repeated for the umpteenth time, "Roll it again, Blondie."

While fantasizing about pouring boric acid down his throat, she ran the phone call recording for the umpteenth-plus-one time.

Everyone thought she was vanilla. A pushover. At work she was the nerdette good girl anyone could go to in order to get the job done. Just like she'd been at home growing up with four brothers—doing their homework and their chores. Born and raised with low self-esteem, she'd do anything it took to make things peaceful in the traditional nuclear family home she'd been raised in.

Little did they know that after work the good little nerdette was compelled to go to clubs and pick up lovers who didn't know who she was, where she came from, or what she did. Lovers with whom she could be herself—or a version of herself that she could slide in and out of as easily as she slid in and out of their beds.

No one suspected her of being such a vixen—least of all the genetic freak that ran her department.

Yes, she was creeped out by Corn, not just because he was gross, but also because she was in love with someone else at The Centre—someone who didn't even know her name—the only other person there who also called her Blondie.

Daphne was startled out of her thoughts when she finally heard Cornelius yelling, "I said stop!"

She froze the audio.

The imp ordered her more calmly. "Now go back three seconds."

She dialed the sound back exactly three seconds, asking as she did, "Except for the fact it's totally weird, what was the significance of Jarod saying, 'Ice cream is good'?"

"It's not what *he* says, it's what *someone else* says right after," he corrected.

She replayed Jarod's audio and listened.

"... And by the way—ice cream is good."

Daphne strained to hear what Corn heard and finally did. Very faintly in the background was a pattern of sound that Corn informed the world was "A public address system of some kind. Strip it out and enhance it. It will tell us where the Pretender is."

And that, he thought mouth-wateringly, *will make all my dreams come true.*

Chapter 32

WHEN THE BELL rang the woman behind the door of the two-story colonial wanted to ignore the intrusion. But she didn't. She couldn't. Every doorbell ring was a reminder to Cassandra Hearns of her prayer: that her son would return again one day to that very stoop. When she opened the door he'd be smiling and clutch onto her like he'd never let go. Despite the anxiety it represented, the doorbell could never be ignored—it brings with its chime the greatest possible sorrow and the greatest possible joy.

Both emotions were on her face when she opened the door to find the man wearing a conservative grey wool sports coat straight off the rack from Sears. The jacket made Jarod look like any other mid-level professional, in this case that of a police detective. He flashed his badge. "Cassandra Hearns?"

Her lips quivered as she asked, "Did you—find my baby?"

"Ma'am, my name's Jarod Coto, I'm a detective with the Boone County Police Department—about 30 miles south and I want you to know I'm not here with news about your son—good or bad." Jarod then held up a copy of a missing persons flyer with a picture of Luke and *HAVE YOU SEEN THIS CHILD* printed boldly across the top. "But this ended up on my desk and I'd like to help if I can."

Cassandra Hearns had sent this flyer to every hospital, police station, fire department, social services office, church, homeless shelter, media outlet and every other facility she could think of on the Eastern Seaboard. To anyone that a washed away child could wander upon if they had survived.

Jarod sensed her mind easing which allowed her to notice his face for the first time. He projected a trust through his eyes and smile that made her feel safe.

"Strangers showing up at your door these days must be unsettling."

"Excruciating." She took Jarod's flyer, then stepped back. "Please, come in."

As Cassandra led Jarod into the living room he realized he'd been in before—at least virtually. It was the same room in which the Christmas video Jarod studied had been recorded.

Cassandra stood by the fireplace, its once roaring flames now nothing but cold ashes. She looked at the portrait over the mantel: her son sitting in her lap, her husband standing behind them—a smiling all-American family. "We moved from the city to raise Luke in a place where he could be safe." Cassandra looked from the missing persons flyer to Jarod. "I know sending this out was a reach but—well, sit down."

She sat on the couch and began flipping through a binder of news clippings on the coffee table. "When the 2004 tsunami devastated Sumatra, there was an eight-year-old Indonesian girl who was swept away by the rushing waters. Her parents searched and searched for her, but finally accepted that she had died." She lightly touched her fingers onto the girl's delicate face, her eyes filling with tears. Not tears of sadness but of hope.

"But she hadn't died. The girl washed up many miles away, disorientated and starving, with no memory of hers or her parents' names. Taken in by strangers, she lived the life of another child for the next seven years—always wondering who she *really* was. When she was fifteen she remembered the name of her village and returned to it, searching for her family."

Cassandra met eyes with Jarod. "Luke needs to know we haven't given up."

Jarod touched her hand comfortingly—"We can't ever lose hope for our loved ones—ever. If he's still out there, I know he hasn't given up either."

At the sound of the back door abruptly opening, Jarod felt Cassandra flinch, her emotions shifting from hopeful sadness to nervous anxiety.

"Is something the matter?"

"No—it's—my husband." With trepidation, Cassandra stood and looked at the passthrough door to the kitchen and it didn't take long for Jarod to understand why.

In less than four seconds Jarod heard Roger Hearns fling open the door to the liquor cabinet, grab a bottle, open the freezer and shout—"Where's the goddamned ice!?"

Cassandra cringed—"I'm sorry, Honey, the maker broke. Repairman will be here tomorrow. First thing."

"What the hell am I supposed to do tonight, damn it?" Roger Hearns slammed the freezer and stormed into the living room. Shocked to see Jarod, he stopped in his tracks. The Pretender was shocked too. Roger was unshaven, his body gaunt, brow deeply furrowed and the whites of his eyes were a bloody roadmap of despair. Luke's father was no longer the vibrant man Jarod had seen in the Christmas video but a man devastated by loss. Roger looked from Jarod to his wife and barked. "I told you not to let another goddamn reporter into our house! Why don't you vultures leave us the hell alone!?"

Cassandra cringed.

"I'm not a reporter." Jarod calmly flashed his badge. "I'm trying to help find your son."

Eight weeks of self-torture welled up inside of Roger Hearns. He was a man fighting not to shatter. He then looked to the floor as he quietly spoke to Jarod.

"There's nothing the police can do for us either." Before Jarod could respond, the cell in Roger's pocket rang. He stole a look at his watch and swallowed hard. He whipped out the phone, stared at the screen. "I have to take this." With a shameful look to his wife, Roger walked back through the kitchen, the phone still ringing. Cassandra stood frozen and watched as Roger grabbed the scotch and headed outside to the secluded pool deck. She spoke more to herself than to Jarod. "Every day at the same time he does the same thing. But I'm one to talk …"

Jarod knew what Cassandra did every day at the same time. He could only wonder about her husband's self-destructive ritual and decided then and there that he would. Jarod quietly spoke up, "If this is a bad time …"

Emotionally exhausted, Cassie tried to force a smile that wouldn't come. "Detective, there are no good times anymore."

Jarod took in her pain—the depth of which seemed bottomless. He knew there were moments when the right thing to do was say something comforting and others when the best way to express your empathy was with silence. This was one of those times.

Cassandra glanced out through the French doors, eyeing her husband on the chaise lounge poolside. He was arguing into his phone until it appeared he was hung up on. He stared into thin air and began medicating his own suffering. "Since the accident he's nearly become a recluse. Only place he goes is to work and back. I can hardly get five words out of him. In many ways he's as lost to me as Luke is."

"I came today to find out about Luke. Anything you can tell me about him, his likes, his dislikes? Even the simplest thing might help, in case, like the Indonesian girl, your son is found and doesn't remember who he is?"

The mention of Luke's name in a hopeful context brought a spark back into Cassandra's eyes. "Would you like to see his room?"

Jarod smiled—inside.

Luke's room was exactly what he wanted to see.

It was exactly where he wanted to go.

It was the reason he was there.

There were things in Luke's room Jarod expected to find, but there was also something *special* he was looking for.

Chapter 33

THE INSTANT JAROD entered Luke's room he was overwhelmed with emotions he had not anticipated. They were mostly of joy but were tinged with sorrow. The Pretender spent a lifetime imagining what a boy's actual bedroom would be like and this one had everything a boy could dream of—everything he'd been denied as a boy.

It was a treasure trove of boyhood and everywhere he looked there was something—*wonderful*.

The bedspread had a picture of a flying robot with a maroon, manlike body, a gold face and a glowing triangle in the breast armor above his heart—*wonderful*.

Two other delightful characters hung from the swirling blades of the ceiling fan. One was an astronaut (whom he would later find out was named Buzz Lightyear) who smiled out broadly from under a half dome space helmet as he perpetually chased his friend, a lanky puppet in a cow-boy hat and calfskin vest, around and round and round. *Wonderful*.

Near the foot of the bed was a multi-purpose TV stand complete with video games and accessories, three game consoles, four game controllers, two guitar controllers and dozens of DVD/Blu-ray games. *Wonderful*.

Jarod had to spin 360 just to take it all in. He could only imagine the endless joy the boy who'd grown up in this room must have had here. There were bats and balls. There were monsters and masks. Light sabers, movie posters, trophies and books, games and comics—and toys and toys and toys and toys!

Everywhere he looked there was something—*wonderful!*

But there was one very special object that captured Jarod's attention the most, one that circled the entire room, twisting and turning, over and above and around itself. It was the model train set Luke had been given in the Christmas video.

Much to the surprise of Cassandra, Detective Coto, with a rush of delight, dropped down on all fours and gave the elaborate train set an exuberant *up close and personal.* As a person who had once built a scale model of the entirety of Manhattan, Jarod was impressed with the realism of its countryside panorama and the excitement Luke must have had as he built and enjoyed this amazing thing of play. Jarod turned and looked up, his bright eyes falling on those of Cassandra's. He pointed to the train's joystick controls, "May I?"

This was the first time something happy had happened in the room in quite awhile and Cassandra found a smile emerging through her pain. She nodded 'Yes.' "It would be nice to hear it again." Jarod grabbed the controls and was about to turn the train on but paused to observe Cassandra walk toward the far wall where two built-in bookcases were bisected by a window with a bench seat.

From the shelf on the right, the one overflowing with sports trophies, she picked up a tattered old teddy bear that had once been her little boy's favorite. As she looked at it reflectively Jarod got the sense that she probably came in here and held it like that when she needed to feel something in her hands that had been in Luke's.

As she sat at the window seat Jarod turned the train's power switch to *on*—then pushed the joystick forward. The sleek Maglev engine started slowly, *clickity-clack, clickity-clack,* but then began to pick up speed as it chugged around the track. Jarod followed with his eyes as it meandered past boulders, a stand of evergreens and then across a suspension bridge. As it made a turn, Jarod flattened down on his belly as he imagined Luke must have to watch the train go under the bed, only to emerge on the other side through a cornfield and farm with a big red barn and its farm animals.

Jarod stood jubilantly. "Luke must love this thing."

For the second time in as many minutes Cassandra was taken aback by this man. "He and his father would spend hours in here with it. Just the boys." Cassandra peered out at the window to Roger. "My husband adored his son and Luke adored his father. I guess that's the way it is between all fathers and sons."

Cassandra looked at Jarod as if to gauge his level of adoration for his father. Her look stung Jarod's heart.

Jarod couldn't remember much about his childhood before The Centre—his memories distant and fading. Somewhere in the recesses of his mind he recalled his mother's hair was red and that she and his father used to sing him a nonsense nursery rhyme about a barefoot goose, but little else. Even though he had no other memories there was one thing Jarod was sure of—"We all love our fathers—and our mothers."

As the train continued to circle Luke's room, Jarod stood and searched with his eyes for that special something he was there to find. On the left side of Luke's room, Jarod noticed the boy's computer desk and asked a question he already knew the answer to: "Was Luke a good student?"

Cassandra smiled as she rubbed her finger gently atop the bear's head, remembering just how bright her Luke is—"Straight A's—especially gifted in science and math, just like his father." Cassandra gazed out the window and down at the pool area at Roger pouring another scotch.

Jarod crossed over to look at the items on the shelves she was sitting between. The objects on the bookcase to her left, Jarod was already familiar with. They were the reason he'd known how intelligent Luke was before he'd asked. The shelves were full of crude electronic devices and science projects Luke had made with his father. Jarod immediately recognized them. They were like the items he had recreated at his living quarters at the offshore windmill turbine.

Nikola Tesla's electronic devices.

On the top shelf was the cream of the crop—a small shiny metal orb that when infused with electricity would shoot man-made lightning bolts across to a metallic column standing near it—a mini version of the magnifying transmitter. Next to it was a framed newspaper clipping and photo of Luke, smiling proudly, standing in front this same orb holding a first place ribbon from the Bissonet Plaza Elementary School science fair.

Next to that was a child's magnetic play set—identical to the one Jarod had left behind for Sydney in the toy chest.

Jarod had been fascinated with both the Tesla science projects and the magnets since he'd first stumbled across the story of Luke's tragic vanishing on the Internet.

A story Jarod could relate to on so many levels.

A mystery Jarod had been compelled to solve.

"Your son appears to have quite an imagination."

"Luke isn't a typical kid. Like every boy he loves his toys and games, but what he loves most are his train and his experiments. Because those were the things he had in common with his dad—the things they did together.

"Since the first day Roger took Luke to work with him, when he saw what his father did, nothing made Luke happier than trains and science. Luke said that day was the day he became a big boy." Cassandra looked at the bear—"My little man was only six when he said that—and he meant it. After that day this guy's been collecting dust."

Jarod smiled back at her and asked a second question he already knew the answer to. "What does your husband do?"

"Roger's a transportation engineer specializing in train safety. He's got projects all over the world. He's very in demand for what he does—or at least he used to be. When he could focus. But now …"

Cassandra again gazed down to her husband, his face in the palms of his hands. "My husband blames everything about this on himself. It's killing him—killing us." She then put the bear back on the shelf—and that's when Jarod found what he was looking for.

It was a tiny little toy.

A red, half-inch by one-inch by four-inch tall rectangular plastic column with the head of the green, very muscular half-man half-monster that Jarod had seen on Luke's pajamas in the Christmas video.

He was surprised that it had been sitting out in front of his face the whole time and he'd just now noticed it. He was more surprised when he picked it up and accidentally pulled the green monster's head back and from beneath where his neck would have been, had he had one—a small rectangular shaped piece of candy emerged. Embossed on the side were three letters P-E-Z.

"Your son is a fan of Mr. PEZ?"

Cassandra chuckled for the first time in forever. "Thanks, detective. Not a lot of humor around here these days. The Hulk is Luke's favorite."

"The Hulk?"

"You know—the genius guy with the superhero inside? The Hulk PEZ is Luke's good luck charm. Carried it with him everywhere he went— he must have forgotten that day."—*and his luck ran out*—she thought.

Cassandra checked her watch—it was almost 4 o'clock. In eighteen minutes she had a ritual to attend to at the river. She stood, "Do you mind letting yourself out when you are done, Detective?"

"No, ma'am. And I'll let you know if I find anything at all about Luke." Except for the train it was extremely silent in the room after she left. Jarod took the controls and ticked the joystick to full power. The train sped up, going faster and faster until the *clickity-clack* went silent as the wheels of the train lifted off the tracks—the Maglev now *floating above them.*

Jarod remembered on the Christmas video the amazement on Luke's face as he looked from the floating train to his bright-eyed father smiling— "It's flying!"

As the Pretender looked down at the shattered man by the pool, he gripped the Hulk PEZ into his hand and then slipped it into his pocket. While he knew Roger Hearns was lying to his wife, keeping a secret of some kind, Jarod felt this was not the right time to confront the man. That would come in due time.

For now, Jarod had gotten everything he'd come for.

Chapter 34

WITH ITS TWO powerful Rolls-Royce BR725 engines, The Centre's sleek new black Gulfstream G650 could reach a speed of Mach 0.925. The most advanced business aircraft in the sky, it came standard with advanced safety features and next-gen technology designed to improve pilot situational awareness and safety, with an EVS II Enhanced Vision System, Heads Up Display, the Synthetic Vision-Primary Flight Display package, a Triplex Flight Management System, Automatic Emergency Descent Mode, 3-D weather radar and Advanced Flight Controls. None of which Miss Parker gave a shit about.

What she did give a shit about was that Jarod had escaped The Centre, stolen a hundred million dollars and was making her look more incompetent by the minute. She, Sydney and her team of six Sweepers—all former special ops-like members of a Centre mercenary unit—descended into JFK airport. As the G650's state-of-the-art landing gear scorched rubber as it touched down hard, Miss Parker had only one thing on her mind: catch the Pretender.

~~~

His appearance at the Stock Exchange proved that Jarod had been in New York. And the call from Cornelius Miss P just finished, as she and her team entered her favorite hotel in Manhattan, led her to believe Jarod was still nearby. As she marched her entourage across the expansive lobby, she filled Syd in.

"In between whining because I wouldn't let him come along on this field trip, Cornelius the freak had one good thing to say. He managed to lift ambient pages and tones from the call Jarod made to you and confirmed it originated inside a hospital in the New York, Jersey, Connecticut area. He's narrowing it down now. We'll surprise Jarod when he least expects it."

Syd cocked his head to the side and looked at her, perplexed as to why she still didn't understand. "Miss Parker, Jarod didn't have to show himself coming out of the Stock Exchange and if there were tones on the call, believe me, he wanted us to hear them. It amuses him to watch his opponents chase their tails."

She ignored his assessment as they approached the registration desk.

"Well, if it isn't the lovely Miss Parker." Hornstein, the sycophantic hotel manager fawned over Miss P, and before she'd even made it to the desk, he was placing her electronic room keys on the counter. "How wonderful to welcome you again to the Fountain Grove. Your rooms are ready. Three for your team, one for Mr. Sydney per your reservation a corner suite for you."

"Thanks, Horny, it's nice to be remembered." Miss Parker apathetically tossed him her Platinum credit card.

Hornstein hated the nickname she always called him by, but smiled anyway as he pushed the card back to her. "This won't be necessary, Miss Parker, the rooms have all been prepaid—including incidentals."

"Prepaid?"

"Yes." Horn squinted at his registration screen. "By an Isaac Le Maire. I assumed he was your assistant when he called this morning."

Miss P looked questioningly at Syd, who was stifling a grin. "Isaac Le Maire founded the New York Stock Exchange. Jarod always had a good sense of humor and this is his way of saying ..."

She knew what Jarod was saying—loud and effing clear.

"Mr. Le Maire also had this hand delivered, something special for you, Miss Parker."

From underneath the counter Horny retrieved something, that upon seeing it, caused Miss Parker to exhale abruptly. It was a present wrapped in lavender paper and royal purple ribbon, exactly like the one she'd been given so very long ago by her mother.

Miss Parker ripped open the paper and inside found a child's art toy.

Sydney registered the angst in Miss Parker's face as he asked, "An Etch A Sketch? I had no idea Jarod knew what one of these was."

Miss Parker couldn't answer Sydney aloud. Yes, it was an Etch A Sketch and Jarod knew damn well what it was—especially to her. But it wasn't just the Etch A Sketch that held such meaning for her, it was what Jarod had left on it: an amazingly life-like drawing of Miss Parker as a little girl at the exact age when she was 'Little Miss'—the last age when she was happy.

But the Little Miss drawn on this Etch A Sketch wasn't happy. She was sad, her eyes welling with tears.

Miss Parker bore contempt into Sydney as she said, "You're genius isn't amusing anymore."

Chapter 35

THE SNORING OF Oscar the Rat, curled up in an empty carton of chocolate milk that Jarod had fashioned into a rat bed, didn't seem to bother the angry man with the plastic green face at all.

Which was a surprise since some who knew him thought the angry green man was hyper-aggressive and brutal. Others felt he was cunning, brilliant and scheming. All understood that at one point he'd been an emotionally reserved physicist, a level-headed man of knowledge and science—before the accident. But after his emotional impulsivity, when angered or in danger, he physically transformed into a mutated humanoid with incredible strength and an inability to control his rage.

A Hulk.

Jarod didn't know any of these particulars about the man with the green skin. All he knew was that when you pulled back the plastic head of the version of the misunderstood superhero, you were rewarded with a candy that was delicious.

Jarod loved PEZ and since he had taken The Hulk dispenser from Luke's bedroom, he'd carried it with him everywhere he went.

The green monster was atop Jarod's dressing mirror, staring out at dozens of damsels in distress. These damsels were the type The Hulk would save in the graphic novels he starred in. These damsels weren't real though. They were just images in black and grey trapped behind clear Plexiglas and framed in red plastic.

They were all images drawn on Etch A Sketches of Miss Parker at different ages and all of these Miss Parkers were facing Jarod, as he changed his persona for the second time today. Having just removed the baggy, *straight off the rack from Sears* sports coat, Jarod paused before the mirror, taking a long look at his nude body.

His six-foot frame was toned, muscular and younger than its years. For as long as he could remember he had followed a nutrition and weight training regime that kept his body fat in the 11% range and his blood levels consistent. He also religiously practiced both yoga and an ancient form of Tae Kwon Do that kept him very in tune with his balance and physicality.

And then of course there were the scars.

There were four of them on his form—only three of which he could remember getting. Jarod turned to view the large one on his mid-back where he'd been gashed in a near-death fall during a botched sim when he thought he was around nine.

Jarod then focused on the burn on his right shoulder, remembering the searing sensation he'd felt during the lab explosion during his 15th year of captivity. His eyes then fell to his right calf. On either side of it were puncture wounds left by the fangs of a Rottweiler. Wounds he'd received on the fateful night that prolonged his confinement.

The fourth scar was one that was a mystery to him—small and hook-shaped on the left side of his chest, midpectoral. It was the scar that still caused him pain—pain more mental than physical. As he touched it and wondered how it ended up above his heart, his attention was suddenly drawn to a girl's voice asking, *"What are you doing in there?"*

Jarod began putting on a fitted dress shirt as he looked from the mirror to the screen of his notebook computer where another DSA of him as a child was playing.

A pre-teen Young Jarod was alone in his isolation cubical, a precursor to his dome, working at his desk. He raised his head upon hearing the voice of the young girl and looked to his right as well. There, Young Jarod saw something and someone he'd never seen before. It was Young Miss Parker at ten years old in her white blouse and plaid skirted school uniform. She had snuck into the lab room and closed the door behind her.

Young Jarod sat dumbfounded at his desk, peering out through the Plexiglas wall as Little Miss slowly approached him.

Though still prepubescent, Young Miss Parker was mature and precocious beyond her years. She sauntered slowly toward him with a deliberate provocative nature that was sexual in an instinctual way. Never breaking eye contact with the boy behind the glass wall, she looked at Young Jarod as if dissecting him with her eyes. "I said what are you doing in there?"

"Nothing. I—I live here."

Young Jarod noticed that his breathing had become shallow, his heart beating more quickly. He looked around nervously. Miss Parker noticed all of this. Even at her young age, she liked knowing that the boy behind the glass was uncomfortable—that her mere presence elicited a physical reaction from him. She liked the power of knowing she was in control.

"Dr. Sydney and the others are gone for the day. No one saw me come in. They don't know we're together. So you don't have to worry."

Jarod wasn't worried. He was anxious but also intrigued. He breathed in deeply, then looked at Little Miss P and uttered with fascination, "You're—a girl. Right?"

Little Miss looked at him with a sardonic smile. "And they said you were a genius."

Without taking his eyes off the DSA, Jarod stepped into his slim tapered slacks as he continued to watch the juvenile form of himself look into the eyes of Little Miss.

"What's your name?"

Little MP smiled to Young J, "My father said to tell people to call me 'Miss'—that it's more ladylike."

"My name is Jarod."

Little Miss began playing with her hair as she eyed him coyly. "I know who you are. I heard my mother talking about you."

Jarod was lost in this beguiling creature. He'd never seen a young female before—at least not that he remembered—nor did he know when he might ever again. So from her penny loafers to her piercing eyes, he made sure to take it all in. He noticed her one flaw, her only flaw, was a recent cut on her knee.

"How did you hurt yourself?"

Miss Parker smiled, "I tripped over my toy chest."

Jarod's young face scrunched with curiosity. "Toy?"

"Yeah—it's something you play with." Little Miss stepped closer to the glass. "You know how to play, don't you?"

"I'm not allowed to."

Little Miss enticingly raised her delicate hand and extended it out toward the young Pretender's face—the only thing stopping her from touching him was the glass that separated the two young beings. Her tiny brow furrowed. "Why do they have you locked in there?"

Young Jarod slowly brought his hand up and placed it finger for finger to meet hers.

Jarod remembered that moment so clearly in his mind. He remembered that he'd felt warmth through the glass—*her* warmth. He got slightly lost in the memory, but then refocused on the computer screen.

Young Jarod looked into Little Miss' eyes. "I don't know."

"What do they want you to do?" she asked, moving her face closer to the glass.

"To be other people."

Jarod put on a paisley blazer, his transformation from local detective to big city doctor complete. He turned off the DSA, took a PEZ from The Hulk and left him to keep watch over the snoring rat and the Etch A Sketch Miss Parkers.

Chapter 36

MISS PARKER'S FAVORITE mixer was ice. Like her father, her favorite drink was bourbon. As a child she'd lie in bed and 'listen' to him drink.

Yes, listen.

Late each evening, long after she'd eaten dinner alone and long after she'd supposedly gone to sleep, she secretly stayed awake waiting. On the nights he had come home after an incredibly long day at work, her father usually arrived around midnight. She knew the sound of his driver's car like she knew the sound of her own heartbeat—the heartbeat that skipped when she first heard his Jaguar in the distance and then raced when it pulled into the circular drive in front of the house.

As a girl, she'd smiled as she counted out from memory the six steps on the crunchy gravel, the three wipes of his size 13's on the welcome mat and the two seconds until the front door would open with a slight creak. His deep voice would then follow—a voice that would mumble parting words to one of the many nannies Miss Parker burnt through like cordwood growing up—the nannies who'd taken care of her all day and couldn't wait to leave for the night. She was happy when they were gone. That meant it was just him and her in *their* home.

She'd then listen for the 16 steps he took crossing the porcelain tile of the grand foyer and then nine more down the main hall, the last one accompanied by a slight squeak as he turned at the doorway to his study. Seven paces more over the old yellow pine floor and he'd reached the bar.

Identical to the one in his Centre office, it was custom made of Kentucky white oak and served one thing and one thing only: Maker's Mark. There'd be a few seconds of silence until she'd hear the cabinet nearest to the sink and freezer open. *Clank,* a tumbler would be placed on the marble countertop, followed quickly by the opening of the freezer door and the *clink, clink, clink* of three ice cubes dropping into the glass—always three— never more, never less. The end of his routine was the *gurgle, gurgle, gurgle* of the bourbon and the cubes crackling as they were covered with the silky honey-brown liquid.

Ice was her father's favorite mixer and that's how she drank hers as well. Usually. But not tonight.

With her personal concierge (one of her favorite perks of the hotel) unreachable, Miss Parker was forced to find her own ice. But when she'd arrived at the icemaker on the 14th floor, it wasn't working. All that it spit out was water that ricocheted off the bottom of her empty bucket and all over her black silk, mini-kimono. So much for *dry-clean only*. Too frustrated to go to another floor and too impatient to send one of her Sweepers, Miss Parker drank her Maker's Mark neat.

She sat on her bed, drank and stared at the masterpiece Etch A Sketch portrait that must've taken Jarod hours, days, maybe even weeks to accomplish. The detailed etching was more like a black and white photograph than a mechanical drawing. It was truly a piece of artwork.

And she absolutely hated it.

She poured three more fingers of salvation and intently eyed the sketch, especially drawn to the eyes of the younger version of herself, eyes welling with tears that stared back into her own, creating a vicious cycle of pain and anguish. This was a little girl Miss Parker no longer recognized, but whose hurt she could still feel deep inside in places she rarely let her soul venture.

Why? Why had Jarod gone to all the trouble to capture that instant in her life? He knew what that moment meant to her. What that gift meant to her. The son-of-a-bitch even knew the color of the paper and the ribbon it had been wrapped in.

The brilliant little bastard was making her look at this on purpose. Look into a mirror by design. But why? Was he earwigging her? Was this a misdirect? An emotional breadcrumb that he wanted her to follow to get her off of his trail?

As her mind spun she took a deep gulp of Maker's Mark from her glass and swirled the burning nectar in her mouth. She loved the smokey-sweet essence of the *libation,* as her daddy called it, when he'd poured that first sip for her at age 15. She remembered him explaining that Maker's Mark was aged to taste in white oak, fire-charred barrels rotated from floor to ceiling in barns over the life of the bourbon's aging process. There, the seasonal temperature changes forced the alcohol in and out of the oak itself, from which it extracted both its brownish hue and the perfect amount of caramelized sugars, to give it its unique flavor. Only under that amalgam of time, heat and pressure did it transform into what it was destined to be.

As Miss Parker stared at the Etch A Sketch she felt like she'd been aging in a barrel most of her life as well. Certainly since the day this image of her was captured. As she thought about that, Jarod's words from his phone call with Sydney echoed in her mind, "Nothing gets past her—but happiness." *What the hell did he know about happiness, especially hers?*

The little girl in that sketch thought she'd known about the world, about security and love and all the things that give children a sense of certainty. But that was the day she grew up. Was forced to. That was the day the pressure and heat began building up in her barrel. And she was better off for it. The world was not what she'd thought it was. It was a cruel place and she would never allow it—or Jarod—to hurt her again.

And that's when she saw it, something she hadn't noticed before in the drawing: a tear, frozen in time, about to drip from her eye. Inside the tear was a reflection of Young Jarod. He was at a similar age to the Miss Parker of the drawing and was staring back at her with empathy.

This made Miss Parker think two things. One, had Jarod ever really cared about her? And two, how the hell had he drawn that? And with an Etch A Sketch, no less.

In the end though, what it did more than anything else, was piss her off.

In her anger she shook up the Etch A Sketch to erase the image. She'd have the last laugh on this.

But as she tossed back the last of her bourbon and then turned the Etch A Sketch back over, she was stunned but not surprised; as if by magic the erased drawing reappeared—Jarod magic.

"What are you up to, you bastard?"

Chapter 37

THE L'ENDROIT DE L'Homme Club at Grand Central was the elite hub for the self-important medical professional set to swill gin and congratulate each other and themselves on their Godliness. The ambience of this exclusive society was finely appointed with old world grandeur that whispered of arrogance, conceit and extravagance. It boasted $80 martinis, $1,000 cigars, and Beluga caviar hors d'oeuvres, all served by an exclusively female wait staff, each of whom modeled million dollar bodies—some born, some bought, some sold. The L'Endroit de L'Homme was not only a hedonistic, misogynist nirvana of excess, but like everything else in New York, it was ultimately all about power, domination and control over money, status, women, each other and ultimately, over life and death itself.

A relaxed Jarod sat in Bilson's reserved booth next to the Chief Administrator himself, who proudly lorded over his domain, along with the gruff and always seemingly preoccupied Dr. Su, who clenched his martini glass as if someone was going to take it from him. All three gentlemen puffed on Cohiba Behikes, a difficult to acquire $750 Cuban that Bilson had breezily ordered for them along with their drinks.

Into the cloud of cigar smoke sauntered a beautiful waitress, her tray overflowing with drinks almost as much as her open blouse was over-flowing with cleavage. She did a well-trained, classic Bunny dip, giving the men a tasteful show while serving them another round.

Jarod, or rather, *Dr. Russell*, took in an appreciative gaze of her seductive femininity as she placed a fresh martini in front of him, gently breathing out a

"Thank you" to the lovely creature for her service. As she moved around the table, Jarod exchanged a knowing look with Bilson. The Chief was enjoying the young doctor's reaction to his surroundings, which was precisely the reason he'd brought him here. Dr. B motioned in the air for the waitress to bring the check. Trained to keep the conversation to a minimum and the sexuality to a maximum, she nodded demurely. "Yes, Dr. Bilson."

As she sashayed away, Jarod followed her with his eyes for as long as he could and then perused the rest of the club with a contented smile. "As a wise man once said, 'If women didn't exist, all the money in the world would have no meaning.'"

Bilson took a luxuriant puff of his cigar as he too soaked in the club's opulence, adding, "And as the commercial used to say, 'Membership has its privileges.'"

Su sucked down the last of his martini and then clumsily shoved his Adidas Man fingers in his glass, fumbling for the olive stuck at the base of it. "Think they'd have higher quality olives," he grumbled. He finally grabbed it and shoved it into his mouth, chewing loudly.

Bilson was dismayed by Su's boorishness. "Su loves to complain. Now that he can afford the best, he likes to look down upon it."

Su shrugged unapologetically. "I like the ones with the little onions— not the pimentos—so sue me."

As Su began slurping his second martini, Bilson did a visual comparison between Jarod's savoir-faire and the Asian doctor's more baboonish nature and shook his head. "Class is like Legionnaires Disease, you either have it or you don't."

The waitress then returned, laying a leather folder on the linen tablecloth. "I can take that whenever you're ready." As she walked away, Bilson looked at Su, pointing to the bill. "Know how much this weighs?" Su then stepped right into Bilson's low inside pitch.

"No idea."

"Try picking one up sometime and you'll find out."

Bilson reached for the check but Jarod beat him to it. He looked at his new boss. "It's on me."

Bilson was pleasantly surprised by the bravado of his young surgeon. "Be careful what you're offering—the one thing this establishment isn't, is cheap."

"Neither am I." Jarod glanced over at Su, who was still oblivious. He returned to Bilson with an even gaze. "Besides, I am a man with a diversified income."

"Then, by all means." Bilson removed his hand. Jarod opened the folder. The bill was over $3,000. Bilson and Su looked at each other—both wondering how Jarod would react to the exorbitant tab. But he didn't. Without missing a beat, Jarod pulled out his wallet. When he opened it, it was their turn to react. Inside, Jarod had a stack of crisp hundreds *at least* an inch thick, as well as several credit cards in the colors of rare metals. But the card Jarod pulled out wasn't platinum or gold—it was black—American Express Black—the world's most exclusive charge card, reserved for the wealthiest and most elite. Out of the corner of his eye, Jarod saw Bilson's attentiveness and zeroed in on it. Bilson knew all about The Black AMEX. That it wasn't a card you apply for, but one you must be invited to receive. A prestigious card that Dr. B had tried to get an invitation for himself for many years—but couldn't.

What Dr. B didn't know was that Jarod knew this too.

Jarod placed the card in the leather folder, closed it and handed it off to their passing waitress with a smile. He then turned back to the doctors.

Bilson nodded at Jarod's wallet. "Well-heeled for a young surgeon and knowing what I pay you to be one, it makes me wonder, how did you get a Centurion Card?"

Jarod played coy. "Well, in this challenging economic climate, I'm sure you both know that one needs to be resourceful and consider *all* opportunities to make money."

Bilson gave him an inquisitive look. "You play the odds on Wall Street?"

"I play to win. In fact, I recently manipulated the commodities futures in my favor and made a hundred million." Jarod's answer was delivered completely deadpan. Bilson was stumped, Su disgruntled. After a stunned second of stupid silence, Bilson began to smile at Jarod as if they were old school chums and all in on the joke. Bilson nudged Su. "I told you I loved this guy."

Su's expression didn't budge. His regard of Jarod was more begrudging tolerance to Bilson's affection.

Jarod closed his billfold, took a puff and blew it out playfully. "Let's just say, there are a million and one ways to make a dollar out of fifteen cents in this town and I'll try them all. If they have at least half a chance of success, I can usually cover the other half."

Su flicked ashes into his newly empty martini glass. "Like the Triexapan?" As Su intended, this got Jarod's attention. Su took another puff and focused on the Pretender. "For using a med that pricey, not to mention highly experimental, I assume a 'so inclined' physician—especially one who helped the people at Dharma-Pharmaceuticals develop the drug—gets some kind of *'royalty'* for prescribing it?"

"A small one." Jarod winked at Bilson, "And if you gentlemen are interested in the reported benefits of using Triexapan, I can speak with Dr. Dharma himself about giving the hospital an added *incentive* to use it more often. He's very good about taking care of those who take care of him."

Bilson was pleased. "Yes. Your former employer is a generous man. Dr. Dharma offered that reciprocity to us as well."

Su, lowering his voice for emphasis, added, "Personally."

Jarod raised his brow. "Personally? I thought Dr. Dharma was in Mumbai on sabbatical."

"He came back." Su continued, "Couldn't take the stink." Su then stuffed the last $385 worth of his Cohiba into the liquid remains of his gin. He then spit a piece of tobacco off the tip of his tongue and stared squarely into Jarod's eyes. "And from what Dr. Dharma told us, it doesn't seem that the 'Dr. Russell' who worked with him and the 'Dr. Russell' who is working for us could possibly be the same man."

Chapter 38

SU NOTICED JAROD'S eyes widen ever so slightly.

"No reason to look surprised. I'm Asian—we always do our homework."

The waitress returned with the credit card slip. She didn't realize she was interrupting a covert conversation, but she did read the tension in the air. "Excuse me. I can come back."

As she was turning to escape, Jarod stopped her—"No need to go." Jarod held his hand out for the leather portfolio. "What is your name?"

She gave him the folder. "It's Angela, Dr. Russell."

Jarod opened it and began doing the necessary math for her tip. "Tell me, Angela, how do you like working in a place like this, getting to rub elbows with such distinguished men as these two physicians?"

Angela shifted her weight from one leg to the other, unsure how to answer this, but finally deciding upon, "It's very—educational."

Jarod signed the receipt. "All of life is. You never know what you'll learn next." Jarod took his Black Card and placed it back in his wallet, then continued with the doctors. "So tell me, what did Dharma have to say about *his* Dr. Russell? I'm sure it was educational too."

Su hit squarely. "He said he didn't know *his* Dr. Russell to be such an amazing surgeon."

"I can do surgery in my sleep. So much so, that I sometimes find it a snooze. But when I need to do it to pay the bills, I do. When I worked for

Dr. Dharma I practiced a different kind of medicine. Surgery was not a priority."

Jarod handed the folder back to the server. "Thank you, Angela. You've been wonderful." She noticed the size of the tip he'd left her and almost fainted. "Wow. Thank *you*."

As she happily pranced away, Jarod gave his captive audience of two his full attention and smiled. "So what *did* Dharma have to say?"

Jarod was smiling for three reasons. First, he already knew what Dharma had to say about him. Because second, he controlled both Su's and Bilson's home, hospital and cell phone lines, ensuring that when any of those lines placed a call to Dharma-Pharmaceuticals, the call would be rerouted to a number that Jarod had programmed in. So third, their inquiries were not answered by Dr. Dharma or anyone else at his pharmaceutical company, but by someone else. That *someone else* was one Johnny Boy Creed who, reading from a script that the Pretender had prepared for him, sang the praises of Dr. Jarod Russell, hitting all the right high notes loud and clear.

It was Su who answered. "Dr. Dharma said *his* Dr. Russell was gifted when it came to running FDA approval studies. That he'd devised a system that cut six months off the usual time frame for a trial. But that he was somewhat overambitious."

Jarod went on the offensive. "Was Bill Gates overly ambitious when he left Harvard to create Microsoft? No. He saw opportunity and grabbed it. That's what I do. So yes, it's called ambition. But my having too much of it never seemed to be a problem when Dharma saw that I widened his profit margin enough to move him into the top of the 1%."

"Is that why you left?" Su prodded.

"Let's just say my taste for the finer things in life and my talent for acquiring the means for them far exceed what Dr. Dharma was willing to pay. He wanted it all to stay in his coffers. But his greed was his loss. He'll realize that soon enough."

Jarod studied Su, searching for his angle. "If Dr. Dharma told you I'm not who you thought I was, then why are we here?"

Bilson took a sip of his martini, then moved closer to Jarod. "Because what he told us made us wonder if you were *more* than we'd even hoped for."

Jarod looked at the men but gave nothing.

Su continued, "It made us wonder, that if you were willing to *manipulate the market*, what else would you be willing to do?"

Jarod put both arms on the table and leaned forward. "What else do you have?"

Bilson took control of the conversation. "First, a hypothetical. Under the premise of working towards the 'the greater good,' say that for a select group of investors, you were testing an experimental drug and you knew that giving it to specific patients could cause certain 'side effects' that might be—unfortunate. Would you still give it to them?"

"Are we hypothetically referring to what you gentlemen are doing in the Annex?" The two doctors exchanged an uncertain look. Jarod continued—"That is how you boys diversify your incomes, correct?"

Su's contained reaction broke free. "I see you've done your homework as well."

"I may not have Asian ancestry but I appreciate their pursuit of overachievement."

Bilson took in his measure of Jarod then broke into a grin. "Attentiveness to details is the mark of a successful man."

Jarod joined the grinning party. "And *successful* is what I want to be. With and *for* you."

Jarod scooted in closer and lowered his voice. "So the answer to your hypothetical is: For the *greater good* sometimes sacrifices have to be made. Dharma was too cautious. He wasn't smart enough to realize that human drug trials could be turned into a veritable cash cow. I get the sense you and your 'investors' don't suffer from that kind of limited vision."

Bilson chuckled and took his cigar out of his mouth. "Not in the least." Bilson looked over at Su and raised his eyebrows. After a beat Su reluctantly nodded in the affirmative.

Bilson turned back to Jarod. "Which is why we'd like to invite you to join us in diversifying together."

Jarod settled back in the booth. "Only if the price is right."

Bilson said, "Three equal shares."

Jarod asked carefully, "Why would you lessen your percentages from 50 to 33?"

Bilson became avariciously animated. "For the simple fact we've calculated that if we employ your system we can triple our business. A smaller share, of a much bigger pie. Win-win-win."

"What would we be testing?"

Su broke in. "I've been running a trial on a new psychotropic to control schizophrenic episodes."

Bilson retook the floor. "But to ensure no one beats us to market, it's critical we *accelerate* our trials."

Jarod finished the last of his martini and set the glass down with intent. "The key to my method is efficiency within the study parameters. That's largely accomplished by satisfying the right demographics in test subjects and making sure they are compliant. If there are too many dropouts it prolongs the study."

Bilson glanced at Su for a second too long as he said, "Well, the truth is, efficiency is *exactly* what's killing us—but we have no problem with finding suitable test subjects."

Jarod looked upon the men plainly. "Tell that to someone who didn't happen to see a bogus 'nurse' breaking out of your—infallible security system."

Bilson cleared his throat. "Yes, well, that was highly unusual, but let me assure you, even if she had escaped she wouldn't have gotten far."

He quickly brightened, adding, "And that's what gives us a leg up on the competition. Our guinea pigs belong to us. We get them from a very special source."

Su saw the wrinkle form on Jarod's brow and answered his question before he could ask. "The city's going bankrupt with homeless shelters bursting at the seams with people in need of care, especially for mental illnesses. As a 'public service,' Dr. B performs psych evaluations on the indigent. Those found most in need are committed for treatment in the Annex. So 100 percent of them have *volunteered* as test subjects for meds that will help them in one way or another."

Jarod's brow finally transformed from inquisitive to impressed. Bilson retook control. "The city gets the deranged off the streets and we get test subjects that never drop out."

"Seems very …" Jarod wanted to scream *unethical—illegal—inhumane,* but what came out of his mouth was "lucrative."

Bilson smiled proudly, genuinely sold on himself. "Exactly. And everyone wins!" Everyone, Jarod thought—except the patients.

"So, Dr. Russell, what do you think?" Bilson flashed Jarod an enormous smile.

Chapter 39

THREE MINUTES LATER Jarod emerged from L'Endroit de
L'Homme, taking a last puff off his Cohiba. While he didn't like the taste
the cigar left in his mouth, he did like the taste his meeting with Bilson and
Su had.

He walked to the taxi stand, thinking first thing in the morning he'd
receive all the security credentials needed to get into and out of the Annex
at will. He'd finally be able to get to Room E913 and this made him happy.

For the first time in days, Jarod had nothing to do and a moment to
breathe.

Then someone tapped him on his shoulder.

He spun around and found his favorite candy striper, Tami. She wore
a big grin on her adorable face, a tiny cocktail dress on her tight little body
and was awkwardly balancing on brand spanking new high heels. "Hey, Dr.
J."

"Tami? What are you doing here?"

"I just got off work and was out for a walk and—you know."

Jarod took in her up-do and the goose bumps on her exposed arms.
"Interesting walking attire for a chilly evening."

Tami thought about that and then nervously exhaled. "Well, yeah—I
guess. I mean, I actually got off a while ago and went home and changed
and well, I'm not really on a 'walk-walk'—I mean, I've been walking—
mostly back and forth out here to keep warm, but I'm really on a wait-
walk."

Jarod read her nervousness and found it both cute and curious. "And you just happen to be 'wait-walking' in front of 'the place for men'?"

"Yeah. I mean, no. I mean, I was waiting for a man. I mean, you. I mean, I know you're a man but ..." She took a breath in hopes it would clear her nervous mind, but she was on a jumbled roll and there was no turning back now. "What I'm trying to say is, I overheard Dr. Bilson invite you here for tonight—not that I was trying to be nosey—it just happened that way and well, I knew this is where you'd be. And so here I am."

Jarod said "For ...?"

"Oh." Tami rolled her eyes, *silly me*. Then she reached into her cocktail purse and pulled out and began unfolding a medical file. "I have the results of your DNAP tests." Tami began rubbing her exposed arms.

"That's very nice of you to bring them all the way down here."

Jarod removed his jacket, placed it around her shoulders, almost causing her knees to buckle. "You must be cold." He gazed into her eyes warmly and she fell right inside of his as she returned the stare. "Not anymore."

Jarod reached out his hand to her. "Tami."

"Huh?"

"The report?"

Tami snapped back into the moment. "Oh, yeah." She handed the bent file over to him. As he opened it her eyes continued to glisten.

Jarod quickly flipped through the file, his eyes full of optimistic curiosity, singularly focused on what the information in his hands contained. The results of his DNAP test held the truth about the blood that was coursing through his very veins. The results held the *truth* about who he was.

But when he came upon the last page he realized the *truth* he found was not the truth he expected, the truth he'd prayed for.

Far from it.

The optimism drained from his eyes and was replaced with a cold-blooded rage, the likes of which not even Jarod could've ever imagined possible.

Tami not only saw the fury; she could feel it radiating from him. "Dr. Russell, are you okay?"

Jarod closed the file—very, very far from *okay*.

Chapter 40

IT WAS EXACTLY 3:00 a.m. when Miss Parker instinctively grabbed her Smith & Wesson and painted the ceiling with its laser sight. She was intent on putting a 9mm slug into the blaring loud speaker hidden somewhere behind the plaster. She couldn't find it. Had she found it, the blaring alarm and the annoying voice that had abruptly awakened her moments before, causing a bourbon-induced earthquake to rattle between her ears, would have been silenced for good.

Instead, safe in its hidden realm, it kept repeating itself, *"This is the hotel's emergency fire activation system. Please exit your room and proceed in a calm and orderly manner to the nearest stairwell exit. This is the hotel's emergency fire activation system. Please exit your room ..."*

Calm and orderly—yeah, right. Those were two things that rarely, if ever, described Miss P.

She got up and looked out the window of her 14th-story *non-smoking 'Thank you very much, Jarod'* room to see the cherries ablaze on over a dozen NYFD ladder rigs below. Miss Parker only had one thought: *Well, isn't this just effing perfect.*

~~~

Most of the disoriented people who exited their rooms had the same thought in the back of their minds that every New Yorker had asked themselves since 9/11, a worst-case scenario they'd all run through their minds in detail. The question was simple and yet terrifying. Had they been in one of the World Trade Center Towers on that fateful day, what would they have done? How would they have reacted had they been descending in one of the stairwells as first responders and firemen walked up? But sharing this same exact thought actually made the guests surprisingly calm and cooperative—except for Miss Parker.

She exited her suite fully dressed with a perturbed look and her essentials in hand: her Polyvore carbon fiber briefcase, cell phone and shoulder holster. She met up with her Sweeper team waiting for her in the hallway. They were the only other people fully dressed. She paid them to sweep, not sleep, and they all knew better than to not be *good to go* on her command.

Her glare was to Aires, the Sweeper she'd almost gotten killed on his first assignment and had felt obligated to keep employed since that day. "What's the situation?"

Aires tossed his thumb back over his shoulder. "Trouble seems to be coming from the service area."

As she looked to where his thumb was pointing, her perturbed look turned to a scowl. There was smoke coming out of the same room where the icemaker had ruined her kimono.

Pissed, Miss Parker stood blocking the crowd, until a fireman who was waving guests toward the fire escape exit, whose voice was muffled under his oxygen mask and face shield, ordered her to "Keep moving, ma'am!"

"Ma'am?" She may not be wearing makeup, but how old did this clown think she looked?

"You're endangering others." Miss Parker thought that this junior Red Adair had no idea how endangered she could make them. Ignoring him, she scanned over the crowd to find a disheveled Sydney emerging from his room in a Yale sweatshirt and who, no surprise to her, was the last one in line. Shaking her head with disgust, she snapped and gestured for the shrink to catch up with her below. Leading her Sweepers, Miss P fell in queue with the rest of the guests evacuating out the window and down the fire escape. As they passed, the fireman droned on, "Remain calm and keep moving. Remain calm and keep moving. Everything is under control."

Sydney was about to step through the window when the fireman slammed it shut. "Just one second, sir."

The fireman raised his mask and Sydney's eyes met Jarod's. Syd's emotional relief, his joy, was evident in his voice.

"My God. Jarod."

"I wanted to give you something I couldn't trust to the mail."

Jarod tossed him a USB drive. "Instructions on retrieving The Centre's hundred million. Less my finder's fee, of course." Jarod picked up on the confusion crossing Syd's brow. "The money means nothing to me."

"Then what does?"

Jarod looked Sydney directly into his eyes. "The truth."

Syd was frozen in Jarod's unrelenting gaze. "About what?"

"Who I really am. Did The Centre adopt me? Was I bought? Was I stolen? And where are my Mom and Dad?"

Drawn into the anguish in Jarod's eyes, he felt a pang of empathy. "Jarod, I've told you a thousand times—your parents died in a plane crash in Cincinnati."

"I know what you _told_ me!" Jarod flared, "that I had no other relations, so The Centre took me in. You seared that story into my brain for years, Sydney, but the first thing I did when I got out was to check every detail. Joe and Evelyn grew up on farms outside Cincinnati just as you said. They are buried overlooking the Ohio River just where you said. Everything, every little detail is just as you said! Except for one. Me."

It was Sydney's turn to be confused. "You?"

Jarod grabbed a piece of Sydney's sweatshirt—"I did a DNA profile of me and my so-called parents. It's one of the perks that come with being a doctor. And guess what? Evelyn and Joe had RNA factors in their chromosomes that _aren't in me_. It's impossible that I'm their son."

This revelation truly stunned Sydney, his mind reeling—"I don't understand, there must be some mistake."

"The only mistake was in ever trusting you." Jarod then let go of Syd's sweatshirt—and so much more.

These words stung the Belgian's heart. "If what you say is true, I would never have knowingly lied to you, Jarod, you must believe me."

He always had as a child, blindly so, but now Jarod wasn't sure whether to believe him or not. He wasn't sure of much right now, except that as he looked out the window and saw the first of Miss P's Sweepers stepping off of the fire escape onto the street below, he knew he didn't have much time.

Jarod turned back to his mentor. "I can be a doctor, a lawyer, an electrical engineer."

"And so much more, Jarod."

"Yes, you taught me I can become anyone I want to be—except *ME*. I don't know who I am." Jarod looked deeply into Sydney's eyes, as tears welled in his own. "Please tell me who I am."

"I'm sorry, Jarod. But I—I don't know."

~~~

As Miss Parker arrived at the bottom of the fire escape, Aires watched her disapprovingly as she lit a cig and took a deep pull into her lungs. "Miss Parker, you know, smoking can take years off your life."

"They're the crappy years on the back end—I don't plan to live that long."

As she exhaled the cloud of death something began ticking in the back of her mind. She gazed up at the relatively insignificant amount of smoke wafting out from the hotel above. Her Spidey senses kicking in, she looked around for answers—and that's when she spotted the squirrelly hotel manager, Hornstein who, apoplectic with distress, saw her coming and tried to pre-empt her.

"I'm so very sorry for your inconvenience, Miss Parker. I assure you, we'll have you back in your suite as soon as humanly possible."

"Don't wet yourself, Horny. Just tell me, how'd this thing start?"

"Our fire sensors indicated faulty electrical wiring on the 14th floor ice machine. Which is incomprehensible. The new technician was in just this afternoon to service it."

Miss P gritted her teeth, "Of course he was." She turned to Aires and her Sweepers as the reality that she'd been played again slapped her in the face. "You four block the exits."

Miss Parker looked up at the window next to the fire escape exit on the 14th floor and saw Jarod—staring down at her.

Pointing at the remaining Sweepers, she growled, "The rest come with me."

~~~

Jarod watched Miss P and her Sweepers as they began fighting their way up through the human flow descending the fire escape. The noose was tightening. Sydney read the urgency in his eyes.

"Come back with me, Jarod, I can make everything right."

Jarod yanked Sydney briskly down the hallway toward the elevator bank.

"I'm never going back." Jarod hit the call button with his fist.

"Be reasonable, Jarod—there's no way out of here!"

"That's what they said about The Centre."

Jarod spun his old friend up against the wall. "Now you may not know the truth, but the secret to who I am has to be in The Centre's mainframe archives. I can't get in—but you can."

"Jarod—only people with Miss Parker's security clearance have access to that. And even if I did—if The Centre found out they'd crucify me."

Jarod pressed Syd harder against the wall. "I did <u>everything</u> you asked of me for the last 30 years, now I'm asking you to do <u>one</u> thing for me."

Chaos exploded like incoming mortars. Sydney and Jarod turned at the same time to see Miss Parker and her team tearing down the hall. The veins bulging out of Miss P's neck, "Jarooooooddddd!"

The elevator *dinged.*

The doors began to open.

A panicked Sydney looked at the onrushing Miss P and said with a disarming smile, "Miss Parker, look who's come back." He then turned to Jarod and whispered, "Hit me."

Jarod punched Sydney, sending him flying back onto the rushing hoard, knocking them backward. The Pretender then quickly leapt into the open lift.

Miss Parker fought her way past the obstructive Sydney, reached into her coat and pulled out her 9mm just as the elevator doors began to close.

She had no shot on the annoying speaker in her room, but she definitely wasn't going to miss Jarod. She took careful aim at him, but as she squeezed the trigger, Syd grabbed her wrist—"No guns!"

Her shot flew wildly. Miss Parker rushed to the elevator just as the doors closed, severing her momentary eye contact with Jarod.

Miss Parker turned to the Sweepers, "Find him!" As they rushed off hollering into their earbuds, a furious Miss Parker slammed Sydney against the wall. "Make up your mind, Sydney—be a scientist or a mommy—you can't be both!"

Chapter 41

THE STRANGEST DAY of Jarod's life began with words he'd never forget.

"Goddamnsonofabitchbastard!"

That was the greeting Jarod received as Bilson led him into the psych Annex for the first time.

The string of words may not have been the only thing Master Sergeant Ellwood Doyle was capable of saying, but they were the only words anyone had ever heard him say. The six-foot-eight, 300-pound homeless veteran known as *Sarge* didn't whisper them. The man who was built like a tank and was never intimidated by anyone shouted them—over and over and over again.

"Goddamnsonofabitchbastard!"

Like Old Faithful, for twelve hours a day, every day, the retired Marine sniper with the gray flattop stood on the same spot, next to the same trash can, facing the same wall, his head bobbing up and down, his entire body involuntarily jerking while the same rage boiled inside him.

"Goddamnsonofabitchbastard!"

Jarod recognized the man whose mind had shattered in the sand of Afghanistan the moment he spotted him in the socialization room. But Dr. B didn't. He was too busy exhibiting an unparalleled level of self-infatuation as he showed off the Annex to his protégé, to recognize Sarge's, - or any of the other human's - misery that dwelt here.

But Jarod wasn't.

As they made their way deeper into the room, Jarod's emotions were churning. Though he'd anticipated this space would be unsettling, he wasn't prepared for just how disturbing it was—*especially to him.*

The facility itself was not what was disquieting. Unlike mental wards of old, it was designed in an open space concept. Four well-lit hallways of private patient rooms radiated out north, south, east and west from a central socialization atrium—the focal point of which was a glass domed ceiling held aloft by eight massive colonnades. The room below, bathed in sunlight, was divided into four life-affirming quadrants: the chit-chat area, where Sarge was affirming his life while chit-chatting with the wall; the Games section, designated for soothing competitive interaction; the area anchored by an 82-inch flat screen, cleverly named the TV Room; and lastly, the Quarter for Contemplation. In the middle of it all was a circular glass nurse's hub looking out onto the ward of test subjects. Seated inside, lording over all that surrounded her, was Nurse Kropski, handing out paper cups of pills to the guinea pigs queued at her window.

The nurse with the head too big for her little body was nodding her big *cabeza* in precise automatic gesture for the paper cups of pills they took dutifully.

Kropski reveled in her role of overseer for the people that the *Court of Bilson* ruled mentally incapable of caring for themselves. She took great egotistical pleasure that they were now in her care—but in Jarod's medical opinion Kropski's *patients didn't look well cared for at all.* And that's what Jarod found upsetting.

"Goddamnsonofabitchbastard!"

Besides Sarge, Jarod identified other patients whose files he'd studied the night before.

There was Coraleen Johnson, a middle-aged woman who stared out of deserted gray eyes as she slid along the back wall of the Contemplation area. Tommy Russo, a spastic man, laughed heartily, but Jarod couldn't *contemplate* why; nothing funny was happening in his section of the room.

Nothing funny was happening in any section of the room.

Everywhere Jarod looked, souls were suffering. The pain etched on their faces caused an Old Faithful-like fury to begin bubbling inside him.

"Goddamnsonofabitchbastard!"

To his left, men at the checkers table snickered into their hands as they watched a jittery teen searching under tables and chairs for things that weren't there.

"Goddamnsonofabitchbastard!"

To his right, the 'Walking Dead,' trapped in the world of their minds, wore ruts in the carpet as they strolled aimlessly.

"Goddamnsonofabitchbastard!"

Behind him were the 'Chair Rockers' with wild grins who mumbled as they stared at the gals from The View, spouting words of wisdom none of them were listening to.

"Goddamnsonofabitchbastard!"

But it was what was right in front of Jarod that made him the angriest—and that was Dr. Bilson.

Jarod's rage was deafening. Dr. B was beaming with pride as he casually mentioned something regarding the *care* his test subjects receive being beyond *outstanding,* but Jarod couldn't *hear* the words coming out of Bilson's mouth. No, the Pretender was too zeroed in on the arrogance of the doctor as he looked at the unfortunate people around them—*unfortunate human beings*—as if they where nothing but meat puppets for his financial gain.

Jarod thought of them as something else.

Something he had been for many years himself.

A lab rat held against his will, forced to run through mazes for the intellectual benefit of others, all for a piece of cheese.

His cheese had been the hope of one day discovering who he really was. The cheese for these disenfranchised people, who had traded their freedom for three squares and a roof, was a three drug cocktail of psychotropic meds they'd been assured would treat their 'supposed' illness.

Jarod wasn't so sure about that.

"Goddamnsonofabitchbastard!"

The pills were an atypical antischizophrenic, a second-generation antipsychotic and a new spectrum antidepressant, all of which Jarod had researched down to their molecular level and determined could produce both positive—and negative results.

The antidepressant was a selective serotonin reuptake inhibitor (SSRI's) designed to give relief to symptoms of despondency but also seriously increased risk of suicidal thinking. The antischizophrenic and anti-psychotic blocked dopamine receptors to prevent hallucinations and dis-ordered thought. But these too came with unintended consequences, one of which Jarod thought he saw in a young lady leaning over a water fountain. She was attempting the simple act of quenching her thirst, but because of involuntary movements of her tongue, mouth and arms, the harder she tried, the wetter she got. Jarod recognized these fitful actions as a tardive dyskinesia, an untreatable, irreversible disorder produced by overexposure to psychotropic medications.

Having read the Asian doc's results, Jarod could tell Bilson's testing protocols had been very aggressive in its high dosage approach to the sub-jects and therein laid the problem.

Jarod had spent most of the previous evening researching how over-exposure to psychotropics could cause the very symptoms they were de-signed to treat, permanently altering the brain patterns of the patients.

"Goddamnsonofabitchbastard!"

Bad things were happening to good people and that wasn't something Jarod could participate in—which left him in a quandary. He knew in his heart he couldn't abandon these people to the fate of the monsters in charge of their lives—but his mission here was not to save them—it was to get to the patient at the end of the East Hallway—the patient in Room E913.

As Jarod stared down that corridor at the closed door of Room E913, Dr. Bilson's voice finally cut through. "But as I'm sure you've discerned from Su's records—the trials can be redesigned to run much more efficiently."

Jarod turned to Dr. B and while he wanted to choke him to death, he instead smiled. "I was up all night doing my homework. As perfectly de-signed as your protocols are, Su's execution of them is pathetic."

Bilson bit on Jarod's lure. The testing problems were all, as Bilson had suspected, Su's fault. Jarod continued reeling in his catch. "But don't worry, I already have plans in mind to get it back on track."

"Excellent, Russell. I knew I could count on you." Bilson then noticed something in the room that disgusted him: Dr. Su, who was entering from the security tunnel. Bilson looked down at his watch and then at his chronically overdue associate. "Just like I knew that after being demoted, that petulant oriental bastard would keep us waiting."

As Su walked toward them, Bilson winked conspiratorially at Jarod. "Clean up that imbecile's mess and in the future there'll be greater opportunities around here—and fewer partners."

Jarod nodded, "Consider it done." Su walked up, scratching sleep from the corner of his eye. "Sorry I'm late—long night with a short waitress."

Bilson's fuse was now lit. "The more things change, the more they stay the same."

Before Su could take umbrage with Bilson's patronization, the senior doc dumped on more. "I want you to confer about Jarod's preliminary findings, then initiate his changes ASAP."

Su didn't like Bilson's tone. The Asian doc flicked the eye cheese off his finger. "I'll be happy to—institute the ones I approve."

Bilson didn't like Su's tone.

Before the tension between the two doctors could ignite, a young nurse rushed up and whispered in Nurse Kropski's ear. Nurse K in turn approached Dr. B—"Sorry to interrupt, Dr. Bilson, but we're having the belligerency problem with the Cohasset woman again."

"Goddamnsonofabitchbastard!"

Bilson finally exploded—"Am I the only one who can get anything done around here?!" Bilson pinched the bridge of his nose, then looked sidelong at Kropski. "I'll deal with her." While looking at Jarod, Bilson pointed at Su. "You deal with him." Dr. B then turned and focused his ire on the huge man with the gray flattop, yelling to no one in particular. "Meanwhile, somebody muzzle that crazy son of a bitch—before he drives me mad!"

Bilson marched off down the East Hallway followed by the nurse with the big head. The humiliated Su simmered angrily at Jarod.

"Goddamnsonofabitchbastard!"

Su looked away from Jarod and displaced his anger onto Sarge. He pointed to the young nurse, "50MG of Risperidone IM STAT." As she ran off, Su then waved a couple of orderlies to follow him and the three men approached the shouting Sergeant.

"Goddamnsonofabitchbastard!"

Su stopped several paces behind the massive vet. "Sarge—you know how this works. Shut your hole or we shut it for you!"

His head bobbing, Sarge ignored him.

Su raised his voice and along with it the tension in the entire room. "Last warning, Sarge!"

Sarge's head began bobbing faster—his eruptions coming quicker.

"Goddamnsonofabitchbastard!"

The nurse rushed up to Su, handing him a syringe. Su nodded to the orderlies. The men moved into pincher positions, forcefully restraining the big man. But before he could administer the shot into Sarge, a hand grabbed his wrist. Su snapped a look at the hand gripping him, then followed the arm up to Jarod's glaring eyes. "Is this really necessary? 50MG of Risperidone will put a bear down for days."

"Big boy starts pulling this shit, it doesn't matter what you say—you can't reach into that schizophrenic head of his—the needle's all that works."

Jarod squeezed harder on Su's wrist with his grip hand while taking the syringe from the Asian doctor with his other. "We'll try it my way."

Jarod released Su, then looked to the orderlies. "Let him go."

The surprised orderlies did as they were told and Sarge resumed his bobbing at the wall.

Jarod cautiously walked up to the trash can and threw the syringe inside. He then stood between the receptacle and Sarge. But instead of looking at the old vet, he focused all his attention on the wall in front of his face and started bobbing his head up and down.

As he mimicked Sarge's actions, Jarod didn't see the look the big man was giving him out of the corner of his eyes. He also didn't see the rage bubbling up inside Sarge's body or how it twitched before he blew.

"Goddamnsonofabitchbastard!"

Jarod didn't see any of that—*but he felt it.*

And that was the point.

From the top of his head to the tips of his toes, the Pretender did what he did best. He put himself inside the skin of the man next to him—he *became* the man next to him. He felt everything that Sarge felt. The rage and frustration, the hurt and the pain of a lifetime of witnessing atrocities no one should see and experiencing anguish no one should feel. As he experienced all of that frustration, turmoil and rage build up like a pressure cooker, Jarod tried to hold it inside just like Sarge did everyday for 12 hours. But as hard as he tried to contain it, it could not be. Jarod's body suddenly twitched and the same eruption of pain passed out of his lips.

"Goddamnsonofabitchbastard!"

As Jarod spewed forth so did Sarge.

"Goddamnsonofabitchbastard!"

"Goddamnsonofabitchbastard!"

"Goddamnsonofabitchbastard!"

They dueled back and forth and back and forth and back and forth until they were exhausted and then, as quickly as the eruptions began, they subsided.

The entire room was silent.

Tommy Russo was no longer laughing.

Coraleen Johnson no longer slid along the wall.

Everyone in the socialization room was focused on the two men.

Sarge turned to face Jarod. Jarod returned the glance.

The big man slid a hand over his flattop. "What's wrong with you, Son?"

As the Master Sergeant stared at him, Jarod crooked his finger for Sarge to bend down. When he did, he whispered something into the old vet's ear.

After a beat the vet stood, thought about what he'd heard, then sort of laughed—only he didn't laugh. He went *Harrumph* out of his nose, then grinned at the Pretender and said, "Okay."

Jarod turned to the orderlies. "Sergeant Doyle is going to go back to his room now."

Sarge turned to go. Unsure, the orderlies looked to Su. The stunned Su just nodded. The orderlies parted and the big man calmly walked away. Everyone was staring at Jarod as he faced Dr. Su.

"Sarge isn't schizophrenic—he's suffering from an OCD related disorder and PTSD." Jarod turned to the young nurse. "Taper him off the test meds, five percent a day until clear. They've been exacerbating his condition."

Unsure how to respond, the nurse gazed at Su for guidance. But Dr. S was frozen with uncertainty. Jarod wasn't. "Do it now."

"Yes, Doctor. Right away." She went back to the nurse's hub. The orderlies went back to where the orderlies go. Coraleen began to slide down the wall again. The Chair Rockers resumed their rocking. As everything returned to normalcy in this abnormal place, Su and Jarod were alone now near the wall.

Su was the first to speak. "What did you whisper into Sarge's ear?"

"That I was just as full of fury as he was and if he'd go back to his room I promised to find a way for him to stop feeling such pain."

Without responding, Su began to walk off, then turned back.

"Undermine my authority again and you'll be the one feeling pain."

Jarod was thinking about how that statement was a two-way street when he heard the loud crash.

Chapter 42

THE CRASHING SOUND came from the far end of the East hallway and thinking it may be coming from Room E913, Jarod went running.

As he was approaching E915 the door flung open and a startled Dr. Bilson backpedaled out, his arms up protecting himself from the flying projectiles that flew out from within. The doc managed to side step a plastic water pitcher that shattered on the wall behind his head, but wasn't fast enough to dodge the tray of uneaten breakfast that hit him in his right temple and splattered loose scrambled eggs, mixed fruit and a pudding-like substance all over his Moods of Norway Oluf suit jacket. "Goddamnit!"

Next out of the room was Nurse Kropski, who slipped and slid in the mess as she dodged incoming artillery in the form of a milk box that exploded on the door to Room E914. "Look out she's got another bedpan!" Emerging from Room E915, wielding the deadly toileting device, was the same young woman Jarod had stopped when she was trying to escape the Annex.

The girl with the violet eyes.

Infuriated, Skylar Frisbeed the bedpan right at the little head of Bilson and the big head of Kropski, both of whom ducked in time to save their skulls. "I told you I'm not eating your bullshit food or swallowing your meds anymore. I don't belong here!" With that, Skylar turned and blindly sprinted three steps, smack-dab into Jarod's arms—knocking them both to the ground. Skylar landed atop and face-to-face with Jarod. "Well, ain't this just perfect?"

Jarod's first instinct was to answer in the affirmative. He'd never had a woman in his arms before and he'd damn sure never had one atop him. While he assumed this wasn't the most natural way to find oneself in this physical position, he nonetheless found the feel of her curvaceous body and the sensation of her strength and warmth very pleasing. In fact, as he stared into Skylar's violet eyes and she back into his brown ones, Jarod realized this particular sensation was as pleasing as any sensation he'd ever felt before.

As the same two orderlies that had flanked Sarge rushed up, both now holding restraint gear, Jarod regarded his squirming charge. "Skylar, if I let you up—do you promise not to punch me this time? My jaw is still quite sore."

"Yeah, you're lucky I didn't smack your sorry ass lower."

Jarod released Skylar, who snapped to her feet and raised her hands in sarcastic surrender to the orderlies. "Your mama's must be so proud."

As Jarod regained his footing the orderlies took hold of Skylar's arms. Once he saw the wildcat was secure, Bilson rose from his defensive crouch. The administrator fumed as he rubbed his temple with one hand, while he scraped smashed peach funk off his jacket with the other. Jarod was amused by Bilson's persnickety annoyance and couldn't tell if it was the head pain or the fruit stain which infuriated him more, though he guessed the latter.

Taking his typically 'brave' stance *behind* the orderlies, Bilson assumed control. "Until further notice I want this one restrained to her bed."

Kropski rotated her large cranium toward Skylar. "Happily."

The orderlies were about to carry out Bilson's instructions until Jarod interjected.

"I don't think that would be advisable."

Dr. Bilson rotated his cranium to that statement and its familiarity. "Perhaps you'd have a different assessment had you been the one dodging meatballs and Tater Tots for the last few weeks."

Jarod stepped past Skylar and the orderlies, placed his arm around Bilson's shoulders and escorted him away. "I'm trying to quell a potential 'situation' here." Jarod stopped and, ensuring they were out of ear range, continued. "I've uncovered several patients whose dosage levels Dr. Su has not only flagrantly mismanaged but has also left a paper trail that proves such malfeasances." Jarod let that potential time bomb tick in Bilson's head for a moment then continued. "I'm confident Skylar's irrationality is a reflection of Su's incompetence."

Bilson glared down the hallway to where Su flirted with the young nurse in the chit-chat area. "Damn Gook."

Jarod decided to leverage Dr. B's frustration. "Long story short, a similar non-adherence to protocols at Dharma-Labs caused a series of adverse reactions in patients. Those reactions lead to a whistle-blowing incident from a bleeding heart employee that resulted in a surprise visit from the FDA and a subsequent shutdown. A preventable situation that cost lots of time and even more money." Jarod subtly indicated the orderlies and Skylar. "We don't need that kind of drama here, so until I have all of the dosage issues and testing records 'adjusted,' let me deal with her and patients like her, quietly."

Appreciative of Jarod's concern, Bilson nodded to Skylar. "Jarod, do whatever you have to to get her and this whole study under control."

"You can count on it, Jonah."

In *L'Endroit de L'Homme*-like fraternity, Dr. B double patted Jarod on the shoulder and then, preoccupied with a pudding glob on his slacks, turned his focus to Kropski. "I need to do something about this before the stain sets. Get me some soda water, STAT."

"Right away, Doctor."

As Bilson and Kropski walked back toward the socialization room, the orderlies escorted Skylar back into her own.

As quickly as it had started, the second melee of Jarod's day had stopped—he'd have three more before the strangest day of his life came to an end.

Two would take place in Room E913, but as he stood there staring at that very door he knew there were too many prying eyes in the hallway for him to enter that room just yet.

Besides, Jarod had something else he needed to deal with in the room of the girl with violet eyes.

Chapter 43

"*BETRAYAL* IS THE violation of an expressed or perceived trust by a person or persons with whom a person relies upon for some aspect of his or her life, while *trauma* ..."

Miss P fired up a Pall Mall—"I know what trauma is Syd, and you're going to get a big taste of it if you don't enlighten me as to why—<u>exactly why</u>—your little freak pulled the fire alarm to get face time with you! And don't tell me he did it just so he could squeeze his teddy bear and hear, 'I wuv you, Jarod.'"

Though the smoke had cleared hours ago, the tension in the air was still thick in the living room of Miss Parker's hotel suite. Sydney sat on the hot seat as he had for hours, watching Miss P pace back and forth, her angry steam blowing.

Disregarding her patronization of his relationship with Jarod, Sydney nonetheless answered her questions directly, or as directly as he could, under the circumstances. "Miss Parker, in many ways that's *exactly* what it was. I think he wanted to see me. Look into my eyes. To have human contact with someone he trusted—or someone he wanted to know if he could still trust."

"What does that mean?"

"That's what I've been trying to explain to you." Syd returned to his interrupted train of thought. He would tell her as much as he could but not everything, not until he was certain where he stood in the crazy state of affairs that his life had become. He was talking about Jarod but could just as easily be talking about himself.

"Jarod is in extreme bio psychosocial distress triggered by what he perceives himself a victim of—a condition J.J. Freyd called 'betrayal trauma.' Similar to 'dissociative amnesia,' 'betrayal trauma' is a term used to explain the harm caused by an actual or perceived violation of a psychological contract by persons upon which the victim relies for some aspect of his or her holistic well-being."

As Syd continued he watched Miss Parker sit on the bed and flip open her laptop. On it, Sydney knew, was her personal passcode with access to The Centre Archives Mainframe—the access Jarod needed. As her fingers touched the keyboard Sydney attempted to see what code she typed in. But except for the first key she hit, the number 7, her keystrokes were much too fast for him to commit them to memory.

As Sydney droned on, Miss P was checking to see if her father had sent an email to her private account and was relieved to see that it was empty. She hadn't reported in that they'd missed capturing Jarod at the hotel and hoped he didn't know yet. She'd rather apologize for that after she'd captured him rather than try to explain it now and *now* she needed to return to her pacing.

She had ordered Cornelius work overtime to narrow down the hospital list to find Jarod before he could move on, but was now in her own living hell of bio psychosocial distress as she listened to the Belgian shrink blather on about something called Betrayal Trauma. They'd been going at it for all the hours since Jarod had escaped without a trace. Miss P hated when Sydney psychobabbled, but her father had told her to keep him in the game, so while her fuse was growing short she put up with his droning and tuned back in.

"Psychologist Jennifer Freyd determined that the degree to which events are processed and remembered are substantially higher when the relationship between perpetrator and victim involves closeness, trust, or caregiving. Betrayal Trauma proposes that a victim's recall and recognition of the abuse can manifest in reactive outbursts that can be unpredictable. I'm sure you've experienced some of that in your own life, Miss Parker."

Miss P swiveled to face Sydney. "You quoting Wikipedia to piss me off or to try and impress me, Syd?"

"Google Betrayal Trauma—it's far more injurious than many admit. It violates the victim's understanding of rules, roles, relationships, respect, morals, ethics, and values, which are the core tenets of the psychological contract. And a return to equilibrium requires the individual to redefine one or more of these tenets."

Miss P towered over the exhausted Belgian. "Is that why he met you in the hallway? To tell you he's redefining a tenet?"

Sydney thought honestly for a moment. "I think he met me to say he was redefining his life."

This got Miss Parker's attention. "How so?"

"Jarod believes he's been lied to the entire time he was at The Centre." Syd rubbed his forehead with his hand. "I'm beginning to wonder if he's not the only one."

That was it. Miss Parker decided in that moment she'd kill Syd. She'd have done it right then and there if Aires hadn't entered to announce, "Cornelius is here to see you."

Sporting a Tom Ford, Duke of Windsor-style three-piece grey plaid suit, complete with matching umbrella and eye wear, Cornelius made an entrance worthy of James Bond. "Should have brought me along in the first place—maybe you two wouldn't look so—bamboozled."

Parker glared at his appearance as he knew she would, "You better have a goddamn good reason for ignoring my order to stay put in Blue Cove and maintain the hunt for Jarod."

Corny grinned and explained how he'd stripped the ambient sound down to a level where he actually was listening to a hospital security guard order a Domino's pizza—anchovies and mushroom—to be delivered to the hospital's Burn Center. "Of the 80 plus hospitals within a 30-mile radius of where you're standing right now, Miss Parker, only 23 have designated Burn Units." He then failed to stifle that giggle she hated and often made fun of whenever he failed to stifle it—"Ironic."

"How so?"

"He wanted his pizza extra crispy."

Miss Parker decided she was going to kill him too.

Cornelius grinned again, selling—"It also seems prudent that given Jarod's many talents and his recent successes with them, erring on the side of caution is a good thing."

She just stared at him—he knew he still hadn't *made the sale.*

"Why risk Jarod tapping into and monitoring Centre communications when I could eliminate all risk of that by being on site with you the instant I narrow these Burn Units down to <u>one</u>?"

He had a point. Miss P hated when Corn or most anyone else, *had a point.*

"And Kismet—the hotel was able to make you my neighbor, *neighbor.*" And with that he opened her adjoining room door, revealing his adjoining room—his travel computer rig already set up and good to go.

"Then what the hell are you waiting for?" And with that she crushed her latest cigarette out into the *Thank you for not smoking* plaque mounted on the wall just above her bedside table and promptly ordered every last one of them out.

Chapter 44

STANDING AT HER hospital room window, staring out at the freedom that existed nine stories below, Skylar didn't look at all to Jarod like someone who could've been diagnosed as a paranoid schizophrenic. For the first time since Jarod met her, Skylar was calm.

Jarod wasn't.

Truth was, of the two people alone in this room, he seemed to be the only one carrying on internal conversations with 'other inner personalities.' The conversation was fast and furious and all about how intriguing Skylar was to him. The more he spoke to himself about her, the more he realized he felt a unique anxiety, an anxiety he'd only experienced with one other female long ago, an anxiety he didn't understand but needed to.

The nervousness had begun the instant Skylar had fallen atop of him in the hallway. Jarod thought it would have ended when she stood up, but not only had it lingered, each time he'd looked into her eyes since—it had gotten stronger.

There was a truth within Skylar's violet eyes that Jarod found beguiling, a truth inside of *her* that he wanted to understand. Better. Much better.

Jarod stood next to her bed, pretending to read her patient chart but was actually looking above it—staring at her. He was lost in the way the sunlight through the window cast a soft glow around the delicate silky hairs on her smooth cheek—the soft little ones you rarely are close enough to see. He was enticed by her long elegant fingers and how unconsciously, she slowly caressed herself with the tips of them—from the nape of her neck, across her shoulder, down her bicep and finally to her forearm, where they traced the wings of her angel tattoo.

When she looked up, she caught Jarod staring. But she didn't look away. Comfortable in her skin, she held his gaze for a long time.

A very long time.

Jarod realized her gaze was making him nervous again.

When he was fretful like this as a child, Jarod found the one thing he could do to compartmentalize the cause of his anxiety was to change the subject in his mind and talk about something else. He focused in on her tattoo. "Does your angel have a name?"

"Not one that would mean anything to you."

"You never know what means something to someone."

She looked at him pointedly. "Why are you in here?"

Jarod thought that was a good question. Especially since one of the voices in Jarod's mind was yelling at him to get out of her room as quickly as possible—*the person he was here to see—the job he was here to do was in the room next door.* But the other voice was whispering to him to stay right where he was—*and explore the feelings he was experiencing.* Listening to the whisper, Jarod pulled a stethoscope out of the pocket of his doctor's coat.

"May I listen to your heart?"

"Why don't you listen to yours and let me outta this mad house?" She lifted her chin slightly, pursed her lips. "Or are you like them and think I really belong here?"

"I don't know, yet." Jarod placed the tips of the stethoscope into his ears and patted the edge of the bed. She arched her eyebrows in a good way and then sat. Jarod gently slipped his hand up the back of Skylar's shirt and listened through the diaphragm.

Her heartbeat was strong and perhaps a beat or two fast, but he couldn't really tell. Her skin soft like satin, the warmth of her body felt like sunshine and her hair smelled of flowers, the combination of which had his heart pounding in his ears louder than hers.

Jarod reluctantly removed his hand and tried to regain his composure. "Do you ever hear voices telling you things to do?"

"Just the one telling me to get the hell outta here right now." This amused Jarod. He'd heard that voice in his head a million times when he was in The Centre—it didn't have as colorful a vocabulary, but it espoused the same message.

"Do you ever find yourself having delusions?"

She raised an eyebrow. "I don't walk around pretending I'm a doctor, if that's what you mean."

Jarod looked at her. Her violet eyes were cutting right through him and he couldn't tell whether they had pierced the veneer of his Pretend or if she could read the light reflected in his eyes that said he wasn't who he was Pretending to be. He was frozen until she completed her thought. "Not like that effete pig, Bilson or his incompetent side boob, Hong Kong Su-ey. What worthless posers those dirty A-Holes are."

Jarod gave inquisitive. "A-Hole?"

Skylar rolled her eyes. *Is this big clown for real?* "Assholes? Hello? We on the same planet here, Doc?"

"Don't call me Doc, call me Jarod, please."

"Look, *Jarod please*—if all this is some kind of mental pop quiz, let me save you some time. I'm not a paranoid-schiz. Okay? I don't hear voices, I don't suffer from hallucinations and don't think I'm any better or worse than any other person taking a ride on this blue marble. And for what it's worth, neither are half the other dregs in here. We were all scratching our junk in a shithole city shelter when Dr. B came in promising if we answered some questions we'd get three hots and bedbug-free cots for a few months. Now we're just pincushions for whatever they want to stick us with. I'd rather take my chances back out on the streets—but that useless stretch mark won't let me outta here."

"I think you're right."

"That Dr. B is useless as a stretch mark?"

"No. That you're not paranoid or schizophrenic."

For the first time since they met, Skylar didn't have a smart-assed come back, a sarcastic roll of the eyes or a *what a dipshit this jackass is* look on her face. She was just—real. "Seriously?"

"Yes. I don't think there is anything wrong with you at all." Jarod then grabbed her med chart and started making notations. "I'm going to halve your dosage daily until you've been weaned."

Her joy bent to confusion. "Why can't we just cold turkey it and get me the hell outta here?"

"Abrupt cessation of SSRI's can cause severe withdrawal symptoms. It will take a few days this way, but it will be much healthier for you." Jarod finished writing and looked up. As his eyes again met hers, she showed a type of smile Jarod knew well. A smile of joy mixed with sadness.

"It's been a long time since anyone heard me." She reached out and took his hand. "A long time since anyone cared."

She squeezed Jarod's hand and he let her. "Don't forget about me, Jarod." Lost in her violet eyes, Jarod didn't think that was possible.

"As soon as you are healthy I'll get you out of here. I promise."

He gently let go of her hand and walked toward the door.

She called after him. "It's Sal."

Jarod stopped and turned.

Skylar raised her forearm with the tiny tattoo. "My angel. I named her after my mom."

Skylar then turned her glistening eyes and attention back outside the window—to a freedom she soon hoped to feel.

Finally calm, Jarod quietly opened her door and stepped out.

Chapter 45

THE EAST HALLWAY was quiet.

It was also empty.

For the first time no one or no thing was between Jarod and his ultimate goal—the person in Room E913.

Jarod took the two steps to that door, reached for the knob, then paused.

He'd been thinking about this moment for several weeks, anticipating what he was going to say when he saw him for the first time.

The Pretender thought about why he had come to New York in the first place. He thought about Cassandra Hearns and the pain she endured daily from the devastation of her husband and the loss of her son Luke.

Luke was the reason Jarod was here.

The missing little boy was all Jarod was thinking about when he finally grabbed the doorknob to Room E913 and went inside.

Unlike everywhere else Jarod had been in the Annex, it was dark in this room. Blackout curtains over the windows were closed tightly, the only illumination coming from the glow of the monitors surrounding the hospital bed. Still, their amber radiance was all Jarod needed to recognize the patient under the covers.

Jarod smiled. He'd searched for him exhaustively and finally here he was. The one person who could bring joy back into the faces of a distraught mother and father who thought they had lost their only child forever.

He was smaller than Jarod thought he'd be and from his ordeal, looked older. He was also very frail and still.

To keep him alive, an I.V. infusion pump sent nutrients through a feeding tube into his nose and drugs and saline into his veins. The other machines surrounding him monitored just how alive he was. There were ones that kept constant track of his heartbeat, breathing rates and blood pressure—the most important of which was the EEG that kept constant track of his brain activity.

Jarod read the medical chart at the foot of the bed and opened it. Not surprisingly, it didn't list a name for the patient, just that his condition was 'comatose.' Jarod knew his name, of course; what he didn't know was the severity of his damage.

The Glasgow Coma Scale's indication of the extent of brain injury varies from a minimum of 3—severe brain injury and death—to a maximum of 15—mild or no brain injury. Jarod noted that the patient's intensity had been steadily improving from the dangerous level of 5 when he'd arrived to his current semi-comatose level of 11.

Reading on, Jarod discovered that Dr. Bilson had tried many treatments to awaken him, including glucose shock, several different anti-brain swelling procedures, as well as an induced hypothermia technique. But nothing had been successful and he remained in a minimally conscious state.

But that wasn't good enough for Jarod.

The Pretender stepped bedside, looked down at the helpless being and with an open hand, reared back with all his force and brutally slapped the patient's face.

His head flopped sideways and his lids flickered open, revealing two sunken eyeballs gazing up at Jarod.

One was real.

The other was made of glass.

The patient was the Libyan terrorist, Kaj.

Jarod didn't know if the eyelid flickering was an involuntary nerve response to the stimuli of the slap or Kaj was actually awakening. Either way he was anxious to get some information out of the head of the man who had

five weeks earlier escaped his torturers only to end up comatose after a
violent car crash on a highway in West Texas. The information Kaj had in
his mind was all that mattered to Jarod. He took the one-eyed Libyan by the
scruff of the neck and shook him forcefully. "Where is Luke?"

Kaj's lids began blinking rapidly. Clarity of focus began materializing in
his good eye as if he were trying to escape his mental fog. But as quickly as
it appeared he'd come to, he started to drift away again. "Talk to me! I
know you kidnapped Luke. Now tell me, is he still alive?" Jarod attempted
to shake Kaj into consciousness, but his fight was in vain. The eye made of
glass just stared out at nothing while the Libyan's real eye, clouding back up
as before, floated back into his head.

Jarod dropped him onto his pillow at the instant Nurse Kropski entered, holding replacement I.V. bags. She stopped in her tracks upon seeing
Jarod.

"You're not supposed to be in here."

Unlike Kaj's mind, Jarod's was firing on all cylinders. He spun toward
Kropski. "Well, it's a damn good thing I am! I could hear him choking from
the corridor."

"Choking?"

"Yes! Aren't those monitors hooked up to your station?"

"Yes, but—"

"*Yes, but,* nothing! Cheap words aren't going to save someone from
asphyxiation if you're asleep at the wheel!"

Drawn by the commotion, Dr. Bilson rushed in.

"What the hell is going on now?"

Jarod spun to face him. "That's what I want to know." Bilson was surprised to see Jarod in here as was Su, who also arrived, late as always. Jarod
continued. "I was in the hallway when I heard this man struggling!" Jarod
looked pointedly at Su. "I thought he might be <u>another</u> patient hyper-
reacting to his dosage levels."

Su moved toward Jarod, fit to be tied. "He's not!"

Bilson stepped in front of Su, trying to calm the situation. "This
patient is not even part of the test."

Jarod tossed Kaj's patient chart onto the bed. "I can see that. What I
don't see is how he fits in here."

Bilson didn't take his eyes off Jarod—"Nurse?"

Kropski had hoped she'd faded into the woodwork but hadn't. "Yes, Doctor?"

"Go check your monitor relays for this patient. Make sure everything is working correctly."

"Right away, Doctor." She was turning to leave when Bilson went on. "And Su, make yourself useful and go help her."

Su flicked his teeth with his tongue and held in his contempt, following her out.

Bilson then closed the door and walked toward Jarod. "At times our financial partners request we care for—one of their own." Jarod watched Bilson as he picked up the patient chart. "They don't like questions to be asked—so I don't ask them and neither should you." Dr. B replaced the chart into its slot at the foot of the bed.

Jarod remained quiet for a beat, then gave Bilson a sidelong glance. "Are there any more *surprises* I should know about?"

"No, Doctor. Stay clear of this man and all will be fine."

Jarod had no intentions of staying clear—this patient held the secrets to where a missing boy was—and one way or another Jarod was going to get that information out of him.

Jarod nodded to Bilson—"No problem."

"Good then. I'll take over from here."

"And I'll get back to work."

As Jarod exited the room he could hear Bilson making a cell phone call and quickly pulled out the cell he'd rigged to tap into Bilson's calls like he did before to cover himself with Dharma.

The call was short, businesslike. A man's stern voice simply answered—"Bilson, go" to which Bilson replied, "He may be waking up." There was silence until Stern Voice grumbled—"Clear your schedule." Bilson replied, "Then I'll see you soon," but didn't get all of it out before Stern Voice hung up.

Jarod knew someone else was now coming for Kaj—someone else wanting to know what was in the terrorist's mind just like he did. Jarod knew exactly who it was and also knew he was desperately running out of time.

Chapter 46

BEFORE THE PHONE call from Dr. Bilson, the man in his office in West Texas had been having a shitty day. But as he hung up and thought about what the arrogant prick of a physician had just told him, he felt as though things might be changing for the better.

He pressed a red button next to his phone, then reached up to rub his itchy eye, but his fingers didn't make it to the source of his irritation. They were blocked by the black patch he'd forgotten he was wearing—the patch that was a constant reminder of why he was having a shitty day to begin with.

O'Quinn hadn't had a good one since the Libyan terrorist had used his eyeball for an ashtray. Since then, the bald man had suffered from a chronic irritation caused by his damaged cornea that had healed poorly and felt gritty when it rubbed against the inside of his eyelid. The surgeons had told him the maddening memento of his failure would go away—eventually, they just weren't sure when.

A double knock came on the door. O'Quinn looked over in time to see the man with the face like a butcher's dog enter his office. The mutt's paw was still in a cast from where Kaj had almost severed it when the terrorist had smashed the interrogation room door on it during his escape. B Dog's full attention was on his master. "You rang?"

All O'Quinn said was "Pack a bag."

Chapter 47

TO OSCAR, IN his white lab coat, Jarod looked like a mad scientist.

The Harlem Rat was poking his chubby head out from beneath the gossamer fabric of Jarod's makeshift sim room on the upper loft and peering down to see his human roomy had transformed the kitchen into a research lab. Illuminated by the hanging lamp, Oscar could clearly make out the Bunsen burners that flamed beakers of multi-colored bubbling liquids, various racks of test tubes full of various concoctions of various ingredients that his human was examining under an electron microscope on the dinner table directly below him.

Curious as to what his bunky was up to *this time*, the chunky mammal decided to go investigate in a more up close and personal way. Oscar climbed out from under the sheet and took a running leap toward the chain of the lamp hanging from a ceiling beam. With a perfect four-paw grab, he caught the metal links, then shimmied downward tail first. Letting go he slid across the slanted copper shade, then free fell to the table below. He landed between two stacks of medical books atop a fruit-fly neuron chart, identical to the one Jarod had left for Sydney at the wind turbine station.

For several hours before Jarod had begun the mad scientist routine, Oscar had watched his flatmate study the chart as well as the text. The furry rodent had no idea what the human was concocting or why, nor did he really care.

About that.

What Oscar did care about was the fact that Jarod had been so obsessed with reading these books while mixing his cocktails that he had forgotten to eat—and more importantly, had forgotten to feed his *housemate*. The rat decided he needed to know why, so he scampered atop the open book to get a better look at their subject matter.

Unfortunately, Oscar couldn't really read, but if he had been able to, he would've realized his little paws were on a highlighted section that described what had so captured Jarod's attention.

Needed for the comatose to regain consciousness is a synapse connection between the cerebral cortex and a structure located in the brainstem called the reticular activating system. The experimental technique, known as trans-cranial shock stimulation, sends Nano drugs penetrating into these cells to excite the synapse responses to shock-awaken coma patients. Tested on chimps with mixed results, the technique is still years away from human trials.

As Jarod worked at the microscope, inspecting his serum for impurities, he was thinking of a million things—foremost among them was how Kaj was going to respond in less than an hour.

Satisfied with his serum, Jarod opened the lid of a cylindrical ten-inch long stainless steel container and from inside removed two 20-gauge syringes. He placed the razor sharp point of one needle into the liquid and pulled back the plunger to fill it.

Finishing then with the second syringe, Jarod gently replaced it and its mate into their container and fastened the lid. He wanted them safe until they were needed. They were his key to unlocking the door to Kaj's mind.

As Jarod swiveled to his red iPad and turned it on, his thoughts quickly turned to Luke. From the get go, the desire to find him was an intuitive drive that Jarod could not have turned away from had he tried. The story of the missing boy had pulled on his heart in an instinctive way he knew had roots in many emotions.

These were emotional wells that Jarod drank from every day and from the very moment he'd read about the tragedy of the Hearns family, he was compelled to discover the truth.

As the security cam recording Jarod hacked from the Bissonet Plaza Elementary School sprang to life on the iPad, Jarod found these same emotions surfacing again. Even though he'd watched and reviewed the image hundreds of times now, the feelings it brought up in Jarod only became stronger and more personal.

While waiting outside on the street curb for his father to pick him up, a van pulled up next to Luke. At the instant it did, a fat man wearing a blue Adidas running suit slowly limped by as if he'd been jogging and came up lame. He nonchalantly passed in a way so that Luke was between him and the van. And in the instant as he wiped by in front of Luke—the boy seemingly vanished.

At first Jarod had thought there had been some glitch in the camera—but when replaying the tape one frame at a time he saw it was simply a masterful move.

As the fat Adidas man limped by, a middle eastern man slid open the van door and pulled Luke inside and closed the door in such a smooth subtle way that unless someone was watching intently, you'd have never noticed he was gone.

The Middle Eastern man then hopped into the driver's seat and with one look to his fat partner, drove away.

Sometime ago Jarod had frozen the image of that look, blown it up and discovered through the NSA database this driver was a Libyan terrorist and kidnapping expert named Kaj Rahamzada.

Three minutes after the kidnapping, three minutes after the van containing Luke had driven away, Roger Hearns pulled up in his BMW. As he was looking around for his son, the fat man in the Adidas suit walked back from the other direction. He was no longer limping. He leaned into the BMW's driver window and whispered something to Luke's father. Whatever Adidas man said registered and Luke's father began to argue and then panic. He then threw the BMW into gear and roared away.

Adidas waved frantically to someone off screen and a Cadillac roared up. Adidas man jumped inside and the car chased after Roger.

Oscar scurried over the table and placed his front claws onto the stainless container next to Jarod's arm, hoping to get the attention of the homo-sapien. He was hoping his roomy would 'help a rodent out' and give him a bite of something, but it was not to be.

The Pretender was too preoccupied in his thoughts.

Jarod hadn't positively determined what had happened in the 18 minutes between Roger Hearns driving away, chased by the men in the Cadillac, and when he was fished out of the Tourne River by a 'passerby.'

But he had his suspicions, suspicions that had been reinforced while driving in the Beemer two nights ago. Being chased would explain the reason Hearns would have been going so fast on a rainy road. But it didn't explain the accident itself.

During the long left curve approaching the bridge and while his car was being pulled to the right, Jarod was forced to do a counterintuitive move to recreate the accident, one that took all of his strength yanking the steering wheel to the left to make the car crash through the railing and fly into the river.

Jarod considered all the possibilities.

Did Luke's father go off the bridge on purpose? This seemed unlikely.

Did the Cadillac chase vehicle force him off the bridge? Since the police report didn't indicate damage to the rear of Roger's BMW from another car, this too seemed unlikely.

Which left the scenario that the BMW went off the bridge accidentally when trying to elude his pursuers as the most likely one. Jarod's sim on the bridge supported this *accidental* scenario as well. Especially since Hearns was so quickly fished out by unknown 'passersby'—likely the occupants of the Cadillac who wanted him alive to give the shaken engineer a warning they would kill his son—and God knows what else.

Jarod also surmised that since the evidence at the scene so strongly supported the *accidental* scenario a credible Roger Hearns had laid out to the police, that explained why the small town police force never steered their investigation in any other direction or thought to look at the school's security footage.

The fact that Luke's father had lied to the authorities about having picked his son up from school and then losing control of his car proved to Jarod that Roger was involved in something way over his head. Jarod hadn't been able to figure out what that was—yet. The only thing he was sure about was that neither the attitude of the Roger on the Christmas video nor his actions when Jarod was at the Hearns household had come off as a man who was malicious. He appeared to Jarod as a father who loves his son deeply. A man who is truly distraught but also very afraid of the man in the Adidas sweat suit and whatever threats he made to him. Jarod would figure out Luke's father's reasons for being fearful and for not revealing the whole truth, in due course.

After he'd identified Kaj, Jarod hacked into the Department of Homeland Security's clandestine traffic cam system that was set up after 9/11 to secretly keep watch on all the car traffic on the eastern seaboard. Truth-be-known it was a nonexistent system Jarod had helped devise. In less than six days Jarod had managed to track down the safe house in Newark Kaj had taken Luke to after the kidnapping. But Jarod had arrived there seconds too late. As he was rounding the corner, he saw three men hustling Kaj into a black sedan and driving away. One was ramrod straight and bald, another had the mug of a dog and the third a face that was reminiscent of—well, a penis.

Jarod found traces of Luke inside but they were days old, telling him the boy had long since been moved away.

From Newark he'd trailed the men who'd taken Kaj to a small adobe cabin in the desert outside El Paso. Here too, Jarod had arrived late. He'd come upon the remains of a fiery car wreck—from which three people had been transported to a hospital. One for a broken arm, another for a seared eyeball and the last had been life-flighted out suffering brain trauma.

It had taken Jarod seven weeks on the wind turbine platform to track down Kaj, the victim with the brain injury who'd been sent to a hospital in NYC called Guardian General.

As Jarod took off his lab coat he surmised that O'Quinn wanted to know the same thing he wanted to know, a piece of information inside of Kaj's head.

Jarod reached into his pocket and brought out the Hulk Pez. Pulling the monster's head back, he placed a candy in his mouth. He then pulled the head back a second time and offered the next piece to Oscar, who happily grabbed it and began munching away.

The Pretender placed the Hulk atop the medical books so he could keep watch over the lab. He then headed out to find an answer to the question that had been nagging him for weeks.

Where was Luke?

Chapter 48

HIS MATTED BLACK hair spiked like stalactites over his pocked and elongated forehead. Just below were black eyes deep set and piercing, like onyx caves too perilous to explore. His mouth was frozen in a snarl, his oversized teeth gnarly and corroded, all framed into a thick leathery head and neck.

While the drawing on the cinder block wall was crude in terms of art-istry, this rendering of The Hulk was skillful given it was wrought by the hand of a ten-year-old boy.

Luke Hearns shifted his rear on the stained linoleum, examining his finished work. For a moment the dark basement he'd endured for some weeks now was his Louvre. His fingers were black from the cinder bits he'd pulled from the fireplace on the opposite wall from his cot to create his rendition. And like most red-blooded American boys, he wiped his fingers on his filthy pants.

Unlike most red-blooded American boys, Luke had been kidnapped. And while drawing his hero instinctively gave him strength to go on, inside Luke was scared and lonely.

Though he didn't know the names of the phases, nor was he conscious of passing from one to the next, since he'd been taken Luke had been moving through the emotional stages of his trauma.

The first had been shock—the emotional equivalent of doing a header off the Jungle Gym—a violent violation of his safe world and right outside his very school no less. The event itself had been blocked in his mind at first, but with each passing day grew in clarity. He found it disconcerting that the more he relived the event and remembered more about it, the less scary it became. He didn't know why, didn't even wonder, it just was.

Before long he began to find an unsettling acceptance of his dilemma, one that fueled the longing he felt for his parents. Despite working hard at keeping his mind off these feelings with mind puzzles and internal riddles, something his scientific brain was very adept at, Luke could never completely shake the question that ached most in his heart: Did his parents have any idea what'd happened to him? Did they think he'd run away? Been stolen?

Did they think he was dead?

The thought of being dead made him want to cry. But he was afraid if he didn't get out of here soon, that was exactly what he was going to be.

Dead.

And that realization caused Luke to slide into a different emotional stage. Anger. Who were these people who took him? And why him? What were they going to do to him? What was taking his parents and the police so long? And worst of all he was left with the feeling that there was nothing he could really do about any of it.

Or was there?

When he'd awoken, a plan had begun to gel, his mind raced wickedly prompting his drawing. He knew that the snarl on his hero's face was the inspiration of the plan he'd concocted and was now feeling the strength of it coursing through his veins.

After so many weeks in captivity he barely remembered the first day of his ordeal or the first place they had taken him.

But he did remember the itchy black hood they put over his head when they moved him the second day to where he's been staying ever since. Before they even took the stinking thing off he'd felt the dampness and knew he was in a basement somewhere.

For weeks Luke explored every inch of his captive space, searching for an escape. The two blacked-out windows were not only too high to reach, but each was covered over with a layer of thick wire and then encased behind steel bars. A single door was at the top of the stairway and he'd discovered the obvious on his first day—that not only was it locked, but that posted on the other side was his 'prison' guard—a cruel, chubby, sweaty man who always wore the same Adidas running suit and had B.O. stinky enough to gag a maggot.

Before being taken, Luke was sure he'd never seen the man who grabbed him at school or the guard on the other side of the stairway door. In fact he hadn't seen his actual kidnapper since that second day they'd brought him here. Luke thought both were Middle Eastern, though didn't have the benefit of an accent to help him narrow it down. Neither the man with the weird eye nor his Adidas Man guard, despite seeing him three times a day when he brought food to Luke, had ever uttered a single word.

But that didn't matter anymore. It was time for action. Isn't that what The Hulk would do? The thought had shaken him awake and there and then Luke decided it was time he took action too.

Luke had begun to track the times of his meal deliveries virtually down to the minute using a silent count that he then translated into approximated hours and minutes. Both the timing and the food was always the same: cereal for breakfast, bologna for lunch and soup for dinner. He'd had the first two and now, with only a few minutes until his supper delivery, Luke was prepping himself for a very different scenario than just his usual bowl of Campbell's.

Suddenly footsteps approached the door to his basement prison. Luke stared at his drawing to gain the strength The Hulk always inspired in him. At home it was as simple as swallowing a PEZ from his dispenser. One of those and Luke was ready to take on the bad guys. But he didn't have his PEZ with him, so alternatives were needed. His eyes bore into his hero's and before long, Luke could feel the change inside him starting to happen.

The basement door was nudged open with his captor's Adidas. Pausing on the top step, as he did with every meal delivery, he locked the door behind him before heading down with the tray. Early on, Adidas Man would surprise Luke with a stealth-like arrival, but after awhile he dropped the silent entrance and pounded down the stairs overtly—what the hell could an 80-pound kid do anyway, right?

~~~

The portly man in the running suit landed and rounded the corner, spotting the kid hiding under the covers in his cot. Adidas Man grinned, set the food down on the table and quietly grabbed the covers and yanked them back, intending to scare the boy, only to find piles of wadded up old newspaper instead of Luke.

Adidas Man's eyes went wide and before he knew what hit him, Luke surprise attacked him in a way that would've made The Hulk proud: With a growl Luke dropped feet first through the false ceiling tile he had hidden above and landed next to the table. Adidas Man spun for Luke, but before he could grab him, the boy picked up the hot soup and tossed it into the chubby man's face. As Adidas Man screamed in pain, Luke jumped on his back. The man spun like a bronco and Luke was about to be thrown off until the man glanced up and Luke blew a handful of fireplace ash into his eyes. The now blinded bronco stumbled and went down when his foot caught the cot leg.

In a flash, Luke ripped his captor's key ring from his belt and scrambled up the stairs to the door. Luke fumbled the keys momentarily, his breathing harsh as his fingers raced through the keys, finally finding the right one, sliding it into the lock.

CATHUNK, the bolt sprang. Freedom! But just as Luke shouldered the door open, he felt the stubby creature's claw around his ankle, dragging him roughly down the steps a thud at a time, back into his black lagoon.

Adidas Man was laughing now, literally holding Luke in mid air by his ankle. He then brutally tossed him onto the cot that scooted three feet under the momentum force of his landing.

That's when Adidas Man spotted them: two additional black ember drawings of Luke's on the lower section of the wall, smaller than the green monster, but just as detailed. They were drawings of his two kidnappers, visual clues the boy was leaving behind should the authorities ever need evidence to catch and nab his abductors.

Luke hurt all over as he recoiled on his cot, staring at the approaching man. While Adidas Man admired the kid's guile, he grabbed the water bottle from Luke's breakfast tray and washed away the drawings of Kaj and himself with a yellow smile on his face. As he turned to head back up and out, the Hulk drawing then caught Adidas Man's eye. He gave a splash of the water on that one too, then tossed the water bottle to the frightened boy.

The smelly man then talked to Luke for the first time. "You're alive because I decide you live. Do this again and I'll change my mind."

Adidas Man then disappeared back upstairs with what Luke thought was a chuckle.

But Luke was not laughing, he felt defeated. Hearing the deadbolt latch, Luke inched his way over to his drawing of his hero, black streaks now running down its smeared face.

It appeared The Hulk, like the young boy who'd drawn him, was crying.

Chapter 49

WHILE DESCENDING FROM 27,000 feet, O'Quinn's frustration had turned to anger—and angry was not a good way to pilot a jet.

Especially with only one good eye.

Truth was, with no depth perception and only 50 percent of his peripheral vision, the bald man had no business behind the controls of any jet, particularly one as powerful as the Hawker 850XP that had whisked he and Dog half way across the country in less than three hours. But O'Quinn was on a mission and when on one he never trusted anyone to get the job done right—except for himself. Certainly not the idiot sitting next to him with his paw in cast. No, this was a job for O'Quinn to handle personally.

Because it *was* personal.

It was time to finally see Kaj. Talk to him. To get what he'd wanted out of his head: the location of where the kidnapped boy was, and then make *that effing camel jockey suffer for what he'd done to him.*

When Kaj fried his eyeball, O'Quinn lost more than just half his eyesight. Though loath to admit it, his vanity had been damaged, his ego dealt a blow and his self-confidence shaken—particularly when it came to a certain aspect of flying.

Taking off with one eye wasn't an issue. Nor was cruising at altitude. Those were the easy parts.

Landing was another matter.

If misjudged, the potential for a concrete-related 'sudden deceleration event'—i.e. a fiery crash and all the joy that promised could very easily become a reality. Though hidden by pride-induced bravado, inside the bald man's gut his self-doubt was nervously churning as he lined up for final approach to Teterboro Airport.

The butterflies were as bad as the ones he'd felt when he'd made his first carrier landing back in his Navy days. In that instance the angst was caused by rough seas that saw his touchdown zone rising and falling by 30 feet every few seconds.

Tonight his landing target was stable—which was the good news. The bad was, having lost the ability to perceive the world in three dimensions, O'Quinn couldn't accurately determine how close he was to the end of the runway he was now in a rapidly descending glide path toward.

He focused his one good eye sharp as a needle, hoping to judge the distance correctly. His plan was to flare the jet as speed bled off and touch down as smoothly as possible. But the best laid plans of mice and pilots went up in smoke as he suddenly realized he was right on top of the runway and that he was coming in too hard, too fast and too steep.

He immediately pulled back the engine throttles, retarding power levels, yanked the yoke, attempting to flare up but didn't have enough time and *Wham!* his landing gear slammed onto the tarmac with a jolt that sent pain rippling through Dog's fractured bones and a lightning bolt through O'Quinn's good eye.

Neither of which O'Quinn gave a damn about.

What he did give a damn about were the two doctors, neither of which he had much respect for, who were leaning against a limousine at the end of the private runway. As he taxied up to them, O'Quinn could see they were holding a bottle and glasses.

A duffle bag over one shoulder, O'Quinn bounded down the jet stairs, his Dog obediently behind.

~~~

Led by Bilson, the doctors, each holding a glass of champagne, crossed the tarmac to greet them. "Gentlemen, so good to see you. After a long flight I thought you might enjoy some liquid refreshment." Bilson then offered the flutes. "It's a lovely Clos d'Ambonnay 1995 ..."

O'Quinn spiked him with a scornful look—"You think we flew across country for a friggin' glass of bubbly?" Both Su and Dog snickered silently as the sting of these words shattered the Doctor's ego. Bilson began to flail.

"Ah—ah—of course not, Mr. O'Quinn. I was just—"

Before Bilson could finish, O'Quinn held out his duffle to the chief administrator, making it very clear who was the Alpha in this pack. With uncharacteristic subservience, the doctor took it and then, proving dung rolls downhill, instantly passed it to his dog, Su.

O'Quinn and Bilson moved to the limo. "How long's the Libyan been awake?"

As the medicine men double-timed it to keep up, Bilson explained, "He's not really 'awake—awake.' He's made slow but marked progress, vitals stronger, occasional motor activity. But he's only had one instance of consciousness, though we personally didn't witness it."

O'Quinn stopped next to the car and turned—"If you didn't witness it, then who did?"

"One of the nurses."

Dog barked, "Skinny bitch with the melon head?"

Bilson nodded.

The driver opened the car door. O'Quinn bent to step in until Su shrugged, "And the new guy."

O'Quinn stopped on a dime and rose back up to face Bilson. "*New guy?* What effing *new guy?*"

"We brought in an additional physician."

O'Quinn drilled his finger into Bilson's chest. "The Libyan was sup-posed to be isolated. You brought someone else into this thing?"

"No, of course not—not *this* thing—the testing thing—he could make us a lot more money. Dr. Russell doesn't know anything. Trust me."

O'Quinn flexed his jaw. In his line of work he knew better than to trust anyone. He turned to the driver—"Get us to the goddamn hospital now!"

Chapter 50

THE SECOND JAROD emerged from the security tunnel the hairs on the back of his neck began to tingle as if something cold were blowing on them. It was after midnight and with no good excuse for being in the psych Annex at this hour, he needed to get in and out without being noticed. The tension played on his face as he slid into the shadow of the potted ficus just left of the threshold of the socialization room to assess the situation. His senses on fire, Jarod's eyes darted around the room, taking it all in.

The dimly lit space looked totally different than it had in the morning. The bright sunlight was replaced with a greenish-blue glow reflecting off the Manhattan sky that caused distorted shadows on the support columns holding up the atrium dome above. Apart from the occasional distant moan echoing from one of the lit patient hallways, the usual angst-filled energy was replaced with an unnerving calm.

Except for Coraleen Johnson, who slid along the west wall, there were only four other people in the room Jarod could see. The spastic Tommy Russo was in the game section beating himself at Monopoly as he laughed at the private jokes in his mind. In the TV room two Chair Rockers were bobbing in place in front of the muted flat screen transfixed by Guy Fieri on *Diners, Drive-Ins and Dives,* as he learned to make chicken fried lamb chops with creamy gravy. The last person was Nurse Kropski who was inside the nurse's hub, oscillating her huge head above her tiny body to keep an eye on them all.

When Jarod looked at her he felt the tingle again on the back of his neck and that's also when he heard the tapping sound. He looked around to find the source, only to realize it was his own fingers anxiously drumming on the stainless steel syringe container. Nervousness was not something the Pretender often felt. But tonight it was pounding in his chest. He knew that he wasn't supposed to be in Kaj's room and that if he were seen entering again, red flags would go up and his entire Pretend could be blown.

Jarod quickly devised a plan to time his movements through the room to the oscillation of Kropski's head. As the nurse scanned left, he'd move right from one pillar to the next until he'd made it around to the east hallway.

As he watched her, waiting for the opportunity to proceed, he heard the finger strumming again. But this time it wasn't coming from him. It was coming from the shadows on the far side of the ficus next to him. As he peered through the leaves, the contents of Jarod's stomach lurched. That's when he heard the whisper.

"Goddamnsonofabitchbastard!"

Sarge emerged from the darkness. Jarod was stunned. The giant of a man had been standing three feet away from him the whole time and Jarod hadn't seen him. Sarge curled his lips into a kindly smile. "Better stick to doctor'n. You'd never make it as a sniper." They looked at each other in silence until Sarge stole a glance at Kropski. "Recon mission?"

Jarod was taken aback. Sarge hadn't just hit it—he'd hit it out of the park. The Pretender nodded. "Sort of, Sir."

"Don't call me 'sir'—I work for a living."

"Yes, Master Sergeant." Jarod looked into Sarge's eyes. Only twelve hours of reduced psychotropics and his eyes were already more lucid and thoughtful. "You appear to be making progress."

"Damn right." Sarge's expression brightened. "Without their juice— I'm good to go—as in ready to rotate outta this shithole." He cocked his head to one side and squinted. "And I thought Fallujah was a weird place."

"You'll be out of here soon."

"You can count on that." Jarod turned but Sarge grabbed his arm. "Go slow, son, slow is quiet." Sarge winked. "Semper Fi. I got your six."

The former sniper then emerged from the shadows for all to see and headed off in the opposite direction from Jarod.

The Pretender watched as Kropski's eyes latched onto and followed the retired Marine's movements. Jarod smiled. Semper Fi—*always faithful* indeed. Sarge was leading her look away from Jarod and buying him time to make his move, and move Jarod did, from one column to the next to the next finally slipping unseen into the East hallway.

Eighteen steps later Jarod was at the door to Kaj's room. Room E913.

Chapter 51

KAJ LAY MOTIONLESS in his bed. The only sounds in the room were his steady breathing and the subtle beeps and tones of his vital monitors—heartbeat, breathing rates and EEG.

Jarod crossed to the bed and pulled an iPod out of his pocket. One by one he quickly unplugged the monitor contact wires from Kaj's body and reconnected them to the digital device he had modified earlier. Jarod did this to send normal readouts to the relay screens in the nurse's hub, as he was confident Kaj's actual vitals were about to go on a ride.

A very wild ride.

Jarod untied Kaj's gown and pulled it down to expose his pale chest. He then flipped the cap off the stainless cylinder and slid out one of the syringes with the 20-gauge needle and stared down at his latest patient.

The last time Jarod was in this room he'd managed to get Kaj conscious but not cognitive. What he'd brought with him tonight—if it worked—should excite his synapse responses in a way that would shock-awaken Kaj from his coma—hopefully for a period long enough for Jarod to get the information he desperately needed.

Unsure of the correct dosage, Jarod set the hypodermic to release only half of the Nano drugs. He then wrapped his fingers around the shaft of the syringe like Jack the Ripper would have gripped the hilt of a dagger and in one swift motion plunged the five-inch needle through the Libyan's sternum and directly into his heart.

Kaj's back arched as if he was being electrocuted as neuron lightning bolts erupted in his brain. The terrorist's vital monitors spiked like seismographs to a massive 9.0 quake. His body convulsed. His face became a twisted scowl and his weathered hand reached out and clutched onto Jarod's arm as if it were the railing on the devil's staircase.

His monitors then subsided, Kaj's face relaxed and his lids popped open with shock.

While his glass eye twirled in its socket, Kaj's good eye found some focus on Jarod's looming face. His dry lips trembled. His tongue peeked out weakly, then retreated like a scared turtle's head. The right side of his face spasmed briefly, then switched to the left side, his cheek billowing uncontrollably.

Jarod leaned in close, his voice steady and direct.

"I want to know about the boy. Luke. Tell me what you know about him and his father."

Kaj could only manage consonants, slurred S's, some stuttering T's, puttering incoherent P's until his eyes began to close as unconsciousness fought for control.

Jarod depressed the syringe plunger, sending another quarter of the Nano meds straight into Kaj's heart. Instantly Kaj's EEG and heart monitors flared, his body jolted again in a way that literally left him gasping for breath. His good eye popped back open and came into focus on Jarod.

"Wa—wa—water."

Having anticipated this request, Jarod extracted a small Evian bottle from his jacket and gave the terrorist a sip.

Kaj's good eye darted back and forth. "Where—where am I?"

"You're in a hospital. Where is Luke? The fat man in the blue Adidas suit—does he still have him?"

"Fat man—Adidas ..." Kaj began drifting away again. Jarod slapped his face like he owed him money. Kaj's eyes opened as wide as saucers. "Tell me, damn it, is the boy alive?"

Kaj regarded Jarod with utter confusion—"Who—are you?"

"The person who can either save your life or leave you to the bald man who put you here. Now tell me about the boy you kidnapped—is Luke alive?"

"If I'm alive, he's safe—if something happens to me—he dies."

"I wouldn't expect anything less. Who is the bald man?" As he asked this question, Jarod saw Kaj's face register fear.

"His name is O'Quinn—and if he knows I'm here ..." Kaj looked pointedly into Jarod's eyes, "then I'm not the only one who should be afraid."

Having seen O'Quinn in action, Jarod knew that to be true.

"Who is he? Whom does he work for?"

Kaj's vital monitors were slipping into negative territory along with his energy. His voice was shallow and breathy. "Bad people."

"My guess is you kidnapped Luke for this O'Quinn and his bad people, then held out for a better price."

Something flickered in Kaj's eye and Jarod knew his theory was correct even before Kaj shrugged. "Business is business."

"What does O'Quinn need the boy for?"

The terrorist tried to answer but his speech began to slur. "The boy—is the key."

Jarod leaned in face to face. "The key to what?"

"The key—to ..." Kaj's good eye began rolling back up into his head. Jarod rose up and shook him forcefully. "Don't you leave me."

Jarod forced the remaining quarter of the meds into Kaj. The resulting surge triggered the Libyan's abs to contract, causing him to bolt up into a seated position and his EEG and heart monitors to ping and beep off the charts. Kaj's good eye floated back down and into focus. Jarod grabbed the terrorist's face and turned it toward his. "There we go. Now tell me. What is the boy the key to?"

"He's the key to—to—everything. Everything O'Quinn has planned for the 28th—28th of October."

So little time, Jarod thought.

"What exactly is O'Quinn planning?"

Kaj shrugged. "I—only know—thousands will die—after that O'Quinn won't need the child."

Kaj's drift back into the coma was accelerating.

Jarod pulled the empty needle out of Kaj's heart and took out the other syringe. "You're not going away yet." Jarod adjusted the dosage so

Kaj would get a hundred percent of the Nano med in the first jolt. He wrapped his fingers around the syringe, his thumb on the depressor and was raising his arm to slam the second dose into his chest when the loud voice rang out.

"Goddamnsonofabitchbastard!"

Chapter 52

SARGE WASN'T WHISPERING his famous statement this time. He was shouting it at the top of his lungs.

"*Goddamnsonofabitchbastard!*"

The second time it rang out, his words were followed by a scream and a crashing sound.

Jarod moved to and opened Kaj's room door just enough so he could see down the hall into the socialization room. Sarge had tossed Tommy Russo's game of Monopoly against the wall, an act the laughing man had not found funny. Tommy was now throwing chairs at Sarge, who continued to yell at him.

"*Goddamnsonofabitchbastard!*"

Jarod wasn't sure why Sarge was acting the fool until he saw that behind him, four men had just entered the socialization room: Bilson, Su, O'Quinn and the Butcher's Dog. Jarod realized Sarge wasn't acting the fool—*Sarge had his six and was being faithful.* And it was about to cost him.

Bilson yelled at Kropski—"Get the goddamned orderlies and 50MG of Risperidone IM STAT."

O'Quinn's jaw pulsed as he began to get worked up. He stared at Bilson. "Are we invested in the wrong hospital—the wrong partners?"

Bilson looked exasperated. "Of course not, Mr. O'Quinn."

Tommy R took this cue to toss another chair at Sarge. The big man ducked it and it nearly hit O'Quinn. The man with the eye patch shot a look of contempt at Bilson. "Then what kind of operation are you running around here?"

Before Bilson could answer, four orderlies rushed up. Two subdued Tommy before he could throw another chair, the others took positions on either side of the big Marine who looked at them and shouted again.

"Goddamnsonofabitchbastard!"

Bilson turned to Su. "What the hell's going on?"

Su didn't react, didn't as much as lift an eyebrow. "Perhaps his aggressiveness is tied to his meds being reduced."

Bilson almost blew a gasket. "On whose authority were they cut?"

Su answered in a low voice full of sarcasm. "That would be the authority *you gave* to the new guy."

As Nurse Kropski returned with the shot of Risperidone, O'Quinn turned to Bilson with a derisive sneer.

~~~

Jarod rushed back to Kaj, who had now slipped back into unconsciousness. With no time for the second shot, Jarod gathered his syringes and container, then began switching the vital monitor cords back to their proper machines.

At the same moment he did that ...

~~~

The orderlies grabbed Sarge and Bilson plunged a needle into the big man's neck. The 50MG of Risperidone immediately knocked him out. As he tumbled into the arms of the orderlies, alarms began blaring in the Nurse's hub.

Bilson spun around, "What now?"

Big Head rushed up. "The patient in E913—his vital monitors are going crazy."

The pissed O'Quinn rushed down the East hall, Bilson, Dog and Su on his heels, then burst into Kaj's room.

But Jarod wasn't there. Only a comatose terrorist lying in silence—the keeper of secrets that could save or destroy the lives of thousands—and the life of one little boy.

Chapter 53

DURING THE THREE seconds between Dr. Bilson sticking the needle into Sarge's carotid artery and the time the big man collapsed into the arms of the orderlies, Jarod had slipped quietly out of Kaj's and silently into Skylar's dimly lit one.

Standing with his back against the wall between the closed door to the hall and the open door to her bathroom, Jarod took note of the sleeping form under the covers on the bed. As he did he could hear O'Quinn berating Bilson as the four men ran past Skylar's door and entered Kaj's. Controlling his breathing, Jarod ran the actions of the previous few minutes through his mind, hoping he'd covered his tracks well enough so that his presence in the Libyan's room wouldn't be detected. He thought he had but realized that either way his priority now was to find a way out of the Annex before he was discovered.

As he ran through his limited options he heard a word whispered that had never been spoken to him before—but one that triggered the reaction intended.

"Boo!"

A bolt of liquid electricity raced though Jarod's system as he spun toward the voice coming from inside the dark bathroom, specifically from a shadowy figure standing inside the shower stall. Before Jarod could react, the specter struck a match. As the yellow flower formed, it sent a glow that illuminated the figure's eyes.

Eyes that were violet.

Jarod sighed, taken aback for the second time this night by someone who had unknowingly been right next to him. As Skylar emerged from the bathroom she read the consternation on his face and her delicate lips curled into a sly grin.

Jarod tossed a glance at the bed to what he realized now were pillows formed to appear to be her sleeping body. "I've taken to sleeping in the shower." Jarod turned back to her, raising a curious eyebrow. "Sometimes after a few too many martinis Dr. Bilson would come back late at night and check a certain patient's 'vitals'—if you know what I mean."

Jarod thought about what he'd seen Bilson doing to Tami in the hallway and could only imagine what he did to women he kept drugged up in the Annex. But before he could complete this picture in his mind, Skylar shrugged it off. "People are rarely really who they present themselves to be." She tilted her head, regarding him pointedly. "Like the fact I was making believe I was a nurse—or you pretending to be a doc. What's up with that?"

Jarod didn't know how to answer her. So he blew out the match before it burned her fingers. They stared at each other for a long moment without speaking.

Illuminated by the moonlight through the window Jarod found Skylar more disarmingly attractive than he had earlier.

Much more so.

But Jarod had other things to focus on and walked quietly into the bath. There he swept his eyes around all four sides of the mirror over the sink as if trying to decide something. He then forced three fingers of his right hand under the corresponding corner of the mirror and began to pry. Skylar appeared in the doorway.

"You gonna tell me the truth?"

Jarod looked over his shoulder. "It's complicated."

"No shit, Sherlock. So what's it have to do with the nameless veg head next door?"

Jarod snapped off a three-inch triangle from the looking glass. Coming back into the room he gave her an inquisitive look.

"What? You think you're the only one who plays peeping Tom around here? I snuck over and read Mr. Drool's chart day one."

Even under the tension of the moment Jarod marveled at Skylar's moxie. But he was too busy to engage, he was scanning the room for something he could use. He spotted it on the food tray that was on her bedside table and headed toward it.

Skylar wouldn't give in to his silence. "Don't blow me off. What do you want with him?"

Jarod sat on her bed, grabbed the plastic fork from the tray and then began securing the broken piece of mirror between its prongs. "Nothing I can talk about."

"Really—not even to know where *the boy* is?"

Jarod looked at her for a long time but didn't speak—but she did.

"I'm not deaf and even a dead roach in that wall could have heard you screaming at him two minutes ago."

Jarod stood and quietly crossed to the door and knelt down. Holding the handle of the fork, he slowly slid the mirror face up into the gap between the bottom of the door and the tile floor.

In its angled reflection Jarod could see that not five feet away stood Dog and Su, both looking into Kaj's room and the events happening there. Nurse Kropski rushed into the odd view, holding a sheaf of papers she showed Su. "Readouts from the Libyan's monitors. He's comatose now, but he was definitely conscious for a few minutes." Su motioned into Kaj's room and she took the readouts and entered.

Jarod rubbed his hand through his hair. Confirmation that Kaj had regained consciousness would trigger a series of tests that could take hours to complete. Sooner or later during that time someone would come into this room and then—well—Jarod couldn't allow himself to be discovered.

The Pretender was trapped and desperately needed a way out.

He stood and moved urgently to the window, looking for an escape route—any escape route.

"Sorry, Doc, but freedom through that window is in your dreams."

He turned to face her, knowing she was right.

She moved toward the door. "I've been figuring how to bust out of this Alcatraz for months and it can't be done—alone." She pulled it open enough to see the Asian Doc and Dog still sniffing outside Kaj's room. She looked over her shoulder—"If this blows up in my face I want you to know two things. One, Doc or not, Sal would have liked you."

"And two?"

"You owe me one."

Sky grinned at him, then flung open her door, bolted into the hall and did what Skylar does best: cause a disturbance. In three steps she was nose to nose with the Butcher's Dog, poking his broken paw as she yelled— "What the hell's up with you? People trying to sleep around here, bitch."

Jarod peeked out of the door in time to see Skylar toss a thumb toward Kaj's door. "And this moaner—if nobody else will put a sock in his loud flapper, I will."

She turned and marched toward Kaj's room.

Su and Dog jumped to block her. "Hey, you can't go in there!"

"And whose gonna stop me? You, Chubby Chan? Or maybe the one-armed bandit?"

She bolted into Kaj's room—the two men on her tail. Jarod heard her voice as they all disappeared inside. "Well, if it ain't Big Head and Dr. B? Who's the pirate?"

Something crashed against the wall and Jarod used this as his cue to make his move. He slipped out of Skylar's room and in less than twelve seconds he had crept through the shadows on the far side of the atrium columns, made his way into and through the security tunnel and was inside the main hospital elevator going down.

With the help of two people Jarod barely knew, he'd managed to get into and out of the Annex just in the nick of time.

But time was running out and the job of saving Luke had just gotten much more difficult.

Chapter 54

AS A RESTLESS Miss Parker stared out her hotel room window down at life on 54th Street, she crumpled another dead pack of Pall Mall's, ripped open a virgin carton and torched up a fresh stick of relief.

Random thoughts had been flickering in her brain for the past hour until a singularly unexpected one silenced all others. This one burrowed furtively into her psyche. It snuck up on her really, when her eyes caught a lilting curl of smoke that danced in the air until she sensed it closing in around her like a noose; *cigarettes are the thinking girl's way to a socially acceptable suicide.*

Suicide.

She'd lived that damage for almost 20 years. She stubbed out her smoke, trying to shut out that thought, that word, but the more she tried to hide from it, the stronger the word became and more impossible to ignore. She finally gave up, asking herself the question: *Where the hell did that come from?*

And why?

She knew she wasn't suicidal. Far from it. She finally convinced herself that the whole thing was nothing more than one of those brain tricks that have a way of earwigging people. Weak people.

And she wasn't weak.

Far from it.

So she chalked it up to rebounding off a night of less than two hours sleep.

Of course Parker's lack of sleep wasn't helped any by the fact that she awoke at 3:00 a.m. certain that Corny was trying to pick the lock on her side of their adjoining room door. So sure of it, she even checked the tumblers at daybreak for signs of attempted forced entry, but found none. Still, the very idea of *that thing* creeping into her space or worse, into her bed, made her skin crawl. Though at the same time she would've certainly welcomed any excuse to shoot him.

Lighting up a new smoke, she discovered that the particular brain trick earwigging her this a.m. wasn't finished with her yet. Instead it insisted on stirring up in her the multiple anxieties she fought so hard to keep compartmentalized: her professional failures, her endless paternal disappointments, the emotional scars that wouldn't heal and the anxiety to end all anxieties—that life was starting to pass her by.

But what was beginning to piss her off was the notion that directly or indirectly she knew in some way or another these circuitous anxiety wires all intertwined and lead back to one conduit: Jarod.

While she never drank on the job, this morning's brain trick was forcing her hand. She quickly drained a Maker's from the mini bar without a single wince or regret.

Her agonizing thoughts began to ebb. She hated herself for even contemplating any of them. Self-analysis, voluntary or involuntary, was a sure sign of weakness and something she'd learned to fight off from her brilliant, tough-love mentor Fabiana Rouleau during her teen Centre Indoctrination years.

Brain tricks? Not this girl. Not today.

She seemed convinced until one last drop of doubt refused to dry up and go away: If self-analysis was a sign of weakness, which Parker believed, then why did she continue to awaken during the night, unable to shake off Syd's annoying diatribes about *tenets* and how Jarod was *redefining his life*?

She found herself again eyeing the humanity down below—vendors selling fruit, young wannabes heading off to auditions, a cop directing traffic and limo drivers leaning on their cars waiting. How simple those lives seemed to her at that moment and how complicated her own suddenly felt. Was it possible, even remotely thinkable that it was time for her to *redefine* her own life?

The banging on her adjoining room door rescued her from this consuming vortex of thought. She even pulled the drape across the window to shut it all out as an exclamation point.

She screwed her game face back on and yanked open the door, finding both Corn and Syd on the other side. Corn was grinning, Syd was not.

"You'd better have something good."

"The tastiest mint you'll ever find on your pillow," Corn said, no doubt having worked on that line for days.

She just stared.

"I got him. Jarod, er, Dr. Jarod Russell is practicing out of Guardian General Hospital down on Second," Corn gushed, certain this would be his golden ticket to making this field trip with Miss P. "Shall we go get him?"

She immediately crushed his hopes—"Yes—but you'll be here guarding the mini bar." Her verbal slap caused a sudden flush of red on Corny's pale pallor. She then ordered him to alert the Sweepers and arrange for the vehicles to be brought around, which he dutifully obeyed, trying his best to keep his tail—and the rest of his equipment—from shrinking between his legs.

Parker grabbed up her holster and strapped it on for battle. And just like that, in a matter of mere seconds, she'd once again put *redefining her life* back on hold.

Chapter 55

THE ANGELS FLANKING Guardian General's emergency room entrance were smiling favorably on this bright morning. Today walk-ins and admissions were low and the scream of sirens had been all but silent on this crisp autumn morning cusping the brink of an early winter.

But perhaps the calm foretold the storm, for the smiling angels seemingly quaked at the growing, thundering rumble of a twin engine American Eurocopter EC135 that suddenly shattered the morning calm from above, angling its descent toward the Guardian's rooftop, then vanishing from sight as quickly as it had appeared as the eaves swallowed it.

The angels hadn't seen it coming.

~~~

As Jarod walked through The Village his surroundings may've been sunny, but he was anything but. Not even the skateboarders weaving in and around pedestrians doing their amazing tricks, nor the sight of the Empire State Building in the distance could cheer him. His mind and heart were heavy on this morning, roiling with regrets, doubts and anticipation.

His recent encounter with Syd and close call with Parker and her Sweepers at the Fountain Grove Hotel, mere miles from where he was now, yielded very little for the risk involved. The upside had potentially been there—gaining new insight about his parents and origins, but in hindsight he knew now he'd let his emotions overplay his hand and should've better anticipated Sydney's reticence to reveal anything if, in fact, Syd did have any new insights.

Now he was in a position that left him little or no wiggle room: He'd revealed his location to Parker but could not flee the city since the clock was ticking down on Luke Hearns' life and the innocent lives hanging in the balance of O'Quinn's October 28 event. Jarod knew inside Kaj's memory was the key to it all and that without that knowledge, well, Jarod didn't want to think about that. The injections had only yielded fragments of scattered information from Kaj, so Jarod knew it was desperation time—time for more drastic measures—that there was only one other course of action: Today was absolutely the day he needed to take control of Kaj.

While confident of the technique he'd use to access Kaj's memory, implementing it would not only require preparation, but also absolute control over his patient and the environment. After all, it was a procedure if done incorrectly could very well kill him.

Jarod had never taken another human life before, but he knew if that was the cost of saving Luke's life, so be it. In fact, truth be told, Jarod was surprised just how much he was okay with that, given what was at stake.

And because of what was at stake he'd decided to change the plan he'd been working from, from the get-go.

As he turned the corner onto Second Street, the sight of Guardian General and the Annex behind it brought an even deeper darkness to Jarod's demeanor. There was something in the air today, a feeling crawling around inside of him that he couldn't expel, one that grew stronger as he neared the entrance to the emergency room.

But he was a Pretender and despite his mood he found a smile, the one that belonged to Dr. Jarod Russell, because smiles were who Dr. Russell was—and for the next few minutes anyway, he'd need to be that whiz kid MD that Manhattan medical insiders were all abuzz over.

Today, Jarod knew that would only get him just so far. He then felt around for the two capped syringe vials in his coat pocket, this time both containing a sleep-inducing agent.

It was time. He touched the angel's wings and walked inside.

Chapter 56

JAROD MOVED SWIFTLY through the hall, just down from where the hospital's food service kitchen churned out, delivered, picked and cleaned up several thousands of meals per day. Best of all, he was virtually anonymous down here where the *wage apes*, as Bilson referred to them, toiled and rarely interacted with the upper echelon medical staff.

He glanced at his watch. Breakfasts had been distributed to patients an hour earlier and the cleanup team would soon be mobilizing to gather the meal trays throughout the hospital, and that meant show time for Jarod.

Slowing his pace he pulled a patient file out of his backpack to appear busy—his line of sight just over the pages to the food crew's service door, anticipating the emergence of someone vital to phase one of his plan.

He closed the file as the food service team began flooding out, most with cell phones in hand heading upstairs to light up their nicotine habit in the designated smoking courtyard workers aptly nicknamed *Newark East* for the smoky haze that hovered over it like the filthy city just over the Statue of Liberty's broad shoulders.

Last out, just like he knew he would be, was the man he'd been waiting for: the albino orderly, Ponytail Jude—the only food service team member designated to work in the Annex.

Jarod's eyes honed in to study Jude's pink eyes and alabaster skin, the pronounced limp from his disabled left foot which folded inward and slightly curled the ankle under, his hunched gait from a degenerative disk disorder and his battered, faded ever present fedora Leonard Cohen himself gave to him back in '69.

Within seconds, Jarod had the whole Jude *package* etched in his mind. He also knew the first thing Jude would do is head straight for the men's room across the hall where the talkative Jude had once killed 20 minutes of Jarod's time describing in detail his peanut-sized bladder and frequent urination that he was certain came from a batch of tainted magic mushrooms.

As Jude disappeared into the bathroom, Jarod swept the hall with his eyes to ensure no one was following the albino inside. Assured he was alone, Jarod dropped the file into a trash bin and walked quickly to the men's room door.

Jude was in final drip mode at the urinal when Jarod entered and quietly locked the door. Zipping up, Jude turned, nearly colliding with Jarod. "Hey, Doc—whatta you doing down here in the cheap seats, man? I thought—"

With no time to waste on more of Jude's repeat tales of naked mud baths on acid at Woodstock, Jarod gently plunged one of the two syringed needles into Jude's shoulder. As he emptied it Jarod whispered, "You'll be okay. Just relax." Jude actually smiled—he'd been off drugs for decades, but Jarod's surprise *fix* was clearly a welcome surprise for this former Kesey bus rider.

Jarod caught Jude's limp body, eased him into a stall and carefully sat him onto the closed commode for a blissful nap. He helped himself to Cohen's fedora, locked the stall and slid out from it underneath.

At the sink counter Jarod opened his backpack. He pulled out a contact lens case, leaned his head back and quickly applied both. Gazing into the mirror, Jarod's eyes were now a shade of deep pink. Extracting a long white ponytailed wig, a food service jumpsuit and a tube of Broadway-grade white concealer, Jarod began his transformation.

Chapter 57

WITH A SILENT Syd riding shotgun and a windowless Centre-issued van trailing behind, Miss Parker steered her Town Car quickly through the streets of Manhattan.

Anticipating victory, Miss P was beyond excited. For her the sensation of the hunt was better than an orgasm. And since she hadn't managed to achieve one of those in much too long, she was intensely enjoying the buildup to this variation. She'd learned early on, even during mundane Centre tracking missions, that the aura of *the pursuit* literally made her body tingle. In the case of chasing Jarod, her *tingle* was more akin to a seismic jolt. Even with her lack of success thus far, it was, like with sex itself, the antici-pation of the win that moved her Richter needle.

She steered her ride up to the green loading curb at a safe distance from the Guardian's emergency room entrance. With a deep pull on her Pall Mall she clocked the entire scene: an idling ambulance parked some 60 feet up ahead by the entrance, a collection of pitiful patients in wheelchairs congregated in the hospital's mini-park behind her position and a shift of arriving nurses headed inside. Her conclusion? Nothing out of the ordinary.

She reached for the door handle, but Syd stopped her. "I can't stress strongly enough that we must retrieve and return Jarod to The Centre, peacefully."

"There is no *we* Sydney—just me. Now be a good boy and stay in the car."

She climbed out. As her boots hit the ground she pocketed the keys in her stylish overcoat and took another drag of her cigarette. Syd eyed her with disdain through the windshield. She threw a glance back at the van and in unison Sweepers emerged. She'd opted for her six best. Each one so tuned in to the gospel of Miss P they may as well have been dangling from her nimble fingers like cans on a six-pack ring.

Miss Parker popped the clip from her Smith & Wesson to ensure it was full. She felt that tingle intensifying, her seismic needle starting to twitch as she barked orders to her Sweeper team—"You five surround the perimeter; Aires, you're my shadow. We keep this one nice and quiet." She slapped her clip back in place. "If anyone's making noise it'll be me. Now synchronize." The Sweepers each dutifully checked their earbuds and headed to their respective assignments.

A concerned Sydney took in her predatory demeanor through the windshield, then he leaned toward the open driver door window—"The Centre wants Jarod alive."

A circuitous curl formed at the edge of her smile. "Preferably, Sydney. Preferably."

Without so much as a glance back, she headed for the entrance with Aires, crushing out her Pall Mall on the wing of one of the angel statues poised there.

Chapter 58

KROPSKI TOSSED BACK four aspirins as she watched an East Indian EMT roll his empty gurney through the chaotic yet curious schizophrenics in the socialization room. Her giant head was killing her. And it wasn't from the lump she'd received from Skylar's well-placed bedpan days earlier or the craziness of the last ten hours in this hospital. It was from the voice echoing in her mind as she hung up and tossed her cell phone onto the desk with disgust.

She knew people joked behind her back that she never left the security of her nurse's hub, but none of them knew that she had a damn good reason why. That reason had been a pain-in-her-ass sleepless three hours she'd spent in her crappy two bedroom, one bath apartment the night before.

The ass pain's name was Agnes Kropski, Nurse K's 80-year-old widowed mother, the beast of a woman who'd genetically cursed her daughter with the massive skull and mini body that had made her youth a struggle and who now, after having moved in, was turning her only child's middle age into a living nightmare.

Or more aptly, a *dying* nightmare.

Momma K suffered from old age and some kind of undiagnosed disease that left her increasingly senile. Daughter K suffered through nightly cleanups of her babbling mother's incessant bouts of diarrhea.

If that wasn't enough to push Kropski's frustrations over the edge, Bilson had ordered her to change every test patient's regimen dosages to levels he personally adjusted and emailed to her at dawn.

"Prick," she muttered. As she lumbered her sleep-deprived body up from her nurse's throne, her new dosing orders in hand, her phone rang. She spiked a look at it; it was mommy calling again.

Oh, the problems a well-placed pillow wouldn't solve, she thought, heading off to take her frustrations out on another bitch who'd been making her life miserable.

Chapter 59

IT WAS THE irritating itch in her legs, not the needle in her arm that woke Skylar up. When her eyes came into focus she was staring at the hag nurse with the Jack-in-the-Box head who was injecting more drugs into her. Skylar tried to move, but something was stopping her. She remembered hallucinating off and on all night—figments of *men arguing about secrets and lies and dying* had danced in her head. But this wasn't a hallucination. She realized she was restrained to the bed and then remembered she had been since Bilson ordered the orderlies to drag her back in here last night.

Kropski's scowl, and whatever they'd been pumping her with for the last eight hours, quickly made the itch a distant memory. Still, she pleaded her case. "What are you doing? What is that?"

"Well, Miss Smart Ass, since you won't take your pills, you get liquid form now."

"I'm—I'm not supposed to—call Dr. Russell—he changed my meds."

Kropski looked down her nose at her charge. "I don't work for Dr. Russell. I work for Dr. B, and after last night's escapade he's tripled your dose." She pulled out the needle, "And I'm going to ensure you get every drop."

Nurse K patted Skylar's leg and then exited.

Skylar fought for memory. After the last dosage she'd had only minutes before the hallucinations started. She only had minutes now.

Chapter 60

HIS PALE HANDS gripped the push bar of a food cart. Perfectly mimicking Jude's limp step, limp step, limp step, Jarod hobbled behind, dragging his crippled left foot.

He'd become Jude in every way—even down to the shy man's habit of facing the floor allowing his flowing white locks and brimmed fedora to conceal most all of his now albino face.

His cart was three feet high, four feet long and had refrigerator-like doors on the side. Inside the walls were grooved so that in each compartment 16 trays could comfortably be slid in, two per shelf with four-inch height clearance between, and stowed for transport. With all the trays removed, the cart was more than large enough to conceal a Libyan terrorist.

He felt good as he shuffled past nurses, orderlies and hospital staff, happy to see they paid him no mind when he passed by—something he'd counted on.

He felt even better when he arrived at the elevator bank at the *T* intersection of the two main corridors. The first part of his plan would be successful once he was inside the lift and the doors had closed.

But as Helmuth von Moltke once said, 'No plan survives first contact with the enemy.' And while it wasn't the enemy Jarod spotted on the other side of the elevators walking his way, it was still something he hadn't counted on: Cute and cheery Tami was heading right his way.

Jarod pushed the *up* button several times. Tami grinned and stopped face to face with him to say, "Morning Jude." Hiding under the brim of his hat, Jarod nodded silently, anxious for the elevator to get here. He knew he could fool people with a wave, but a verbal discussion in close quarters was potentially disastrous.

Ironically he was saved from this possible calamity by one that was even more serious when a woman's voice rang out from behind. It was a woman's voice that made his stomach lurch. A voice that said, "Excuse me, nurse?"

A voice that belonged to Miss Parker now standing mere inches behind Jarod.

He slowly closed his eyes and calmed his breathing as Tami looked over his shoulder to address her—"Oh, I'm not a nurse, Ma'am, I'm a candy striper."

"And I'm not a 'Ma'am'—candy striper—I'm a 'Miss' and I'm looking for this man."

A delicate hand with a square-shaped platinum ring on the pointer finger suddenly appeared over the Pretender's shoulder; it held out a phone with a photo of Jarod prominently displayed on its screen.

Tami looked at it and then back over Jarod's shoulder to Parker and Aires. "Oh, you mean Dr. Russell."

Jarod eyed the elevator's readout indicating it was still five floors away from him.

"Yes. Where can I find Dr. Goodbar?"

Tami didn't like the sarcasm in Miss P's voice nor the predatory glean in her eye. A tinge of jealousy crept into Tami's voice—"Are you a *friend* of his?"

Miss P caught Tami's subtext and decided to play with her—"Yes. A *very close one.*" Parker smiled.

Though naïve, Tami knew that usually meant—*I'm more than a friend and it's none of your goddamned business.* Secretly hating that it might be so, but more than holding her own, Tami pointed down the corridor, "His office is the last door on the right. And if he's not there he's probably in the Annex. Would you like me to show you the way? I'd hate for you to get lost."

Four—three—two—Jarod was holding his breath, eyeing the numbers.

"No need. This is a surprise reunion. Besides, I'm sure you and Edgar Winter here have lots to chat about."

Parker winked at Tami, then soberly told Aires to stay put and keep watch. She then turned tail and hurried toward Dr. Russell's office solo.

Tami's mother had always taught her to think before speaking and so while she managed a "Have a good day" to the departing Parker, what she was really thinking was, *screw her and the broom she flew in on.*

Ding. The elevator doors opened and Jarod pushed the cart on and boarded. He watched Tami staring off at Miss Parker.

Alone and now rising, Jarod could ill afford any relief of his first passed test as Jude, knowing now that Parker would soon be right on his handicapped heels.

Chapter 61

JAROD STEPPED OFF the elevator on the ninth floor, the security tunnel to the psych ward directly ahead. His instinct was to run through it as quickly as possible, but his Pretend called for him to move slowly.

Pushing Jude's cart, he limp stepped toward the security doors. He slid his ID through the first card reader and when the door clicked open, easily made his way into the first chamber. He then realized he'd already made a mistake. Jude always dragged his cart through because the retinal scan was next to the door. Jarod was surprised he'd forgotten this little move. It was the reason why Skylar had almost managed to escape the day he met her. When Jude dragged his cart through, it had blocked open the retinal scan door, the one she'd caught with her foot when she was dressed as Nurse Kropski and was doing her own Pretend, trying to break out.

He'd be sure to remember that as he brought the cart back out—the cart that would be full of Libyan terrorist instead of trays.

When he'd reached the threshold of the socialization room the night before, Jarod had frozen when he'd gotten a bad feeling in his gut. When he reached the threshold now, the feeling was worse—much worse.

The room, though filled with patients, was pin drop silent. Sarge wasn't yelling his usual phrase at the wall. No one was talking in the chit-chat section, the games and their players had all frozen in place, the Chair Rockers stood still. Coraleen Johnson had even stopped sliding down the wall and, like everyone else in the room, her attention was on the East Indian EMT who was rolling his gurney past the nurse's hub. The gurney was no longer empty. There was a body on it now, a body covered with a sheet from head to toe.

One of the patients had died.

Jarod flashed with fear that someone had OD'd from the psychotropics. Needing all of his focus, for the moment all he could do was make a mental note to shut this place down. But for now it had to be all about getting across the socialization room and getting to Kaj.

Paradoxically, the tension in the room worked in Jarod's favor. Not only were the patients focused on the dead body, but as the gurney stopped at the nurse's hub so the EMT could sign release papers, so was Kropski.

Without hesitation Jarod seized this opening and began his limp step across the room. He was more than half way when Big Head glared at him. "You're late, Hippy Dippy—been stepping over your damn breakfast trays all morning," she barked.

"Sorry," Jarod mumbled, glad to have a reason to hang his head even lower at her scolding.

Safely traversing the room, Jarod gave one look back at the stretcher with the covered dead patient, then entered the East hallway.

He quickened his gimpy stride as he pushed the cart down the empty corridor toward Kaj's room, his quickening pace matching his escalating heart rate. But as he neared the room, it felt like his heart stopped beating altogether. Something was wrong.

Very wrong.

Kaj's door was open and his bed was empty.

The world fell away, he felt as though he were in free-fall.

From behind Jarod a cackling laugh erupted, startling him back into the moment. He spun to find Tommy Russo spastic and laughing as always, but this time the giggling man had tears running down his face. "Dead"— cackle, cackle.

"What?"

Tommy shifted from foot to foot—cackle cackle. "Sleeping man dead."

Jarod's world began spinning. He grabbed his shoulders. "Talk to me, Tommy, when did he die?"

"Just this morning"—cackle, cackle—"He died. Sad." Jarod released Tommy, who stumbled away.

Jarod was stunned. He had missed it—*limped right by it*—the body on that EMT's stretcher was Kaj's!

Jarod spun to race out, halted by another voice—"Jarod!"

The scream had come from Skylar's room.

Jarod burst in, finding her restrained to her bed. He rushed over and began releasing her.

She looked up to him through disjointed eyes and yet smiled. "I knew I recognized that voice." She then touched his pale white cheek. "The face—not so much."

"It's a long story." Jarod began removing the final leather band. "Bilson do this to you?"

"He wasn't down with what I said to him last night. Go figure. Thought he'd teach me a lesson."

Freed, Skylar's movements were amped but oddly staccato—the psychotropics starting to wreak havoc with her body and mind. What began as an itching sensation in her left thigh was now racing through, a numbing starting to consume her. "I'm sorry, Skylar."

"Not your fault. I'm a big girl."

He rushed to the door to check the hallway, and seeing it was clear, pulled his food cart in. "Let's get you out of here."

He reached for her, helping her stand. She squinted, trying to grasp a thought. "What about the guy next door?"

"I blew it with him. He's dead. I'm not going to do the same with you." He opened the side door of the food cart.

She fought to clear her mind, searching for a memory. As it started to form she slapped Jarod's hands away. She was pulling on what she had thought earlier was a hallucination—*figments of men arguing about secrets and lies and dying*—realizing it wasn't a hallucination—the voices had belonged to Dr. Bilson and O'Quinn as they argued on the other side of her wall during the night. "He's not dead."

Jarod froze in his tracks. "I heard them—they decided to fake his death and transfer him—somewhere else—'somewhere safer.'"

It suddenly all made sense to Jarod. "Did they say where?"

Skylar searched her memory, but it was getting cloudier. "Yeah—no—I don't know. Seems like the bald freak with the eye patch told the ugly guy with the broken arm to call and arrange the transfer with Helix or Tretex or something like that. I'm sorry, I can't remember the name right now—but I think it's who they work for."

Jarod looked out of the door and down the hall.

Across the socialization room he caught the final glimpse of the EMT pushing the gurney across the threshold and into the security tunnel.

Jarod's mind raced and so did his body—back to her.

"Come on."

"No. Go. Do what you have to. I'll be okay. Those bitches can't do anything to me."

Jarod shook his head and swept her off her feet. "I'm not leaving you." He gently placed her inside the compartment of the cart and looked into her eyes. "For once—be quiet."

He slammed the cart door and then set out, limp step, limp step, limp step, down the hall toward the socialization room.

Chapter 62

PARKER RACED OUT of the Jarod-less Dr. Russell's office and stormed down the corridor back toward Aires. "Anything?"

"No, Miss Parker."

Back at the elevator bank, the frustrated Miss P spun 360, taking in the scene. Jarod was here somewhere and she knew it, she felt it and she damn sure was going to catch his ass this time. Spotting a passing nurse, she grabbed and turned her around.

It was Gloria and she was none too happy to have a grip around her arm. She looked at Miss Parker's hand and then coldly into her eyes.

"You want to keep that claw attached to your body, you best let up and right now."

Parker knew when not to press an issue and released her. "I need to find Dr. Russell, he's not in his office and it's urgent."

"Pretty boy's never in the ER anymore." She pointed to the elevator bank. "Try the ninth floor—he's likely in the Annex."

Gloria bulled past Miss Parker, who stepped to the elevator and slammed the *up* button. She looked at Aires—"Stay here. If Jarod comes out of this elevator and you want to ensure your balls remain attached to your body, make sure he doesn't get out of the hospital."

"Yes, Miss Parker."

As she boarded the elevator she barked into her earbud mic— "Perimeter, hold your areas, he's in the Annex, I'm going to flush him down. Nobody faces him but me."

~~~

Syd paced nervously around the Town Car, listening to Parker's admonition over his earbud, finding concern both in her words and her tone. He knew she wanted to face Jarod personally. The question was—what would she do when she did? In the back of Sydney's mind words he and Miss P exchanged earlier swirled. *"Miss Parker, the Centre wants Jarod alive." "Preferably, Sydney. Preferably."* With these words echoing, Sydney threw an impatient look at the hospital's entrance, contemplating his next move and fearing the consequences of inaction.

~~~

On the roof O'Quinn paced next to the American EC135 medical transport Eurocopter and checked his watch, impatiently glancing at Bilson and Dog, who flanked him. His earbud beeped. "Dojame, go."

~~~

Outside the Annex security tunnel waiting for the elevator, the EMT, Dojame, spoke into his earbud and glanced at the covered body on the stretcher next to him—"Smooth down here. Subject is sedated and stable. On our way up."

~~~

O'Quinn swirled his hand in the air at the chopper pilot to turn rotors and almost smiled at Bilson and Dog.

~~~

Limp step, limp step, limp step. Jarod-as-Jude pushed his cart into the socialization room and nearly ran over Nurse Kropski. She was heading into the hall he'd emerged from, which Jarod thought was a good thing.

His head was down and she didn't see his face as she complained about him watching where he was going. When she passed him he looked up and began doing just that.

The good news was her absence from the nurse's hub would make his getaway easier. The bad news, as Jarod looked back over his shoulder, was that she was heading for Skylar's room.

Limp step, limp step, limp step. Jarod picked up his pace as he crossed through the TV room where the Chair Rockers were now back in rhythm. In fact since the dead man was no longer among them, their usual angst had returned. It was about to get worse.

Limp step, limp step, limp step.

Jarod was halfway to the security tunnel, just passing the nurse's hub, when Nurse K came running back into the socialization room. He couldn't see her eyes, but he could feel them burning on his back. He couldn't see her lips, but he knew instinctively they were forming the words about to be shouted out of her mouth. "Jude! Stop!"

Jarod-as-Jude didn't stop. He spotted an orderly looking past him to Nurse K yelling for the orderly to, "Stop that man!"

The orderly focused on Jarod and the Pretender's limp step, limp step, limp step, suddenly turned into limp step, step step, step run, run, run, run, as he raced with his cart straight for the orderly. "Hold on!" Jarod yelled to Skylar as he slammed right into the orderly. The big man went flying into and through a ficus.

The patients who minutes earlier had been quiet as church mice erupted into bewildered chaos. But no one was as bewildered as Kropski when she realized Jude wasn't Jude—but Jarod.

His Pretend inside Guardian General was blown, but this was the least of his problems.

Jarod rushed into the security tunnel. With lightning speed he whipped his ID card through the reader on the first door.

Click!

He burst through and drug the cart with him into the first chamber.

As Jarod leaned his left eye into the retinal scanner, through his right he spotted the EMT wheel the stretcher carrying Kaj into the elevator.

Click!

Jarod burst through the middle door and pulled the cart with Skylar inside behind him.

He was sliding his ID badge through the reader of the final door when the red light above the Annex tunnel began spinning and flashing accompanied by a low tone alarm.

On the Annex side of the tunnel several security guards and Kropski arrived at the first security door.

But Jarod's focus wasn't on what was behind him, it was what was ahead.

Click!

Jarod ripped the ID scanner off the wall and bolted out of the chamber. The orderlies, being unable to unlock the door, would buy him miniscule time.

As the chamber door began to close behind him, the elevator with the EMT and Kaj inside began closing.

Jarod rushed toward it with everything he had, then launched himself as the doors joined together, shutting him out.

Skylar kicked open the cart door and groggily crawled out. Jarod repeatedly pressed the elevator call button when he looked at her.

"He took Kaj up."

"There's a chopper pad on the roof."

Jarod looked at Skylar and though the effects of the psychotopics were starting to kick in even more, she could still read the indecision in his eyes.

Big Head and the orderlies arrived at the last chamber door. Locked in, the big men began shoulder-pounding the Plexi door while Kropski glared at Jarod and Skylar.

Skylar grabbed Jarod's arm. "What are you waiting for—go!"

"I told you I'm not leaving you."

"You didn't."

Jarod reached out and gently touched her face. He stared deeply into her violet eyes. He found himself compelled to kiss her, but there was no time.

Ding!

The other elevator opened and out bolted Miss Parker.

Chapter 63

MISS PARKER WAS stunned to be staring into the eyes of the Pretender and said the first thing that came to her mind—"A friggin' Etch A Sketch?!"

Parker reached into her holster, but Jarod slammed the cart into her, knocking her back into the elevator.

Ding!

The other elevator arrived. Jarod shoved Skylar inside of it and pressed the *down* button. The doors began to close on the lift. As they did, she saw Parker struggle to her feet, bolt out of the other elevator and sprint in hot pursuit after Jarod, nearing a stairwell door.

Big Head and the orderlies finally burst out of the security tunnel. Nurse K pulled her cell phone and punched in a number.

Parker keyed her earbud as she sprinted toward the stairwell Jarod vanished into. "He's heading to the roof. Hold your positions. I'm going to flush him down. Be ready!" When she got to the door she found Jarod had jammed it shut. "Damn it!" As she slammed her shoulder into the door ...

~~~

Upon hearing this, Sydney, still outside on the ground floor, shot an anxious look up at the rooftop—still unsure what to do.

~~~

Jarod pushed himself quickly up the flights of steps to the roof. From below he could hear Miss Parker now bashing at the door while from above he heard the growing sound of helicopter rotors. He pushed on ...

~~~

The chopper blades wickedly sliced air approaching full power. O'Quinn raised the sheet from the face of the stretchered body to get a look at Kaj himself. He was breathing and soon he'd be talking. Satisfied, O'Quinn signaled Dog and Dojame to load the gurney onboard.

Bilson killed his cell phone and with a look of concern leaned into O'Quinn. "We've got a problem."

Jarod reached the last flight up to the windowless roof door. He cautiously nudged it open for a clean eye line to the landing pad across the roof, spotting Bilson, Dog and O'Quinn outside the chopper, the latter two with their guns already leveled at him.

In the half instant that the first yellow bursts appeared from the barrel tips of their guns, Jarod thought Big Head, *big mouth*. Then with lightning reflexes, he dove back as all hell broke loose.

Heavy gunfire rained down, splintering the roof door like paper. Jarod hit the floor, rolled away down the steps out of the line of fire as shards of wood splinters showered all around him.

~~~

Smashing through the stairwell door on the Annex level, Miss Parker reacted to the heavy gunfire above her and raced toward the sound of trouble ...

~~~

Jarod heard the crashing open of the stairwell door down below and Miss Parker's footfalls on the stairs. He knew she would be on top of him in seconds.

The artillery onslaught went silent. Jarod crawled up the steps to the tattered roof door and peeked out through the gaping bullet holes. Squinting through the dust and debris air wash from the revving rotors, Jarod spotted O'Quinn, the last to board the chopper and made his move—bolting out onto the roof toward the whirlybird.

O'Quinn spotted him first and then, along with Dog, again opened fire. Bullets chewed chunks of rooftop gravel just behind Jarod's heels as he dove for cover behind a large air conditioning unit.

From his new position Jarod saw Miss Parker charge onto the roof, gun poised. She scanned for Jarod but didn't spot him, then swung her gun at the chopper. In that instant Dog unleashed a torrent of gunfire at her.

Diving for cover she fired back best she could, but their auto mags were too much for her.

Dr. Bilson was terrified. He ran to the chopper and tried to get in, but O'Quinn slammed the door shut and barked to the pilot.

"Go, go, go!" The chopper revved, then slowly started to lift away. Frantic, Bilson ran across the rooftop, disappearing into the other stairwell.

Jarod had no time for the dirty doc; his focus was on Miss Parker picking herself up. This time she spotted him.

"Jarod!" Parker screamed, firing two intentionally wide shots at him to let him know she was blocking his only escape.

He eyed the helicopter with hopes fading. Jarod knew it was now or never. He dashed toward the rising chopper, the rotor wash buffeting his strides. Parker reacted, but the same rotor wash made her aim impossible.

Only seconds to spare, Jarod leapt up and precariously grabbed onto the landing skids underneath the rising copter.

O'Quinn motioned the pilot to try and shake him off and the chopper began jerking from side to side as it drifted over the divide between the main hospital roof where it took off from and the Annex roof two stories below it.

Parker steadied her aim, the copter now directly above her, buffeting her brutally.

Jarod locked his arm around the skid and clung on with all his might but dangled in the wind under the viciously shaking copter as it banked 90 degrees and started to fly away.

Parker fired and hit exactly where she was aiming: right next to where Jarod's elbow was locked around the skid.

Jarod looked down as Parker's second shot hit even closer, forcing him into a difficult choice.

He unlocked his arm from the skid and let go.

Chapter 64

WHILE IT ALL happened in an instant, the world seemed to be rushing up at Jarod in slow motion as he free-fell down toward the Annex's huge atrium dome.

Parker swung her gun down following Jarod's trajectory, but before she could get aim and fire, Jarod compacted his body. The impact sounded like an explosion when he hit and plunged through the glass dome.

The socialization room was nearly empty when the glass above shattered as Jarod fell through, his 30-foot fall finally broken as he landed on one of the sofas with glass showering down all around him.

Survival mode at full throttle now, he rolled up to his feet but with a deep moan, then quickly did an inventory of the pain. Luckily, he was not seriously hurt—cuts, abrasions, but no broken bones. He glanced to his right where a stunned Big Head's big mouth was agape.

If she'd thought cleaning up her own mother's loose stools was the hallmark of a bad day, Jarod's arrival was a downright sign from God the worst was still to come. "What the fu—?"

As she grabbed a security phone and started barking into it, Sarge walked up next to her. Jarod allowed himself a short smile, seeing that Sarge was giving him a full military salute.

Fighting through the pain, Jarod then dashed back out through the security tunnel, its broken doors now wide open—his limping gait now painfully real.

~~~

While Jarod had been inventorying his injuries, Miss Parker had been weighing her options—to head back down the stairs or follow Jarod through the hole in the atrium's roof he had so generously left her.

She looked down over the railing; it was a two-story drop and a 20-foot horizontal jump to the Annex rooftop and the open dome beyond. She'd done longer drops before, having trained for such situations since age 14 and her intensive Centre Indoctrination. But she'd never made a leap that far.

At that moment she recalled the words of her mentor Fabiana, that were driven into young Miss Parker whenever doubt became the enemy - *Courage is nothing more than blind will.* And at that moment, with the thought of another of Daddy Parker's admonitions on the failures of re-capturing Jarod, Miss Parker ran at full speed toward the edge of the building, eyeing the point on the rooftop where she'd plant her foot and spring-propel herself over the edge.

But at the very instant she hit it—she slammed on her brakes and skidded to a halt.

What am I, crazy? Use the damn stairs.

Miss Parker rushed to the stairwell and descended three steps at a time, covering six flights in less than 30 seconds.

She rushed out into the hallway, spotting Jarod dashing out of the security tunnel door and into the far stairwell. In pursuit, she again keyed her earbud—"He's in the south stairwell heading down! I'll sandwich from above, we've got him! All Sweepers to the main corridor—now!"

Chapter 65

OUTSIDE THE EMERGENCY room entrance, Sydney's head craned up. Parker had just said she had Jarod trapped in the South stairwell and he was outside the south side of the hospital.

Idling in neutral, helplessly, while Jarod and Miss Parker squared off inside, that single thought kept repeating itself in Syd's mind: *"Miss Parker, the Centre wants Jarod alive." "Preferably Sydney. Preferably."*

Sydney could idle no longer and made a decision. He rushed into the hospital.

Chapter 66

AIRES ALREADY HAD his hand poised on his firearm, arriving at
the ground floor south stairwell door. He rushed in and began climbing up.

Jarod scrambled down the south stairs several steps at a time, then instantly stopped as he caught sight between the rails of Aires heading up
from below. He then looked up, hearing Parker descending from above.

Jarod was trapped.

Then he saw it: High on the wall next to the lighting fixture, he spotted an air intake vent. He leapt up onto the railing edge, stretched his hands
out, unfastened the panel and nudged it aside. With one hand he unclasped
and removed his belt.

Parker caught the blur of a live body on the landing just below. She
smiled gleefully—the Pretender was hers for the taking. She whispered into
her earbud, "We have him trapped between floors in the south stairwell.
Rendezvous at the bottom for transport. Aires—proceed slowly up, we'll
contain in the middle."

That's when everything went black.

Though it would only buy him seconds before emergency power
kicked back in, Jarod had used his belt buckle to short out the lighting grid
for the stairwell. As he shrank into the darkness, he hoped seconds were all
he'd need.

Miss P took one cautious step down—"Time to come home, Jarod."

Jarod's answer came from the blackness below—"As much as I
enjoyed our time there together as children, I'm needed out here."

"Too bad there's no way out this time." She took another guarded step.

"Sydney taught me nothing was impossible if I put my mind to it." Then, from the shadows—"You look just like her, you know."

Parker pulled a penlight and shone it above her gun parallel to the barrel. "Seriously, Jarod? You think throwing my mother in my face will help earwig me? You're either really desperate or you don't know me very well."

Jarod could see Aires's flashlight ascending through the darkness from the stairs below. Neither Miss P nor Aires had more than ten steps remaining before they would meet on the landing. Jarod's time was running out.

"I know everything about who you are," Jarod said.

Miss P took another cautious step downward—"What do you know about me, genius boy?"

"I know you loved riding horseback with your mother. I know how much she loved you. I know she was a good woman."

Miss P swept the walls as she crept down toward the landing. Five more steps.

"Wrong, Genius dude, unlike me and Daddy, Mother was weak."

"No, Catherine was strong—and unlike your father—honest."

Miss P found her next step unsteady.

"More lies, Jarod."

"Surprised you're not used to them after a lifetime of lies from your father—especially about what really happened to your mother—lies to deceive you—to keep you in the fold."

She stopped, gathering herself, fighting off his words, refusing to let them get to her.

Her silence told him she was listening, that his words were working on her. "You know I know what the truth is. Maybe if you're nice to me—one day I'll tell you some of it."

Miss P closed her eyes as if to shut it all out. She could be weak here, or she could be strong. Her eyes flashed open and with resolve, she touched her earbud and whispered—"Now."

She bolted down, Aires bolting up onto the landing. With guns and lights, they swept the entire landing, ready to blow Jarod away if necessary.

But Jarod was nowhere—the space as empty as Miss P's soul. She glanced around, confounded.

Aires shrugged. "Maybe he is Houdini."

That's when her eye caught it—the air intake vent on the wall above them was slightly askew. She looked at Aires, gave the silent sign, pointed at her eyes, then to the vent. He nodded in understanding. She mimed for him to give her a boost.

And Jarod watched it all.

From just above and behind them, he strained with every muscle to keep himself flat against the underside of the down flight of stairs above where they stood. Facing down, spread eagle, his weight was held by his feet and hands pushing out against the edges of the stair's steel support beams—Jarod looking like an ill-omened version of Da Vinci's Vitruvian Man.

Aires cupped his hands. Miss Parker dug her boot into it. He hoisted her up to the ajar air vent just as Jarod had intentionally left it. She slid it open and peered into its darkness on the other side.

At their most vulnerable, Jarod released his feet and hands and dropped down below and behind them. Aires craned his neck at the sound, Jarod reached up and grabbed the Sweeper's ankle, yanked it out from under him and then dashed down the stairs.

Aires tumbled as did Parker without her booster. As she dropped, her legs found themselves awkwardly scissoring Aires' head and she both heard and felt the nauseating crack of his neck breaking against the edge of the step under her fall.

He was dead instantly.

Parker crawled up, barely throwing a look at her expendable Sweeper and continued down in hot pursuit of Jarod.

~~~

A perimeter Sweeper, Pedro, rushed down the hallway near the overcrowded ER waiting room, straight for the south hallway stairway.

"Jarod!" In the split second he turned away from the door to glance at the arriving Sydney, Jarod bolted out of the stairwell and was body-slammed by Pedro, sending him flying off his feet. As their bodies crashed into the wall, Jarod's weight forced Pedro's bald head into the cinderblocks with a sickening thud.

Mayhem erupted as patients, visitors and orderlies reacted to the intrusion. Everyone except for Syd, who smiled at the sight of Jarod.

"Jarod, you're alright!" Syd cried with relief as he rushed to help his charge get to his feet. But their reunion was short lived ...

"Not for long!"

Jarod spun around at Miss Parker emerging from the stairwell. "I got him—main corridor," Parker informed her remaining Sweepers into her earbud. "On the floor, Jarod!" she barked.

He looked hopelessly at Sydney.

"Daddy can't help you this time. Get down, NOW!"

Jarod followed her call and hit his knees.

She took a look at the out-cold Pedro and tossed a set of handcuffs to Syd. "Make yourself useful, for once," she ordered, determined not to take her eyes or gun off Jarod.

As Syd reluctantly approached Jarod a loud crash echoed. He turned in time to see Miss Parker's body crumble to the floor—just behind her a groggy young woman holding a thick metal encased clipboard.

A young woman with violet eyes.

She looked at the clipboard and smiled. "It's not a bedpan, but it does the job."

The moment produced a laugh of relief from Skylar until her breathing went shallow and her body started wilting from the effects of the meds.

Skylar collapsed, but Jarod caught her before she hit the floor. She smiled weakly up at him—"You didn't think I'd leave you, didja?" Skylar's eyes then fluttered back in her head as she passed out.

Jarod laid her gently on the floor, then rushed over to the unconscious Parker. He took the gun out of her hand and fished out the Town Car keys from her pocket.

"Jarod!" The Pretender stood and turned to Syd. The Belgian tossed a look over his shoulder toward the other end of the corridor. Jarod's eyes followed it—there were more Sweepers heading their way.

"I haven't gotten what you asked me to, Jarod, but I will. It's the least I owe you." Syd and Jarod shared a split-second silent connection before Jarod urgently swept Skylar up in his arms and rushed toward the exit.

Syd knelt next to Miss Parker, *making himself useful* by attending to her as she stirred back to consciousness. "Where is he?"

"He's gone, Miss Parker."

"Gone my ass!" Miss Parker struggled to her feet as her remaining Sweepers arrived. "Stop him!" Miss Parker led her team toward the exit.

~~~

Outside the entrance, Jarod hit the alarm button on Parker's car key and a black Town Car chirped behind him.

He glanced back into the hospital through the open automated doors, seeing Sweepers and the unstoppable Parker back in pursuit.

He laid Skylar down on the Town Car's back seat, fired several rounds into the tires of The Centre's windowless van, climbed in the Town Car, cranked the engine and threw smoke peeling out, brushing back the charging Parker and her Sweepers as he sped out past them.

"Shit!" Miss Parker could already hear the disapproving voice of her old man ringing in her ears. She kicked the side of the van as Syd, as usual, a day late and a dollar short, sauntered up to her, watching Jarod disappear in the distance. "It's over, Miss Parker."

Miss P lit a Pall Mall and shook her head at the Belgian. "You couldn't be more wrong, Sydney. It's only just begun."

Chapter 67

JAROD PARKED THE Town Car on a remote road near the South Street Seaport to gather himself.

His eyes lit upon the Statue of Liberty just across the water, keeping watch over her children. But despite her soothing presence, Jarod felt anything but free—his heart was heavy, his mind entangled in what seemed to be a thousand thoughts.

He looked into the back seat at the unconscious Skylar, this young woman who'd risked her life to help him. He thought about the pain she would soon endure to detoxify her body from what the immoral Dr. Bilson had subjected her to.

He thought about the feelings this unique woman had stirred in the deepest corner of his soul.

He thought about Miss Parker, her gaping loneliness, her psychological torture at the hands of a dominant father, her seemingly impenetrable emotional armor and how the answers to the secrets surrounding her life's miseries could free her.

The answers that *he knew*.

He also pondered the hollow futility of his gatekeeper, Sydney. At once father figure, prison guard, confidante and conspirator. All of which inevitably lead Jarod's mind to his true origins and the complicitness of Sydney's deceit in the shrouded truth behind it all. Jarod questioned if Sydney would - if Sydney *could* - redeem his actions and overcome his guilt by helping Jarod find the truth he so longed for.

Jarod was angry.

Not because of what had happened to him, but for what had happened to another innocent child taken by a powerful entity to be exploited for their purposes. Though he had but seven days, Jarod was determined to reunite the boy with his family—or die trying.

The Pretender knew that wherever Luke was, he was asking the same question Jarod had never stopped asking himself since the day he'd been taken from his parents ...

"Where are my mom and dad? Where are my mom and dad? Where are my mom and dad?"

Next for The Pretender

In *Saving Luke*, Book 2 in *The Pretender* series of novels, Jarod must draw upon all of his Pretender skills in a race against time to rescue a kidnapped little boy and stop a huge disaster that could claim the innocent lives of thousands.

As their pursuit of their Pretender ramps up, Miss Parker and Sydney must deal with Centre secrets from their own pasts—confronting, personal secrets Jarod reveals to them.

Chasing The Pretender just got more complicated as does the task of determining where everyone's true loyalties lie.

The *Rebirth* of *The Pretender* was just the beginning as it all kicks into high gear in *Saving Luke*!

For all things *The Pretender* and *Saving Luke* follow the link below!
http://www.thepretenderlives.com

Get Saving Luke now!

The Novels may end but in between them

THEPRETENDERUNIVERSE

is always expanding. Come be a part of it at

http://www.thepretenderlives.com

A Personal Thank You From
Steven Long Mitchell and Craig W Van Sickle:

We loved writing the first Pretender Novel *Rebirth* and we hope you enjoyed reading it! We really want to hear from you about the book, and it would really be great you'd send us an email to introduce yourself and share your thoughts. We respond personally to all of our readers.

Be sure to get on our mailing list so you don't miss out on notifications about future books, Pretender related news, updates and contests.

Please send an email to us at *centreinsider@thepretenderlives.com* and introduce yourself, so we can personally thank you for trying our books.